AN AMOS WALKER MYSTERY

DOWNRIVER

LOREN D. ESTLEMAN is a graduate of Eastern Michigan University and a veteran police-court journalist. Since the publication of his first novel in 1976, he has established himself as a leading writer of both mystery and western fiction. His western novels include Golden Spur Award-winner *Aces and Eights, Mister St. John, The Stranglers,* and *Gun Man.* His Amos Walker, Private Eye series includes *Motor City Blue, Angel Eyes, The Midnight Man, The Glass Highway,* Shamus Award-winner *Sugartown, Every Brilliant Eye, Lady Yesterday, Downriver,* and the Shamus Award nominee *A Smile on the Face of the Tiger.* The most recent Walker mystery, *Sinister Heights,* was published in February 2002. Estleman lives in Michigan with his wife, Deborah, who writes under the name Deborah Morgan.

"Estleman is the author who most deserves the title 'Raymond Chandler's successor.' " —*Virginian-Pilot/Ledger-Star*

"Amos Walker [is] one of the last and most durable of those throwback private eyes who still smoke, drink and use the hardboiled lingo in defense of a code of ethics that went out with the stick shift." —*The New York Times Book Review*

"Estleman . . . must be counted among the best of the current hardboiled whodunit writers." —*San Diego Union*

ALSO BY LOREN D. ESTLEMAN

Published by ibooks, inc.:

AMOS WALKER MYSTERIES

Motor City Blue
Angel Eyes
The Midnight Man
The Glass Highway
Sugartown
Every Brilliant Eye
Lady Yesterday

SHERLOCK HOLMES MYSTERIES

Sherlock Holmes vs. Dracula
Dr. Jekyll and Mr. Holmes

DOWNRIVER

LOREN D. ESTLEMAN

ibooks
new york
www.ibooksinc.com

DISTRIBUTED BY SIMON & SCHUSTER, INC

A Publication of ibooks, inc.

An ibooks, inc. Book

Distributed by Simon & Schuster, Inc.
1230 Avenue of the Americas, New York, NY 10020

ibooks, inc.
24 West 25th Street
New York, NY 10010

The ibooks World Wide Web Site Address is:
http://www.ibooksinc.com

ISBN 0-7434-4494-9
First ibooks, inc. printing June 2002
10 9 8 7 6 5 4 3 2 1

Cover design by carrie monaco

Printed in the U.S.A.

To Ray Puechner:

You told me the best was coming.

I had it all along.

DOWNRIVER

1

SUPERIOR ROLLED under a Wedgwood sky, stacking sunlight in long platinum rows and tangling in the broken rocks on the beach. Early in the afternoon a shoreward wind blew passing compact cars across the centerline and teased a pale floating piece of old decking toward land. The plank was worn smooth and poreless and round at the edges like soap. It might have been wandering the lake for a hundred years, the lone survivor of a stove ship carrying coal oil and barrels of molasses and a bonneted lady's Sunday surrey, rotting below Six Fathom Shoal along with skeletons swaddled in black oilskin. It might have been just a piece of old wood.

At that time of day moisture glistened in flat sheets on the gun towers and formed moving columns of droplets like soldier ants on the chainlink fence and on the snaggled teeth of the concertina wire coiling on top of it. The air was wet and clean and smelled of bleached driftwood and sun, scabbed iron and arcing fish. Serving time in Marquette Branch Prison, on the shore of the largest freshwater lake in the world, must be like dying on the first nice day of spring, day after day.

I rested my forearms on the Chevy's roof, watching the gate and letting the sun warm my back and draw the sting from between my shoulders. It was an overnight drive north from Detroit across the straits and through the Upper Peninsula, and I'd made it in twelve hours. From Clare on up it was all pines and pasty stands and straight blacktop like a gash in a green carpet with dotted line flashing under the car, scorching your eyeballs and whiting out your humanity. Now the volume on the radio was up and so was the Tigers' new second baseman, stalling at the plate while he adjusted his gloves and wristbands and helmet and footguard. Twenty years ago Al Kaline used to hit them barehanded over the right field wall into the middle of Michigan Avenue wearing just his uniform and jockstrap, but then he didn't know any better. This one did, and grounded out on the first pitch to end the inning.

The Orioles had men on first and third with two out at the top of the sixth when my client appeared. He was a head taller than the guard escorting him and solid, the way men who have been lean all their lives get to be when they take on weight, wearing a gray suit that fell short of his wrists and ankles and a white shirt with a spread collar. It had to spread to make room for his neck. The whites of his eyes glittered in a charcoal face and the skin of his shaved scalp was tight and black and gleaming. I didn't think much of that. It reminded me of blacktop.

When the gate was open he stepped through, then the guard said something and he turned his body and looked down at him. Ivory teeth slashed the big man's face and he said something back. The gate clanged shut, hard enough to crackle the radio. Outside the fence he set down his cheap overnight bag and stretched, arching his back and straining the suit, reaching up with arms as long as some men are tall; holding that position for almost a minute, like a cat that had been cooped up in the house too long. Finally he unwound himself and spent some time tugging at his sleeves. He licked his lips and smacked them, then he did it all over again. Tasting the air. When he was through with that his big shiny head pivoted around like a gun turret and he looked directly at me. I put up a hand. He scooped up the bag without seeming to bend and came over. As I stepped forward to meet him, the Oriole at the plate broke his bat on a ninety-seven-mile-an-hour fastball and scored two runs.

"You're Walker?" It was a shallow voice, considering how far it had to come to clear his mouth.

"Welcome to freedom, Mr. DeVries."

After an instant's hesitation he wrapped a hand twice around the one I'd extended and turned it right and left, examining it.

"Hope I'm doing it right," he said. "I ain't shook hands since Johnson."

I said he was doing just fine and reclaimed the bonemeal that had been my fingers. Up close his face was fissured with fine lines like old china and he had a close-cropped beard resembling a shotgun pattern. From a little distance he might have been thirty or fifty, but I had done my homework; he had been twenty-two the last time that gate had closed behind him, twenty years before.

"That must have been some conversation you had with that guard."

"Heiny?" The smile cut across his features like yellow jade. "He said he'd hold my room for me till I got back. I told him I was just going out to look up his daughter."

"You better hope you don't come back."

"No chance. I been looking at that goddamn lake every day since they kicked me up here from Jackson. Come November when them waves come walloping them rocks you can hear your name in them. First thing I'm fixing to do after I get me some real threads is buy an oar and then I'm going to put it on my shoulder and start walking inland till somebody axe me what's that thing I got there on my shoulder. Then I'll build a house right on that spot."

"I see they've got Homer in the prison library."

"Oh, we's all readers. That's what they turn out in Marquette, readers and dope addicts. You bring it?"

I reached in through the open window, plucked the paper

sack off the front seat, and held it out. "It's cold by now."

"Sons of bitches took twenty minutes on top of what they had coming to them processing me out." Setting down his overnight bag, he took the square Styrofoam container out of the sack, found the tab, and freed the fat hamburger from inside. "I been wondering about this here fast food," he said, handing back the litter. "When I went in it was short order or wait."

I watched him make easy work of the sandwich. The advertising said it took two hands, but his weren't the hands they had in mind. When it was gone and he was using a fistful of paper napkins to wipe special sauce off his beard and fingers, I asked him how he liked it.

"Well, it's fast." He gave me the same look he'd given me from the gate. This close he was staring almost straight down. "Elon Royal said you was a big man."

"Elon Royal never played center for the Pistons."

"I didn't neither. They was scouting me when I went down."

"How is Elon? I haven't seen him since before he tried crashing out of Jackson."

"Isolation. They found a extra toothbrush poked under his mattress last week."

"I heard they make you be good up here."

He wasn't listening to me. He had his head cocked toward the radio. It was the bottom of the sixth and Detroit had a man on. "Norm Cash was fouling them off the day they wrote me up. Sucker on the mound must of made a dozen pitches. This big sergeant had a Japanese radio."

"Cash is dead."

"I heard. You know what they took me down for."

"Armored car robbery. During the riots."

"Conspiracy to commit," he corrected. "They said I bombed a building to turn heads while my partners hit the car. A man got killed and they threw the City-County Building at me on account of I was the only one they caught alive. Eighteen to thirty for starting a fire in a condemned building."

"You didn't do it?"

"Oh, I threw the bomb. Bomb. Fucking Thunderbird bottle full of paint thinner with a burning rag stuck in the top. The place was three years past due to come down. Rapists was using it, dope dealers. My favorite cousin OD'd. Anyway they put the fire out in ten minutes and me in for twenty years. I didn't even know the armored car was there."

"But you knew one of the robbers. The one they killed."

"Davy Jackson. Little Davy. Shit, I went to school with him, when I went. He got himself shot down and they give me a piece of that too. That's the law; someone you stick up a place with gets killed, you're on the hook for murder. Only I never stuck up a place in my life."

"After you called I read up on the case," I said. "It was a hot time. Forty-three people were killed in a week and a lot of real estate got turned into ashes. They were afraid it might start up again and so they were more lenient with most of the people they arrested than they might have been otherwise. Not with you, though. They set yours aside as a special case, a punk trying to turn a major tragedy to his personal advantage. Even so they offered you an easier time of it if you agreed to name your accomplices and tell them where the money was."

"If I had accomplices I would of told them. If I had money I'd of bought a real lawyer instead of the kid P.D. they hung on me. Why'd I want to knock down no armored car? I had a shot at pro ball and I was going to be married. Well, they took care of both of them things; my girl hooked up with somebody else and I broke the free-throw record in slam sixteen years ago. My life's shit. Okay, I did arson, but I had a clean record before that and any other time, any other summer, I'd of got probation. What I got was half my life in a room on the lake."

He'd laid it all flat, his voice rising only once, when he spoke of his chance to play for the Pistons and the girl he'd planned to marry. But his eyes were glistening. I reached in and turned off the radio.

"If it's clearing your name you want, you need a lawyer,

not a detective. I could have told you that over the telephone if you'd let me and saved you my expenses here and back."

"Forget my name. Everyone else has. I want the money."

"What money?"

"The two hundred thousand dollars they stole out of that armored car. I paid for it and now it's mine. I want you to find the ones that done it and get it from them and bring it to me."

2

"I'M A LOUSY THIEF," I said, when it sank in. "I return quarters I find in telephone coin slots. It makes me crazy but there you are."

"You don't think I got it coming?"

"More, probably, if you're innocent. It works out to ten thousand a year. These days that's barely a living wage. Say you're telling the truth. Finding them is one thing, getting the money is another. If it isn't all spent they'll be attached to it by now."

"We'll work that part out after you find them."

"I'm not sure I can find them."

"I know where to start looking."

"I thought you didn't know anything about the robbery."

"I didn't at the time. But they turn the lights off here at nine o'clock and you get to think in the dark. About who put you up to what you done and why." He turned his head up the coast in that pivoting motion. "There a library in town?"

"Libraries and museums up to your—well, *my* eyebrows," I said. "Give me your bag, I'll toss it in back."

"Change of clothes and a razor." He handed it to me. "And this."

I looked at the check stretched between his hands. It was signed by the Michigan Secretary of State and made out to

Richard DeVries in the amount of seven thousand dollars. "I guess you saved on haircuts."

"And just about everything else. I don't smoke, so I turned my cigarette allowance back into the inmate savings plan along with most of what they paid me to stamp license plates. Like if they didn't I'd quit and go to work for the other place. You don't need much to get along on in the house of doors. Room and board's took care of."

"It buys a month of my time. For finding the people you're looking for, not for the other. And not if you're planning to twist their heads off and dribble them into the Detroit River."

"I'm a lousy killer. I walk around spiders. It makes me crazy but there you are. Got a pen?"

I produced one and he endorsed the back of the check and gave it to me. "What are you using to live on?"

"I was hoping you'd make me a loan against the seven large."

I set his bag on the floor of the back seat and put the check in my wallet and counted out two hundred from the travel fund. When he closed his hand the bills disappeared. "I hope your cellmate wasn't arrested for uttering and publishing," I said.

"Marquette don't believe in cellmates. I had a Detroit city councilman in Jackson, but they paroled him when he got re-elected."

We climbed into the car. I showed him how to adjust the seat to keep his chin off his knees and started the motor. "So how was prison?"

"Better than no sex at all."

Don't go by your dashboard compass when you get near the city of Marquette. It rests on a shelf of solid iron and in the old days, before modern mining processes made it easier to get ore out of hard-to-reach places in more temperate climates, the glow from the blast furnaces and from the kilns that made the charcoal that fueled them turned the harbor the color of blood. Today, scuttle-shaped carriers still ghost along the violet horizon lugging millions of tons of iron pellets bound for factories in Duluth and Detroit and Buffalo, but the railroads have gone to scrap and kindling and hydraulic machines have replaced most of the miners, whose shades still prowl the crooked shafts in hardhats and blackface. Wooden elevator towers doze on hilltops awaiting the beat of belt-driven machinery and jumbled curses in Swedish and Norwegian and German and Cornish, and everywhere you go in the perforated, grown-over countryside you hear the silent echoes of the gone.

I gassed up at a Best station layered between a rock shop and a combination mining museum and junk store and found DeVries grinning when I got back behind the wheel. "They let you pump your own?"

"It isn't your choice. The friendly attendant with the uniform and bow tie is as dead as Elvis. Didn't they let you watch TV?"

"I stopped when they took off *Gunsmoke*. Ain't we supposed to buckle up or something?"

I showed him how to work his shoulder harness and strapped myself in. "They passed a law. For our protection. You'll see surveillance cameras in public restrooms to protect us from perverts and police barricades to protect us from drunk drivers and dusk-to-dawn curfews to protect us from teenagers. You'll think you never left the joint." We pulled out into traffic.

He let it ride. "You got to remember what it was like in 'sixty-seven. The mayor was white, the cops was white. Malcolm X was dead. About the only place the brothers could hang out and get down was in the after-hours places, the blind pigs. When the fuzz busted that one at Twelfth and Clairmount it was like sticking a boil and the pus running out."

"You were there?"

"Three blocks away in this white dude's basement apartment, drinking Thunderbird. I came with Davy Jackson. The cat was a law student or something at Wayne State. I don't remember how he knew Davy. Andrew something, or maybe it was Albert. We was wasted when we got there. He was living with this skinny dirty hippie blonde. They was toking and Davy and me was drinking and we heard glass breaking. We went out for a look-see and here's this Tactical Mobile Unit going by with its rear window all cracked and pieces of busted glass all over the trunk. The brothers and sisters was on the sidewalk and in the street thick as bedbugs, yelling and throwing bottles. One just missed me and hit a streetlight and busted. I thought it was a bomb."

"Speaking of bombs."

"Not that night. People was running all over the place smashing windows and kicking in fenders. I went home when the sirens started. That was the end of it, I figured.

"Well, all hell's still flying loose when I get home from the junkyard three days later. I was living in my mom's old place on Sherman. She died when I was eighteen. Cancer. Anyway I been stacking car batteries all day, all I want to do is scrub off the crud and crash. Just as I get to the door Andrew or Albert comes cruising past in this rusty old Ninety-Eight with one door tied on and he sees me and stops and calls me over. The blonde's with him, wasted again, or maybe still wasted from before. Next thing I know I'm in the back seat swigging Thunderbird and going to see the Man get it stuck to him."

"You said Albert or Andrew was white."

"You know what them rebels was like; anything, so long as it fucks the Establishment. They was almost like brothers."

I parked in front of the Peter White Memorial Library. Neither of us got out. He was staring at the windshield.

"South of the Ford and east of Woodward it was like the stuff they was showing on the news from Saigon," he said. "I mean Jeeps on the street and paratroopers in camouflage on the sidewalks and snipers up on the roofs. Everything was in ashes. Man, I was tired and high, it looked like the system had fell apart. None of the rules meant nothing. Everybody was burning, why not me?"

"That's kind of a jump. Even drinking."

"Not when you're twenty-two and black and your white foreman has been watching you all week, scared shitless you're going to freak and cut him. Man, it made me *want* to cut him. I was missing out. Anyway I had the bottle. I was in the deep slam before I remembered where I got the paint thinner; Andrew or Albert had some cans in the trunk, he said he painted houses to buy books. I don't remember filling the bottle, but I lit the rag with a old Zippo with a bad flint and threw it. It was a pretty shot, four stories up from the foul line. Sailed nice as potato pie through a busted pane and went *cush*. Building looked just like the one my cousin died in. Oh, it was a sweet fire. I was still admiring it when they grabbed me and threw me down and screwed a rifle into the back of my neck."

"You didn't see the robbery or hear the shots?"

"They was shooting going on all over. That fire was all I seen or wanted to."

"So far you're an arsonist who pulled the kind of sentence arsonists don't usually get and should. I'm having trouble identifying, even with your check in my pocket."

"The neighborhood was evacuated. Maybe I'd of burned a cat, except cats never let themselves get trapped. I ain't saying it wasn't stupid. Didn't you never want to burn nothing down?"

I lit a cigarette off the dash lighter and blew the smoke out the window. "I had a pretty good plan for burning down my junior high school. I didn't like my gym teacher and the principal had it in for me. That's as far as I got, the plan."

"Maybe with a sore back and a bellyful of cheap wine you would of got farther."

"Probably not. But I've never been black in a white world."

"I wasn't out to hurt nobody, black nor white. I didn't rob no place and I didn't shoot no guard and it wasn't me got Davy killed."

"Was Davy in the car?"

"Just the white dude and his dirty girlfriend. I can still

smell her. I never seen Davy till they was showing pictures of his body in court. You got to realize where my head was. I didn't know half of what was going on and I wasn't feeling too clean on account of starting the fire and I never made the connection between Andrew or Albert and the robbery. By the time I did I had bars on my face. I wrote letters. Nobody wrote back. They had their pigeon."

"What's in the library?"

"Let's go in and find out."

The place smelled of books and oiled wood and time in a jar. Sunlight tiled the floor in gold patches and the old rosewood whimpered under DeVries's size fifteens. At that time of day we were alone with a woman in a salmon-colored suit and a gray silk scarf seated behind the information desk. She wore her black hair short and her eyes gray. She was about thirty and looked better than the job called for. When we stopped in front of her desk she looked up from her writing—and up. The desk came to DeVries's knees.

"It's a woman," he said.

"What'd you expect?" I asked. "There are more male librarians than there used to be, but you've still only got two possibilities."

"I mean it's a woman. I thought they was all married to other cons and kept behind glass."

"May I help you?" She shifted her attention to me. It wasn't as far to yell.

I said, "Excuse my friend. He just mustered out of the French Foreign Legion. He carried the camels when they got tired."

"I see." And looking at him again, she did. Living in a prison town they get so they can spot them. Something like sympathy worked under her features. It didn't work too hard. When they smoothed over again DeVries said, "October fifteenth, 1984."

"I'm sorry?"

"I want the Detroit *News* for October fifteenth, 1984. You got it?"

"That would be on microfilm. In there." She pointed at a door.

I thanked her and steered the big man through it. Three of the viewers stood on a library table and the walls were lined waist-high with dated file drawers. July to December 1984 was near the floor.

"She was wearing perfume," he said. "Did you smell it?"

"More likely cologne. Library boards haven't bent that far."

"What's the difference?"

"About fifteen dollars." I took out a box labeled OCT. 84 and we went to the table. He watched me clamp the spool of film in place and thread it through the machine. "I miss the big books."

"Wait till you see what they've done to typewriters," I said. "Say when."

The light projected the transparencies onto the viewing screen at the bottom of the machine. I turned the crank and we watched the days blur past. It fascinated him. They hadn't gone that quickly for him the first time.

"There! Go back."

I reversed the crank. The page we'd just passed slid back into frame. I sharpened the focus. There were several columns on the Tigers, boiling over from the sports section in the wake of the big Series victory. I wondered how the game with Baltimore was going.

"That's him. Albert or Andrew. I memorized the date. They didn't let us keep clippings in the cells."

His pointing hand obliterated most of the page. He withdrew it. The photograph had nothing to do with baseball. It showed Timothy Marianne, the former Ford Motor Company vice president in charge of engineering and design, signing a labor contract on a desk surrounded by his staff and representatives of the United Auto Workers. The caption said it was his first official act as owner-director of Marianne Motors. Since then his angular, black-browed features and thinning gray hair had become as familiar to Detroiters as the Penobscot Building.

"Timothy Marianne wasn't in college twenty years ago," I said. "He would have been in his mid-thirties even then."

"Not him. The one standing on his left. You don't forget a face like that."

He was right. Feature writers made a lot of Marianne's rugged good looks, but the man pictured leaning over his left shoulder in a pinstripe suit and paisley tie was someone to look at twice in a crowded elevator. His hair was black and long for an executive, combed straight back from a modest pompadour behind his ears to his collar. He had high cheekbones and light eyes and a straight nose and lips that curved like a girl's. That fresh look would stay with him well into his thirties and already had, if he was who DeVries said he was.

I said, "It's a place to start. I wouldn't hope too hard. He isn't identified. We don't know if he belongs to Marianne or the union or if he's still with either of them."

"I figure we can get a line on him at his old apartment house on Twelfth. Maybe the landlord can tell us his name or where he went from there."

"I doubt it."

"How come?"

"The building isn't there anymore. Neither is Twelfth Street. They bulldozed that section and renamed the whole thing years ago."

3

DeVries didn't say anything after that. I rewound the film and put it back in the box and took it into the main room, where I gave the librarian the date and page number and asked for a printout. She got up with it and went through another door, moving crisply and silently on low heels. I wondered if during the job interview they made them walk up and down and assigned points according to how much noise they didn't make. While we were waiting I asked DeVries how he was holding up.

"I'm cool. I feel like someone changed the sheets on me is all."

"A lot's different. Cars and movie screens are smaller. Girls are women, when they aren't persons. There are as many telephone companies as telephones. Movie stars are politicians, politicians are doing guest shots on TV. Cigarettes and cholesterol are out. Computers and carbohydrates are in. When a woman you don't know approaches you in a bar it doesn't necessarily mean she's in business. That's for starters. About the only thing that's slowed down is records."

"I know about all that. I read."

"Reading it and seeing it," I said.

"Yeah."

She returned with the printout—a grainy reproduction of

the Marianne picture—and I paid for it and she put it in a manila envelope for us. The sympathy had gone from her face, leaving cool untouchability in its wash. Back in the car I turned on the radio. The game had finished. I had to wait for the announcer to dispose of all the other scores in both leagues before learning that Detroit had dropped it with two errors and a base on balls in the ninth. I flipped the knob. "Where to?"

"Detroit. I got an appointment with my parole officer Friday."

"Today's Wednesday. They don't give you much rope."

"What's rope?"

The way to US-41 took us along a broad, sun-sloshed main stem with fresh pavement ruled in bright yellow. It was lined with clean store windows and parking meters against the buildings to clear the curbs for the plows that removed twelve-foot drifts in the winter. A few tourists were out pushing the season in tank tops and shorts and blue knees and elbows. Hope and pneumonia spring eternal in the breasts of Michiganians.

We were four hundred miles from home as the crow flies, if it flew across the Great Lakes. Our route was considerably less direct and half again longer. The Upper Peninsula, which belongs geographically to Wisconsin, was Andrew Jackson's left-handed gift to Lansing in return for surrendering Toledo to Ohio. There had been some hollering about it at the time because a port on Lake Erie was worth twice as much as a rocky wilderness, but Ohio had more voters. Then the lumber industry started up and copper and iron were discovered in abundance and the hollering stopped. The war with our neighboring state goes on, however. There's no sense in wasting a good hate.

Two miles outside Marquette we passed through Harvey—two blocks of boarded-over storefronts and depressed tourist trade—and turned away from the lake. DeVries never looked back at it. The road opened up and so did I. The only other vehicle in sight was a dot of color in the rearview mirror.

"Marquette's for incorrigibles," I said. "What'd you do that made you too hot to hold in Jackson?"

"Cut my hand." His domed profile was sharp against the evergreens striping past his window.

"That shouldn't have done it."

"I cut it on a guard's front teeth."

"Bad move. They use angry young men for warm-up exercise inside."

"What do you know about it?"

"I've been in jail a time or two. It's the same neighborhood."

"You was just visiting. I lived there."

I said nothing. He tipped his head back against the padded rest.

"I feel like shit. I thought I'd be happy when I got out."

"That's normal."

"There was guys inside didn't want to leave. One of them had to be dragged out when his time was up. I never figured that to happen to me."

"Freedom's scary. You'll get used to it."

It was his turn to say nothing. The dot of color in the mirror had become an old maroon Dodge truck with a plank for a front bumper. It was making good time for the amount of smoke it was laying down behind it. The driver must have put in oil as often as he filled the tank.

"There's something to be said for knowing tomorrow's going to be just like today and yesterday," I said. "We're all looking for that. Living on the edge is too hard on the heart."

"It's noisy out here. That's the first thing I noticed. You don't know quiet till you been on the block. Some nights you can hear the hopes drop."

The truck flashed its lights. I let up on the accelerator and crowded the shoulder to give it room. It swept past with a swish and a click and a clattering of lifters. Smoke tangled around us.

"Guess I got out just in time," DeVries said. "My ears are institutionalized."

"Hang on."

Sixty yards ahead the truck swung into a sliding turn across both lanes, rubber scraping the pavement like nails on steel and gushing black smoke into the gray. It hinged up on its inside wheels, hung there for an instant, and came back down bouncing. By then I was already turning in the opposite direction. My tires wailed and the rear end came around with a snap that sounded and felt as if the car had bent in the middle. DeVries's palm smacked the windshield. When the nose was pointing back the way we'd come I squashed the pedal to the floor. The front wheels spun, grabbed, and lashed us ahead. The steering wheel yanked my arms straight.

The third vehicle, a new black Monte Carlo that had been exposed for the first time when the truck pulled out to pass, was turning, but I'd reacted too fast for the driver and he had only one lane blocked when I tore around in front of him, slinging two wheels up the grassy bank. Just then the fuel injector cut in with a deep gulp; the inertia broke the catch that held my seat in place and it slid back in its track and from then on I was reaching with all four limbs to maintain control from the back seat.

"Hell's going on?" DeVries was gripping his door handle.

I couldn't answer and drive like an idiot at the same time. In the mirror the Monte Carlo had engineered its turn into a U and was coming on. From the amount of smoke I saw behind it, the truck was following suit. Harvey flashed past like a subliminal commercial and then I had a turn coming up and a sign advising me to slow down to thirty-five. The sign wobbled in my seventy-mile-an-hour wake.

I felt the wheels leave the road and knew the instant when they decided not to come back. Gravel sprayed, grass swished, and then we were hurtling down a grade with nothing in front of us but blue Superior.

4

IT WAS ONE of those county sheriff's departments with brass hats and military titles and enough gold braid to hogtie a Democrat. We drew a major.

Not that he acknowledged the title, engraved on a brass bar on his chest along with the name R. E. AXHORN. He was a big Ojibway with iron gray in his short black hair and black eyes in a broad pitted face the color of old blood, wearing a brown leather jacket over a buff-and-brown uniform and a revolver with a cherrywood grip in a holster behind his right hip. He shook my hand and then DeVries's and took a seat in the wing-backed chair facing the sofa we were sitting on, leaning forward to keep his weight off the gun.

The living room was in back of a rock shop belonging to an old man named Coulee who had waded in up to his hips to help tie a rope to my rear bumper and the other end around a tree to keep the car above water until the wrecker came. DeVries and I had managed to rescue the big man's overnight bag and my valise containing changes of clothes and now we were wearing them, growing warm and drowsy in the heat of a small woodstove, our hands wrapped around two man-size porcelain mugs full of steaming coffee laced with bourbon. The coldest winter I'd ever spent was twenty minutes in Lake Superior in late spring.

We were alone with Axhorn and a Corporal Hale, six feet and a hundred and forty pounds of elbows and Adam's apple in a neat uniform, smoking a cigarette at a window overlooking the lake. Coulee was in the shop polishing the largest collection of Petoskey stone north of—well, Petoskey. He had gone up to Eagle River from his home in Dowagiac before the Depression to mine copper, moved to Harvey after the market bottomed out, and hadn't been off the peninsula in sixty years. He had told us all this while we were diving for Chevies.

For a minute Axhorn sat without speaking, bent forward with his elbows on his thighs, circling the brim of his Stetson through his fingers Gary Cooper fashion. Then he looked up at me from under his brows. "You told Corporal Hale you were run off the road?"

"Not exactly," I said. "I lost it on the curve while we were being chased."

"Sure it was a chase?"

"Not if you don't want one."

He stopped circling his hatbrim. "What might that mean?"

"I saw what looked like a trap closing and reversed ends and got out of there. They turned around and followed, scratching up asphalt. Could be both drivers remembered something they'd left behind at the same moment and were in the same hurry to go back and get it. Could be they were in so much of a hurry they both kept going after we went into the water. It doesn't have to be that they heard Hale's siren and rabbited. If the paperwork's easier that way we won't yell."

After a space he said, "Which one of you is the convict?"

"Ex," DeVries said. "Ex-convict."

Axhorn went on looking at me. "That makes you the private eye. I figured."

"What might *that* mean?"

"On TV the big-city eye is always breaking down in some hick county with a crooked sheriff that wants to see the eye on his way. City cops are always clean, it's the counties got their fingers in some pie. Some do, I guess. If you watch enough TV you think they all do."

"Sorry, Major. I guess you didn't pick out all that brass."

"Yeah." He glanced down at his nameplate. "County work's hell. The higher you get the more metal they hang on you and the closer you are to unemployment every time a new sheriff gets elected. Either of you grab a license plate number?"

I shook my head. "The truck was smoking too much and we never saw the back of the Monte Carlo."

"Describe the truck."

"A maroon Dodge beater with a board mounted up front in place of a bumper. Needs new rings bad."

"That's Burt Wakely's rig," Hale said.

"Who's Burt Wakely?" I asked.

"Burt and his brother Hank are old customers at County." Axhorn studied his hatband. "This don't sound like anything they'd get tangled in, though. They'll get drunk and bust up a place or take somebody's car for a spin without exactly asking for it, but road piracy's outside their specialty, or was last I heard. If you'll sign a complaint we'll bring them in for a talk."

"They the kind that talks?"

"In a bar maybe. Not to the law."

"Forget it then. What about the Monte Carlo? Black, this year's model?"

"Probably a transient. The year-rounds in this county like to eat. You can't do that and own a fifteen-thousand-dollar automobile up here. The summer people, maybe. You might have noticed it isn't summer."

"I noticed." I inhaled some whiskey fumes and felt the amber glow spreading through me.

"Maybe you got some idea why Burt Wakely might want to turn hijacker."

I met his polished ebony gaze. "No."

"Your friend don't talk much."

DeVries said, "Where I come from you don't talk till someone talks to you."

Axhorn looked at him. "What's a convict—*ex*-convict, excuse me all to hell—want with the company of a private cop two hours after he's released? I never been, but if I was to make a list of the people I'd care to spend time with straight off the block, that one wouldn't make the first fifty."

"I been in twenty years. Somebody has to show me around."

The Indian waited for more. His profile belonged on a penny. The telephone rang then on the stand next to his chair. He waited politely for Coulee to come in and answer it, then picked it up on the fourth ring.

"Hello? Bob Axhorn, who are you? Okay. That bad, huh? Yeah, I'll tell him." He hung up and looked at me. "That was Andy at the garage. They've got to gut your car and pump out the tank and fuel line. It'll be ready Monday."

"I'm due in Detroit Friday," DeVries said.

"There a car rental place around here?" I asked.

"Marquette." Axhorn glanced at the big watch on his wrist. "They'll be closed now. Long hours are for the tourist season. You can try them in the morning. Lots of vacancies in the motels now."

"You want us to check in when we get registered?"

"I'll find you if I need you. I don't know why I would. It's just another accident involving a crazy downstater as far as the department's concerned. I ought to have Corporal Hale ticket you, but you might take it into your head to fight it, and what I most don't want is to see you hanging around here any longer than it takes to get your car fixed and go home and stay there." He rose in one smooth movement and put on his Stetson. It made him look like a cavalry scout.

I put down my mug and got up. "It's not you, Major. It's just neater this way."

"I don't want to hear it." He looked down at DeVries, hunkered over his coffee in a gray flannel shirt and stiff new jeans that left his ankles bare. "The speech don't change. Whatever you did that took you down don't matter to me. What does is you take it out of this county."

"I hear you."

"Where do these Wakelys hang out?" I asked.

Axhorn regarded me. "They got a shack a mile down White Road off Twenty-Eight east of Harvey. You don't want to mess with them, though. They wrestle them big flatbeds for the lumber company and they're both as strong as black bears and twice as mean. Your big friend might take one of them if he don't turn his back on the other. They eat running backs like you for breakfast."

"Thanks for the advice."

"Don't bother. I'm paid to keep the peace."

Hale put out his cigarette in an ashtray made from a hunk of raw green copper and followed his superior out. We heard Axhorn talking to Coulee, then the front door slammed. I groped in my shirt pocket, remembered I'd drenched my last pack of Winstons in the lake, and let my hand drop. "Any ideas?"

DeVries rolled his mug between his big palms. "Andrew or Albert."

"Would he know you were getting out today?"

"One phone call would of done it."

"It might not have been you they were after. I'm not as popular as I look. Or it could have been an honest hijacking. The world's changed, like I said."

"It ain't changed so much I'll buy that one." He stood. I winced, but his head fell an inch short of the exposed oak rafters. "Let's go see if your money's dry and find a restaurant. I'm hungry enough to eat the asshole out of a skunk."

"More fast food?"

"I ain't *that* hungry."

Coulee was a short wide gnome with a cap of white hair and blue eyes like glass shards in a face nearly as dark as Axhorn's. He was as deaf as driftwood, but he got our meaning finally and gave us back our things, only slightly damp now that they'd been spread out near the stove. Some of the ink had run along the edges of the library printout, but the picture was intact. I offered the old man fifty dollars for his help and hospitality. He surprised me by accepting it.

The sun was setting in Keweenau Bay, tinting the water orange and making black hairy fingers of the points of land and scrub pines stretched across it. Gulls congregated on the knuckles and took off in a dozen directions, dive-bombing the lake and looping back up in a sudden acceleration of wings, their shrill calls sounding like two boards mating. As the water cooled, a chill wind riffled the surface and found its way through our clothes to the skin, as it had with white and black mariners for two hundred years, and with the brown-skinned paddlers of dugout canoes for twenty thousand years before them. The lake was a continual awareness unaffected by eons, changing only when it chose and then lapsing back into the immutable calm it had known since the last glacier. Maybe it wasn't so bad to be a prisoner on its shore. Doing time means nothing where time doesn't exist.

We hoisted our worldly belongings under our arms and went in search of food and lodging.

5

THE MOTEL HAD EVERYTHING except a Victorian mansion on the hill and a nervous taxidermist in the office. In his place was a woman of Coulee's height and general age group in a curly blond wig and man's canvas jacket turned back twice at the cuffs, who gave our waterstained luggage the fish eye and told me I'd forgotten to write my license plate number on the registration card.

"We came on foot."

"Thirty-five dollars," she snapped. "In advance."

When I'd forked it over she directed us to one of six log bungalows on a dirt lot. The only vehicle nearby was a spanking new silver Ford four-by-four pickup with a snowblade on the front, parked under an outside light behind the office. I glanced inside at the tasseled pillow on the driver's seat and the wooden blocks tied to the floor pedals and decided the old lady made her payments with her guests' gold fillings.

DeVries was thinking the same thing. "If it's okay with you I'm sleeping with the lights on tonight."

Our bungalow had two double beds, an Indian rug made by the Taiwan tribe, an obese lamp, and a water closet worthy of the name. The plastic sanitized glasses on the ledge over the sink were the only things in it not nailed or bolted down. Everything was spotless, at least; what the Upper Peninsulans don't spend on luxury goes into clean. I kicked one of the beds. "I guess sleeping with your feet hanging over the end is nothing new to you. Which one you want?"

He threw his bag onto the one nearer the bathroom. "I'm used to sleeping next to a toilet."

I stripped the cellophane off a glass and drank some water. We'd eaten in a family place on the edge of Harvey, complete with red-and-white-checked tablecloths and friendly waitresses and enough garlic in the spaghetti sauce to float the Vatican; my upper tract had sworn a vendetta. When I came out of the bathroom, DeVries was still standing between the beds. He had a look on his face like a little boy at Disney World. "So when do we go see the Wakely brothers?"

"Who said we would?" I asked.

"We walked past three other places looked better than this. If what Axhorn told us is right we're just a brisk walk from their shack."

"*I* am. You're a hundred miles away. If it comes to busting heads, I don't have a parole to worry about. I thought that was why you hired me."

"I been free six hours now. I'm ruint for staying put 'cause someone tells me to. Besides, you heard what the cop said."

"I'm tougher than I look."

"I got you beat there. I'm *just* as tough as I look."

"You're too big to argue with. Get some sleep. It's coming on your bedtime and I need you fresh and dewy-eyed when we take on the Wilderness Family."

He took his bag off his bed, stretched out on it fully clothed, and was asleep inside five minutes, snoring evenly. Sleeping when you're not tired is one thing prison teaches you. I opened my valise on the other bed and got out the S&W Police Special I'd been carrying for eight years. It was dry in its holster and chamois leather wrap I used to keep it from bouncing around in the case, but just for luck I unloaded it and cleaned and oiled it from the kit and wiped off each of the cartridges before replacing them. Then I put it aside and lay on the bed and wished I had a cigarette until it was time to wake my client.

A light fog was rolling off the lake and collecting in the hollows when we turned off the highway and started on foot down White Road. My jacket was still damp; I moved my shoulders around inside it to generate some heat. Under a ragged milkwater moon the big man at my side looked like a shadow cast by me and was making about that much noise. Giants have more practice at being quiet than the rest of us.

The road was fine sand, which is all there is up there besides rock, flanked by sixty-foot pines as silent as cemetery monuments. It was too cool even for mosquitoes. We were the only things stirring in a cerecloth stillness that seemed unnatural. Each tree concealed another ghost clad in peacoat or breechclout, leggings or French tunic. It made me want to walk faster and whistle.

The distance seemed much longer than a mile. It was probably about that. A light hung in the trees like the last pear of autumn, disappearing as the trunks came between, then appearing again closer. We rounded a slight bend and then we were standing at the end of a rutted drive terminating in the sort of slant-roofed board-and-batten hovel that hunters used to build before the area became more popular with vacationers. The battered truck whose driver had tried to seal us off on US-41 was parked in front of it with its plank bumper pointed toward the road. An older white Buick sat next to it with one red fender and its wheel wells gone lacy with rust. No new black Monte Carlos here.

DeVries bent down and whispered, "Think they got dogs?"

"Everyone up here has dogs."

We started up the drive, feeling the ruts with our feet before trusting our weight. The yard, really a bare clearing in the forest, was littered with rusting engine parts and empty oil cans. Keeping the Dodge going was costing them more over the long run than a new truck. Nearing the lighted window I gestured to DeVries to hold his position and covered the rest of the distance in a crouch.

I put an eye to a corner. The air was just cool enough to fog the glass and I cleared a peephole with my thumb. Inside, the place was all one room with a big quilt draped over a clothesline at the back, probably masking the beds. It had a new rug on the floor and some worn furniture and a black-and-white TV set with snow on the screen and a stereo in an expensive walnut cabinet that looked new. I wondered how long it would be before the downstater who belonged to the stereo visited his cottage and found it missing. But I was more interested in the girl who was watching TV.

She was a brunette of about twenty, very pregnant, in a housedress with sunflowers on it, sitting on a stiff kitchen chair with her hands folded on top of her massive belly and her legs splayed. She was barefoot, which seemed appropriate, and the nipples of her swollen breasts were plainly visible through the thin material of the dress. Although she was staring at the screen she didn't appear to be paying attention to what was going on there. If the sound was on at all it was turned too low for me to hear it through the window. I waited until I saw her breathe, then withdrew to tell DeVries what I'd seen, keeping my voice low.

"The men must be around," he said. "Their ve-hicles are here and I don't figure them to be big for walking."

"Keep an eye on the front. I'm going to get a look at what's behind that quilt."

I was almost around the corner of the building before I remembered what I'd said about dogs. A big shepherd with more wolf in it than domestic pet came bounding around from the back, dragging a chain and yammering fit to shake the needles off the pines. Ivory teeth flashed in its black muzzle. I drew the gun and backpedaled, aiming between its eyes. Just then it came to the end of its chain with a wham. It strained forward with its hackles standing, barking and snarling and collecting foam in the corners of its mouth.

"Walker!"

I was wearing my magic stupid ring that night. Walking past the truck I hadn't noticed the open door on the passenger's side, or the hulk passed out across the seat. Now he rose up and off it like some swamp monster, six feet and two hundred and fifty pounds of fat and muscle in overalls, scooping a shotgun off a rack below the rear window. But DeVries's shout had startled him before he could level it at me, and as he was turning in the ex-convict's direction I had six chances to drop him before he remembered me. So naturally I didn't shoot. Instead I charged him.

For all his bulk and obvious drunkenness he had reflexes like a cat's. I was halfway to him when the shotgun swung back around and I could see myself snatched off my feet by the blast, pieces of me flying all over and lighting in the trees. DeVries yelled again—just a yell this time, not a name or a word anyone would recognize—but Overalls wasn't going to be distracted by that a second time. In the light from the window I saw his finger tensing on the trigger. All this time I was still running, my feet touching the ground in slow motion, a running dead man trying to gain as many yards as possible before the whistle.

DeVries's next shout had a new quality: a killing edge. It made both of us stop what we were doing and look at him. He was standing on the sagging boards of the porch with one huge arm bent across the pregnant girl's throat. Her bare feet were off the ground and from the position she was in he had his other hand around her wrist and her arm locked behind her back. She had come outside to see what the commotion was about and DeVries had acted with the speed that would have made him a basketball star if the law hadn't beaten the scouts to him. The girl was grimacing, but in her eyes was the same blank look she'd been giving the television screen. I'd seen that look in hospitals and nursing homes, directed at the walls.

"Lurleen." The name had a dull sound in Overalls' mouth, like thumping a grain barrel.

"I'll break her, man."

I couldn't tell if DeVries meant it. For a man his size, doing it was easier than saying it. I saw the fight go out of Overalls' eyes. They were big and brown in a red face with dun-colored stubble. He looked to be in his late thirties. The shotgun came down.

After a beat I stepped forward and took it out of his hands. He stank of whiskey and caked sweat and dirt. I holstered the revolver.

"Burt?" said Lurleen. She had a little girl's voice.

"Where's your brother?" I asked Burt.

He was still thinking about that one when a man in an undershirt and patched jeans came to the shack's open door from inside. He was as tall as Burt but not as broad. Light from behind him limned his slabbed solid frame and sparkled off the sight of the big automatic pistol in his left hand. He was black-bearded with a white streak in his rumpled hair, a birthmark. His feet were bare. He was younger than Burt.

"You're Hank?" I trained the shotgun on him.

He gestured with the automatic at the bigger weapon. "It ain't loaded. Burt can't be trusted with no loaded gun. One beer makes him crazy."

I swiveled the shotgun aside and squeezed the trigger. It clicked. I lowered the barrel.

"Put it down or I break her," DeVries told Hank. He had moved to the end of the porch to keep both brothers in sight.

"Nigger, if you move I'll shoot your eye out."

We were like that for a while. There was something in the way he held the gun. I said, " 'Nam?"

"Grenada. You?"

I nodded. "Cambodia too. Why the marines? That's strictly volunteer."

"I had some trouble here and walked into the first place I came to and raised my right hand. Next time I'll take the trouble."

"Give it time. It'll fester out."

"This here's private property. Come in here, scare my brother, threaten Lurleen. Who the hell are you?"

"This afternoon somebody driving that truck cut us off on Forty-One," I said. "I figure whoever it was was being paid by the man who tried to close the back door. He was driving a new black Monte Carlo."

"That truck was here all day."

"We're not the law. All we want is answers."

He said nothing. The automatic was cocked.

I said, "I know how things are up here. The farming stinks, the Indians have a lock on the commercial fishing because of the treaty, and the tourist season's too short. The law's spread thin. A man has to support his family, especially with a baby coming."

"Lurleen's our cousin Clyde's girl," Hank said. "He's got six months left in the federal house in Milan. I promised him we'd look after her."

"That was you in the truck."

He made a decision. "I didn't figure you drownded."

"Family's family," I said. "The lumber business is tight. I figure you're laid off to be free in the middle of the week. A man comes up from downstate with money to spend, he asks around and finds a couple of hard local numbers, who's to tell them they're wrong to listen? All we want is his name."

"I don't have to be talking. I can take my time shooting the nigger and then do you. Me and Burt will just haul your bodies back to the bog and dump you in. They won't find you for a thousand years."

DeVries said, "I'll still break her before I hit the ground."

"Let her go," I said.

"No way, man."

"Hank's no killer or you'd be dead. You still will be if you make a move. I'll help him."

"You're working for me!"

"Up to a point. You're standing on it."

After a minute he said, "Shit," and lowered Lurleen to her feet. She ducked under his arm and huddled close to Hank. He made room in the doorway. "Get to bed."

She fled inside. He stepped out onto the porch and pulled

the door shut behind him. He was still holding the pistol. Without the light at his back he looked older; the kind of older that comes on overnight. I wondered if the white streak in his hair was a birthmark after all.

I said, "I'm going to reach inside my coat."

"No, you ain't."

"The heat's on my right side in back. Burt can have it. It's not what I want to get."

He said nothing while saying everything.

"It's a photograph," I said. "It might be the man who hired you to stop us. If you tell us yes or no and maybe put a name to him we'll be on our way."

"I don't think so."

"Lurleen's going to need a hospital in a few weeks. I'm thinking whatever he paid you won't settle the bill."

That got to him, but not in the way I thought. "Mister, how cheap you think we work?"

"It will, then," I said after a pause. "I'm impressed."

DeVries spat, rubbing the spittle automatically into the porch boards. Prison habit. "Redneck talk. I didn't figure to hear it this far north."

I said, "The Dodge needs an overhaul. That's expensive too."

"Talk plain," Hank said.

"I talk plainer indoors."

The forest was quiet. It was too early for crickets. Hank said, "Take his gun, Burt."

A horned hand fumbled under my coat, found the butt, and jerked it out. He relieved me of the empty shotgun too. It took some coaxing, but finally he went over to his brother and surrendered the revolver. Hank stuck it in his belt, took the automatic off cock, and went inside, leaving the door open.

6

THE PLACE WAS COZIER than it looked from outside. A barrel stove kept the temperature in the middle sixties and someone had erected insulation and drywall over the scrap lumber from which the shack was built. Pictures of the fishin' hole variety decorated the walls in drugstore frames—Lurleen's contribution, most likely. She was nowhere in sight, having apparently obeyed Hank's order and retired behind the hanging quilt. Hank and I sat at an oilcloth-covered table with a half-empty bottle of Seagram's and a smeared glass on top. He laid the automatic and my revolver on his side of the table like a riverboat gambler and poured himself a drink.

Burt and DeVries remained standing, the black man hunched a little in front of the door to keep his head from banging the plaster ceiling, Hank's brother by the quilt as if to guard Lurleen. The useless shotgun dangled at his side.

Hank was looking at me with eyes no deeper than cigarette foil. His beard was well trimmed and his hair and clothes clean; the unkempt effect was strictly attitude. When the silence got long I peeled two fifties out of my wallet and set the bottle on top of them. Then I slid the wrinkled envelope out of my inside pocket.

"The man standing on the right." I showed him the printout. "Is he the one who hired you?"

He studied the photograph for a tenth of a second. "Wasn't him."

"Sure? That was taken a few years back. He might have changed."

He splashed some whiskey down his throat. "Take more'n a few years to turn a colored man white."

"He's lying," DeVries said.

"Yeah, I lie all the time when I got the guns."

"Any name?" I asked. "What'd he look like?"

"Like a colored man. He had a black car and green money. He never gave no name. Tried talking to Burt first, but Burt don't like the coloreds. Said if we helped him follow this here big nigger was getting out of the prison and helped stop him he'd pay us enough to put something down on a new truck."

"He say why he wanted to stop him?"

"Talk, he said."

"Believe him?"

He might have smiled in his beard, or maybe not. It wouldn't mean much either way. "You seen this place. Man bought the believing."

"You weren't curious?"

"Some. Not enough to risk scaring him off."

"That's no answer."

"Sure it is," DeVries said.

I looked at him, standing with his hands hanging at his sides. Where he'd been there were no belts to hook your thumbs on and they slapped your hands out of your pockets. "You come from no money you learn to respect it when you see it," he said. "Your belly's empty and somebody offers you a chicken leg you don't turn it over to see did he drop it on the floor."

His eyes were on Hank when he said it. Hank was looking back and there was something there that cut through race and environment, a thing I would never share with either one of them. I felt like a husband at his wife's high school reunion. "I need a description," I said. "Don't tell me again he looked colored."

Hank emptied his glass. "He had gray hair and a thick neck. Nice suit of clothes."

"Tall? Short? How old? Was he solid or just fat? Did he talk like a sharecropper or an arithmetic teacher, and did he have any kind of accent? Did he carry a perfumed handkerchief in his sleeve, or did he spit his tobacco juice just anywhere? Feel free to jump in whenever you like."

Burt said, "Want me to knock him, Hank?" A liverish flush had crept up into the older Wakely's hairline.

"Stay put. Mister, you don't raise your voice in our daddy's house."

I lifted a hand and let it drop. Their story held no interest for me, and probably no surprises. An alcoholic father, maybe both parents alcoholic, and maybe too a death or a desertion and then a steady stream of aunts or uncles who smelled of lilacs and who kept missing their buses and having to stay overnight while the kids occupied themselves torturing small animals in the backyard. No one who raised himself ever made much of a job of it. It would be starting all over again with Lurleen's child. I had a dusty degree in sociology, which meant I could come up with questions for all the answers. It was a runaway hit at cocktail parties, if you liked cocktail parties.

"What happened when you didn't get us?" I asked. "Did he stiff you?"

This time he didn't smile. "He wanted to. Burt wouldn't let him."

"He didn't know the shotgun wasn't loaded, I take it. Then what?"

"Then nothing. We separated there on the highway after he gave us the money. He's halfway home by now, most like."

"I guess I'd just be catching a cold through my mouth if I opened it to ask if you got the license plate of the Monte Carlo."

"Just the last part. D-R-Y."

I looked at Burt and reached up and pushed my jaw shut. His face was still flushed but now it looked like its natural shade. A big proud grin shambled across his features at my expression.

Hank said, "Burt's partial to letters. Word puzzles are his favorite, if the words ain't too long."

"Buy him some out of the hundred." I got up. "Can we go, or are you planning to stuff us and mount us out by the road?"

"I didn't want you here in the first place."

He saw me looking at my gun and picked it up and swung out the cylinder and tipped the cartridges out onto the table. Executing a neat border roll he held it out butt-first. I accepted it and returned it to leather. "If he comes back, save him some trouble. Tell him we're on our way to Detroit."

"He'd best not come back. Burt don't like welchers worse'n he don't like coloreds."

"Burt isn't the one he has to worry about."

DeVries held the door, covering my back. He didn't need weapons. Hank could empty his clip into the big man's chest and still die of a broken neck.

"Redstick ranger," Hank said.

I turned in the doorway.

"Something the colored said." He studied the letters stamped on the side of the automatic. "I asked him why didn't he take the front car, on account of his was faster. He said he'd leave that to us, what'd we think he was, a redstick ranger? Maybe that means something to you."

"Not me. You?"

DeVries shook his head.

"Well, it's what he said."

I said, "Thanks."

"You bought it. Store's closed after this."

When we stepped outside the dog lunged to the end of its chain and set up a howl. Burt came out behind us with the shotgun and swept the stock against the side of the dog's head. It yelped and slunk back behind the shack.

On our way back to the highway, DeVries asked what next.

"Next we sleep. Then if the old lady who runs the motel hasn't cut our throats for what's in our pockets we round up some wheels and roll home. Unless you want to troll for salmon or take in the Mystery Spot."

"Don't you at least want Axhorn to run that plate?"

"I can have that done in Detroit. Something tells me that's where we'll find the owner."

"Figure he's working for Andrew-Albert?"

"I never figure without figures to figure."

"You some detective."

I stopped in the motel office and bought a pack of Winstons from the machine. The old lady was dumped in a chair behind the desk, snoring like a lumberjack. DeVries was asleep on his bed in all his clothes when I got to the bungalow. I sat up smoking in mine until eleven, then undressed and turned in, dreaming of watery graves. I woke up wet the next morning.

DeVries, accustomed to early rising, was already washed and shaved, his shotgun-pattern beard trimmed to Spartan neatness. I did a sloppier job in the light of the twenty-five-watt bulb over the sink. We packed our things and walked to the same restaurant for eggs and sausage. He had a double portion.

"Prison's the only place I ever got all I wanted to eat," he said, letting the waitress fill his coffee cup for the sixth time. "They like you fat there; harder to squeeze through the bars and jump the wall."

"You aren't fat."

"They only gave us twenty minutes to eat."

From there we went to the garage where they had towed my car, spread out now in a hundred pieces on a concrete floor slanting down toward a drain at the back. The seats had been removed and the carpet draped over a pair of sawhorses to dry. Major Axhorn was standing in the middle of it all in the same Stetson and leather jacket with his hands in the slash pockets. It was a dank morning.

"Breaks your heart, don't it?" he said. "Like going to the

emergency room in the middle of the night and a nurse handing you your son's clothes."

"A cop with a son." I put down my valise and lit a cigarette. "I thought you just split in two like amoebas."

"I didn't say I had one. My wife works. Keeps the books on an avocado ranch."

"Someone told me all the avocados in this country were grown in California."

"He was right."

A tall white-whiskered man in a greasy blue flannel jacket and matching greasy workpants approached me, wiping his hands on a clean rag that was greasy when he finished with it. "You're Mr. Walker?"

"How's it look?"

"Fuses all need replacing, and maybe the wiring. We won't know what else till we find it. This turned up under the dash." He pulled my Luger out of his hip pocket and extended the grip. I took it. "Better swab it out and oil it," he said.

I thanked him and thrust it under my belt opposite the Police Special. "When will the car be ready?"

"Sometime next week."

"Last night you said Monday."

"Maybe Monday. Where can we reach you?"

I gave him a card, as if he were really planning to call and I were really expecting him to. I got his card, which was the one that counted, and he stuck mine in his shirt pocket behind a plastic pen holder and went back to the gutted chassis. I asked Axhorn if he'd been waiting long.

"Just about twenty minutes. I figured you'd swing by here before or after you rented a car. That gun registered?"

"My CCW's up to date," I evaded. "What's the squeal?"

"State police found an abandoned black Chevrolet Monte Carlo about three o'clock this morning outside Mackinaw City. Thought you might like to know."

I dropped some ash on the floor and stepped on it. Up there they like you to keep track of fires. "Orphans don't usually turn up that quick."

"Fellow from Lansing come up for a long sailing weekend and found it in his driveway. I got it off the wire when I opened the office and called the Mackinaw City post."

"They run the plate?"

He nodded. "City woman there reported it stolen night before last. Three-oh-six-D-R-Y. Folks started remembering their license plates when the Secretary of State's office started using vowels. You get some good ones."

"Helped the time go faster when we was stamping them," DeVries said. He was hardly paying attention to what he was saying. I raised some dust to draw Axhorn's attention from the big man's excitement. "Could be the car. Those new full-sizes get boosted all the time."

"I didn't say this one was new."

"Wasn't it?"

"Yeah." He surrendered the point. "Man from downstate parks his car below the bridge, lifts one, then dumps it close by when he's done so he don't have to walk too far to get his. That spells professional. That fit in with how you worked it out?"

"We don't have anything worked out," I said. "It might not even be the same car, like I said."

He changed the subject. "Went out to the Wakely place, did you?"

"Nice family. Mean dog."

"Got back all of a piece, too. Must of been that gun on your other hip."

"You've got sharp eyes."

"Comes with being an Indian. Hope I don't got any cleaning up to do down White Road. Lurleen being in a family way she might have an idiot child."

"If she does you can blame genetics. Nobody did any bleeding, although I can't answer for the pooch. It's shotgun trained." I blew smoke. "I thought you preferred to be called native Americans."

"I never heard one call himself that. I think a white liberal invented it. They're the ones fizzing all over about the land that got stole. Only you can't steal land, it belongs to everyone. That was the whole idea. I grew up on the La Pointe reservation, served with the Indian police. We drove the drunks home, talked the husbands and wives out of carving on each other, drove the drunks home, bailed the brawlers out of jail in Ironwood, drove the drunks home. Nobody wanted to be there, including us. It never was that we wanted something, just what we didn't want, and we didn't want to be there."

"So you left."

"I joined the army and became an MP. That choice wasn't there for the old ones and the young ones that didn't measure up. They're still there, getting drunk and carving on each other and going to jail. You stay where they feed you."

I dropped my cigarette and squashed it out. "I was an MP."

"Same job only different. It's always different when they're not your own." He looked at DeVries. "You still waiting to get talked to?"

"Why talk?" he said. "Ain't nobody listening."

"You been in too long. They're listening now."

It was the second time in twelve hours I'd been shoved outside. I elbowed my way back in. "What's the phrase 'redstick ranger' mean to you?"

"Sounds like a slur. I been called most of the others but never that one. Where'd you hear it?"

"Around."

"Yeah?" He waited, then shifted his attention to the polished toes of his boots. "Well, I guess you know it all now. No need for a big dumb blankethead to come around sticking his horns in."

"We appreciate the help," I said. "It just isn't a local fight."

The brim of his hat came up. His face was as calm as a Red Man label. "I live here, mister. This isn't just a place to stretch my legs and pee like it is for you. Next time don't take your fights into my county. I got all I can handle with the natives."

7

"YOU BETTER HOPE you never need Axhorn's help," DeVries said.

We were on I-75 heading south in a new rented Renault that was built about as well as the Maginot Line. Afternoon sun was spreading and the Mackinac Bridge hove in sight, looking at that distance more like cobwebs strung on a row of mop handles than the world's fourth longest suspension bridge. The little motor chugged along on two cylinders most of the time, then squirted ahead on all four without warning before cutting back again with a little Gallic cough. We were saving gasoline but I missed the V-8 dinosaurs they used to sing about on beaches. There just aren't any catchy rhymes for "transverse-mounted engine."

I said, "You have to watch the human ones like Axhorn. Pretty soon you forget they're cops and there you are in a broom closet down at the station telling everything to a tape machine. We didn't have that kind of time."

"Bullshit. You was worried about busting my parole."

"It's something to think about. Even if it's not your fault it doesn't look good for an ex-convict fresh out of the wash to be involved in high-speed chases and confronting known troublemakers in their homes. If they dug and found out you threatened the Wakelys with the girl you'd be back inside quick as spit. If I'd thought Corporal Hale hadn't seen more of what happened on the highway I wouldn't have told them as much as I did. I overcompensated there. One of the first things you'll notice about me is I fall down as often as I get up."

"You looked okay in front of Hank's pistol."

"So did you. We'll make a couple of brave corpses someday."

He tried sliding his seat farther back. He was practically sitting in the trunk as it was. "At least we know it's Albert-Andrew behind it."

"How do we know that?"

"What Axhorn said about the job being professional. Guy palling around with Tim Marianne could hire all the muscle he needed."

"I want to check out something else first."

"What else is there to check?"

"What Davy Jackson's relatives are up to these days."

"Davy got hisself killed trying to take down that armored car. I didn't have nothing to do with that, why'd they care about me?"

"The law thinks you had everything to do with it. Maybe he left behind someone who agrees."

"His folks was shit-poor. They couldn't afford the trip up here, never mind paying somebody to take it for them."

"Twenty years is a long time to get rich in."

"Not in my old neighborhood."

Our tires whistled on the bridge. Last night's fog had cleared and the water of the straits flashed metal-bright between the struts. On the center span we were skyscraper height above the surface, yet it looked close enough to dip a hand in. Here and there workers with coveralls on over their coats hung on the cables like spiders while they scraped and painted the sandy steel. They were there every day all year long except when it rained or snowed, painting and scraping and painting again, never finishing before it was time to start all over. They'd have made good detectives.

On the other side I paid the toll and we negotiated the broad crooked streets of Mackinaw City with fudge shops and billboards advertising tours on either side. Behind us an ore carrier as long as a football field was gliding under the bridge. The gulls were as thick as pigeons. While I followed the signs back to the expressway, DeVries filled me in on Davy Jackson's family. It sounded like "Roots."

We stopped to eat at a Wendy's in Grayling, a fishing and deer-hunting town gone to K-Marts and Ben Franklin stores and chain restaurants, and finished the trip in a four-hour straight shot into Detroit. Our way took us through farm country, flat and green as a crap table, past Amish barns with Quakerly faces painted twenty feet wide on the ends, and past the new Zilwaukee Bridge, still unfinished after five years, rising like Roman ruins out of the low Thumb area, cracked and leaning with a monster crane marooned on top. Detroit had made haste in the middle of the scandal to hire the same engineer for its downtown People Mover project, still unfinished after three years. DeVries liked the farms best.

"I wasn't looking at them much coming up in the bus," he said. "I was busy hoping somebody'd broadside us and I'd be out a window."

"Hard to believe all this will fall apart if a couple of plants close in Detroit."

"That what they say there? Shit."

"It's worth a few million from the governor to say it."

"They put me away for stealing a lousy two hundred thousand."

"What was an armored car doing there in the middle of a riot anyway?" I asked.

"Every storeowner in the neighborhood was cleaning out their till. If you tried to do it yourself the National Guard shot you for looting. It was the modern American Revolution, man. Smash and grab and if you got shot you died for the cause and a color TV set."

"The thing had to have been planned. They had to have known the car would be there at that time."

"What my lawyer said in court. It didn't do no good."

"Who arrested you?"

" 'Guards held me down for a big white dude in plainclothes. I don't remember his name. Cops them days was all big and white."

"They're still big." Dusk was folding down south of the last Flint exit. I turned on the headlamps. The car slowed down. "It's a place to start. Closed cases have a special appeal for me. Nobody's waiting to part my hair with a nightstick."

"Why you want to go scratching around in that? I'm comin' home, I done my time. All I want's what's mine."

"Prison's worse than I thought," I said. "Piping pop rock into your cell can't be constitutional."

"Just find out who's got the money. I'll do what comes next."

"We'll discuss what comes next. Right now I'm most interested in finding out who wants to stop you before what comes first."

"The cops, maybe. Maybe they think I got the money stashed and I'll take them to it."

"In that case they'd have just followed you and tried not to look like cops following an economy-size ex-convict. Stealing a car and laying a trap isn't procedure. Besides, the insurance company would have paid that off long ago, and hiked its rates to cover the loss. It's like the money never existed."

"Makes it all the more mine."

We drove the last forty-five minutes in silence. I tried the radio and got the same static I'd gotten north of the straits. At that time I'd blamed it on the microwave telephone towers they use up there, but it was just the French getting back at us for New Orleans. We swept under a riot of layered overpasses into Detroit, lit by forty-foot lamps on both sides of the expressway to discourage motorized rapists. It was a warm night that far south and music drifted out of a dozen rolled-down windows. I asked DeVries if he had a place to stay.

"Deputy warden gave me a voucher for a dump called the

Alamo on East Jefferson." He patted his shirt pockets, then remembered he was wearing different clothes. "If it didn't get soaked to pieces."

"It's a dump all right. I've got a couch at my place."

"Ain't you afraid I'll cut your throat for the silverware?"

"You haven't seen the silverware."

"I got used to my own company a long time ago. Thanks just the same."

The Alamo made a good case for being forgotten. The name was etched in sputtering orange neon across a plate-glass window with the shade pulled halfway down like a junkie's eyelid and the front door, a thick paneled oak job that had been refinished under Truman, stuck in its casing and required a shoulder to open. Inside, a green brass lamp with a crooked paper shade oozed light onto a waist-high counter with a floor register in front of it to catch coins. It was someone's job to empty it out once a month and pay the electric bill. On the wall behind the counter, next to a life-size acrylic painting on black velvet of John Wayne dressed as Davy Crockett, a sign was tacked reading:

THE ALAMO HOTEL
(Permanents and Transients)
No Pet's
No Children
No Visitor's in Rooms
No TV or Radio after 10:00 P.M.
Enjoy Your Stay

A squashed fly dotted the *i* in "Children."

We were sharing the lobby with a square of trod rug and a wicker chair on a pedestal fashioned after an elephant's foot. DeVries slapped the bell on the counter. It went click. After a minute, John Wayne swung away from us and a cadaver in a shawl collar and brown wing tips came in through a door squirreled behind the painting. He was a tall item of forty or sixty, but nowhere near as tall as DeVries, with black hair pasted down on a narrow skull and fuzzy white sidewalls and white stubble on his chin. When he stopped at the counter with the light coming up at him through the opening in the top of the lampshade he looked just like Vincent Price.

DeVries got out the wrinkled voucher he had separated from the clothes in his overnight bag and smoothed it out on the counter. "They told me this is good for a week," he said.

Vincent Price didn't look down at it. "Ten bucks."

"They said the room's paid for. State takes care of it."

"The ten bucks is for you. Leave the paper."

The big man ran a hand over his beard.

"Welfare scam," I said. "He rents the room to somebody else for the regular rate, then turns the voucher in to the state and gets paid a second time. It happens a lot during the winter when Lansing remembers the tramps and bag ladies on the street."

"I don't want ten bucks. I want a room."

Vincent Price hit the bell, and this time it rang. John Wayne got out of the way of a young, very fat black man in king-size green slacks and a paint-stained gray sweatshirt gnawed off above the elbows, who came in from the back and walked around the end of the counter to stand next to DeVries. He was carrying a Louisville Slugger.

The counterman said, "Take the ten or don't, but leave the paper."

DeVries took the baseball bat away and broke it over his knee. He tossed the pieces onto the counter. The big end rolled off and landed on the floor with a clank.

"Registration card." I waggled my fingers at Vincent Price, who took his jaw off the counter and slid one over. I selected a pen from a coffee cup full of them to hand to DeVries.

The fat man sent his right hook by Western Union. It started two inches above the rug and picked up speed as it rose, his body pivoting behind it with more grace than you'd have thought him capable of if you'd never seen a bouncer in action. DeVries watched it coming, then slapped it aside and stepped in and picked him up in both arms. He started squeezing.

Vincent Price reached under the counter. I pointed the Smith & Wesson at him. He relaxed and laid both hands on top, empty. I switched grips on the gun and clicked the pen. "E-I?" I asked.

"I-E. Big D and V." The big man's voice was strained. Not much, but a little. He was out of shape.

By the time I had the card filled out the fat man had lost consciousness, a large yarn doll dangling in the ex-convict's embrace. I said, "You better let him go now. He doesn't look black anymore."

He spread his arms and the bouncer slid out of them. The counterman looked down at him disgustedly. "You killed him."

Just then the man on the floor took a deep breath and started coughing like a cat. I said, "Nothing wrong with him that can't be cured with ten or twenty yards of tape and no pole-vaulting for a month. Key."

He slapped down a brass one with a green plastic tag. "Eighteen. Upstairs, end of the hall."

DeVries picked it up. "You want to meet here tomorrow, or your office?"

"I had a partner once. It didn't take." I put the gun behind my hip. "You hired me, remember?"

"Who's going to look after the shotguns and baseball bats?"

"I got this old without help."

He rubbed his beard. I was coming to know the gesture. I said, "The parole board says you can't get into trouble. It doesn't say you can't pay someone to get into it for you. I'll be in touch."

"Okay," he said after a silence. "Don't make me come looking for news. I stink at waiting. Marquette taught me that much."

I went out after shaking his hand. He was getting better at it. The bundle on the floor made a lowing noise.

8

Somebody had made a stab at breaking into my place while I was gone. During my routine inspection walk around the outside of the house I saw the gouges under the bedroom window where whoever it was had tried to force it with a pinch bar, but the paint was unbroken around the frame, so he must have given up. Maybe a blue-and-white had cruised down the street or—less likely—a neighbor had spotted him and sung out. It sure wasn't due to any burglarproofing on my part. The decision to live without bars on my windows was a hard one, right up there with electing not to change my sex. Not that there was anything inside worth taking except a cheap stereo, a geriatric TV, two suits, and a shower. The Persian rugs were all out being deloused.

I washed off the Upper Peninsula in the shower, put on a robe, and called my service for messages. A junior partner at a legal firm I sometimes collect affidavits for had called asking me to get back to him, then called again later to cancel the request. A man had tried to reach me saying he was a vampire and wanted someone to act as go-between with the police before he handed himself over; I should return his call anytime after sundown. Two people had called asking for me and then hung up without leaving their names. That would be the last I'd hear from them. It was a comfort to know I had a service and hadn't missed any of this.

I'd made a purchase at an all-night liquor store where an alert salesclerk operated the cash register one-handed, keeping the other out of sight under the drawer. I pulled the bottle out of the bag and corrupted the innocence of a clean glass in the kitchen, wound the Seth Thomas in the living room, put on something hoarse and smoky by Anita O'Day, and sat down in front of the speakers to wait for the mellow. Some men need a drink to wind down after a lively couple of days. I get along just fine on music and a drink.

Two issues of the *News* had been waiting for me on the doorstep. I'd forgotten to suspend delivery, which was why my would-be burglar had thought the place worth a try. That day's, Thursday's, had a front-page piece on Marianne Motors, which was seldom absent from the headlines now that production had begun on the Stiletto, a gunmetal sportabout designed for middle-aging men and women for whom the Corvette was too much car. An insert in the photograph that ran with the article showed the vehicle parked in the middle of a barren proving ground with gull wings raised, looking like a fiberglass bird of prey. The main picture featured a grinning Timothy Marianne accepting a check from a heavy dark-suited bald man who looked like he'd rather be anyplace else. The caption identified him as Hector Stutch, president and chairman of the board of Stutch Petrochemicals and one of the grandsons of Leland Stutch, who in 1901 had mounted an internal combustion engine on a carriage body in his father's barn and thirty years later sold the Stutch Motor Corporation to General Motors for eighty-five million Depression dollars. The Commodore, as old Leland had been known since retooling to produce minesweepers for the navy during the First World War, was reported in good health and semiretirement as Hector's consultant in the family mansion in Grosse Pointe, having observed his one hundredth birthday in February of that year. The photograph had been taken to commemorate Stutch Petrochemicals' investment of seven hundred and fifty million dollars in Marianne Motors.

The check was a dummy. Barons the likes of Stutch and

Marianne didn't get ink on their hands or stand in line at the bank. Someone who made twenty thousand a year tapped some keys and a number followed by a flock of zeroes flew through the ether from one corporate account into another. But that didn't make as good a picture.

The story that accompanied it was more of the same. With his customary flamboyance Marianne had acquired a bankrupt tractor plant downriver, razed most of it, put up a new building, and installed state-of-the-art equipment at a cost far exceeding what would have been needed to start from scratch. This had drawn plenty of criticism from the rest of the industry, but the local economy had benefited from the increased demand for labor and the energetic new magnate was a popular speaker on the chicken-and-peas circuit. He had used his considerable personal charm to wangle large investments at home and abroad, although none was as big as Stutch's. The reclusive Commodore was an unknown factor because of his age, but his grandsons were careful businessmen and speculation ran high that the financial vote of confidence would loosen a great many purse strings on Wall Street. In workingmen's bars throughout Detroit and its suburbs the patrons were singing "All day, all night, Marianne," referring to production at the Stiletto plant.

The media had fallen in love with him, the way they will with good-looking men who speak well and spend a lot of money and glitter when they walk. He had been consulted on everything from presidential candidacy to his favorite Christmas carol and always offered up something quotable that would offend nobody the public didn't want offended. Those editorialists and market analysts who counseled caution were trampled under the same stampede that had swept several local mediocre boxers and clownish ballplayers toward their inevitable Waterloos. It played hell with your faith in the basic wisdom of mankind.

I turned to the box scores to see where the Tigers stood, then read the funnies and my horoscope. I was warned to approach new ventures warily. I bought myself a wary second drink and warily flipped the record on the turntable. When that side was finished I tried some wary TV. It was getting thin by that time.

I caught the last twenty minutes of a colorized version of *Thirty Seconds Over Tokyo*—Spencer Tracy had blue eyes and a complexion like Deanna Durbin's—and then the newsbreak came on just before sign-off. Someone had blown up a restaurant in Beirut and so far three groups had claimed credit for the explosion. The President had caught a fish while on vacation. Local news was dominated by the press conference following the announcement of the Stutch deal with Marianne Motors. Wonder Boy himself broke the news, fielded a few hyper questions from the reporters, then turned the floor over to Alfred Hendriks, his new general manager, and strode out of the room, stopping at the door to look back and wave before passing through it. He had no bodyguards that I could spot. Which might mean that he had some very good bodyguards. In any case I wasn't paying too much attention to Marianne.

The reason for that was Alfred Hendriks. The slim handsome dark man who had taken his employer's place at the podium had aged slightly, but he was the same man who had been photographed with the automaker at the time the contract was signed with the UAW; the same man, according to Richard DeVries, who had handed DeVries a Molotov cocktail to cover for an armored car robbery during the worst race riots in the city's history.

9

I GOT UP the next morning with a stiff neck, some kind of delayed reaction to the dip in Lake Superior. I waggled it, bombarded it under the shower head, took a couple of aspirins, and rubbed in some cream from a tube that smelled like Stillman's Gym. After a cup of coffee and a radio weather report calling for unseasonably high temperatures I put on the blue summerweight and knotted a red silk tie that looked cool and nonabrasive to my freshly shaved throat. By then my neck had frozen up tighter than a fence post. Backing the Renault out of the garage was one for Torquemada.

My office mail was fanned out under the slot in the door with A. WALKER INVESTIGATIONS lettered on the glass. I read the envelopes on my way through the waiting room and dumped them into the wastebasket in the private office. I used the duster on the desk and telephone, called my service to tell them I was in the traces, then looked up a number in the metropolitan directory, and used the telephone again.

"Marianne Motors, executive offices." One of those quality-controlled female voices.

"Alfred Hendriks, please."

"One moment."

I listened to eight bars of the Marianne Motors advertising jingle.

"Mr. Hendriks' office." This one had been inspected even more closely.

"May I speak to Mr. Hendriks?"

"Who is calling?"

"Amos Walker."

"Hold, please."

Second chorus.

"I'm sorry, Mr. Hendriks is in a meeting. May I take a message?"

I said no and told her good-bye. I lit a cigarette and smoked half of it. Then I ran the gauntlet again. I knew the jingle by heart now.

"Mr. Hendriks' office."

I deepened my voice a notch. "This is Adolf Wentz, vice president in Investments at Stutch Petrochemicals. We've run into a hitch and I need to discuss it with Mr. Hendriks."

"One moment, Mr. Wentz."

The jingle was cut off in mid-lyric. "What sort of hitch?"

This was a man's voice, smoothly blended, but not smoothly enough to overcome the wheatfields in it; a toned-down Henry Fonda. "Mr. Hendriks?"

"What sort of hitch, Mr. Wentz?"

"Sort of none," I said. "Adolf Wentz was my algebra teacher in high school. Those German names cut through a lot. My name's Walker. I own a pocket comb with STUTCH PETROCHEMICALS stamped on it, but that's my only connection with the firm."

"If this is some kind of sales gimmick I want the name of your employer." There was no change in his tone. Those were the dangerous ones. Give me a yeller anytime.

"I'm a private investigator working for Richard DeVries. Maybe you remember the name."

"I meet a lot of people. You'd better give me a hint. A quick one."

"Twenty years ago, during the riots. You'd remember him. He's a whole lot bigger than a breadbox."

"Sorry, Walker. I was in England at the time of the riots, studying at Cambridge on the exchange program."

"He says it was Wayne State."

"I was at Wayne State for a year. The wrong year for the riots. I took my accounting degree from Michigan."

"Law, he said."

"Perish the thought. Your Mr. DeSoto is mistaken, Walker. Don't bother me again."

I listened to the dial tone for a moment, then cradled the receiver. Rubbed my rigid neck.

He shouldn't have said DeSoto. Either you remember a simple name like DeVries or you plain forget it. You don't get it wrong unless you try. Or maybe you do. There are just no rules for that sort of thing, only a grumbling in the guts, and I had that.

I decided to let it grumble for a while and got out my pocket notebook where I'd scratched down the information DeVries had fed me about Davy Jackson's family. If any of the slain armored car robber's relatives were still in the area and had a telephone I'd find them in the directory. The ex-convict was right about one thing: Twenty years isn't enough time to go from the smell of cooked cabbage in the hallway to an unlisted number. Not in that place, and not without a gun.

Davy's parents' names were Cleveland J. and Emmaline Jackson. They were together the last DeVries knew, but his knowledge had been left standing in a jar for two decades. There were no entries under either name, but I made a list of Jacksons with the initial C. or E. and one C. J. and started dialing. I got two no-answers, a busy signal, a man with a Tennessee drawl as thick as Graceland who had a cousin named Davy alive and kicking down Murfreesboro way, and two offers not to be alone Saturday night. One of them was from a man named Calvin.

I tried the busy line again. It belonged to C. J. Jackson.

"You get 'er straightened out?"

A man's voice, very slow and scratchy, like a wornout tape. I said, "Get who straightened out?"

"Ain't you fambly service?"

"Not today."

"Hell. I been all morning trying to scare up a pair of crutches for the wife. Dog-damn computer never heard of us, and we been with Welfare since 'sixty-two. Sure you ain't fambly service?"

"Sorry."

"Hell. You think we was fixing to sell them crutches and run off to Mexico."

"Are you Cleveland J. Jackson?"

"Who wants him?"

"Was Davy Jackson your son?"

In the quiet on his end I heard the electronic laughter of a TV situation comedy rerun turned down low. "You a reporter?"

"No."

" 'Cause one called here oncet, said he was doing a piece on the riots. Said he wanted to talk to the relatives of all the victims that was still living in Detroit. I told him to go do it up a rope. He went ahead and wrote the story anyway. You do that I'll kill you. I got a gun."

"My name's Walker. Richard DeVries hired me to investigate the robbery."

"He in jail."

"He's out."

"Dog-damn."

I couldn't read him. He would have had years of practice at not being read. I said, "He says he didn't do it. He wants me to find the ones who did."

"Them 'Guards seen him fire that place."

"He admits to that. It's the robbery he wants me to find out about." I waited. The droid audience on his TV was becoming hysterical. I asked him finally if I could come out and talk.

"Our boy Davy was no good," he said. "I done told his mother but she didn't hear it. He dead, what I want to talk about him for?"

"I think if you didn't want to we wouldn't still be talking now."

"I ain't got the time. I got this crutch thing to chew over."

I lined up my notebook with the edges of the desk blotter. "How tall is Mrs. Jackson?"

Heat was rising in thick greasy sheets from the pavement in front of the Jacksons' house when I curbed the Renault between a gypsy van missing its left front fender and an Opel station wagon with Saran Wrap taped over an empty window. Mine was the only car on the street with all its equipment. As I was getting out with the aluminum crutches I'd bought at a hospital supply house on Michigan, a reedy lad of fifteen or sixteen separated himself from a gang brawling over a soccer ball in a burned-out lot on the corner and slithered over. Some of the shine went out of his eyes when I stood up and tucked the crutches under one arm.

"Watch your car for five bucks," he said. "They been shooting out headlights in this neighborhood."

I onced him over. He was almost my height but forty pounds lighter, in khaki pants and a stained nylon mesh football jersey with the hem hanging to his thighs. He was wearing the skinhead cut that had replaced the Afro while I was looking in some other direction. I turned to slam the car door and grasped his belt through the jersey and pulled him in close, shoving the padded armpieces of the crutches under his nose and bending his head back. He struggled, but his neck creaked and he stopped. There was pink fog in the whites of his eyes.

"Give it over," I said.

It took a little more pressure from the crutches, but after a second he reached behind his back and came out with an air pistol with a heavy plastic stock rigged to look like an auto mag. I leaned the crutches against the car and accepted the pistol. Then I let go of his belt.

"That cost fourteen bucks and change."

"You talk like you bought it." I stuck it under my waistband, giving him a hinge at the butt of the Smith just before I refastened my coat. "If I've still got headlamps when I come out you get it back. Don't bother blowing off steam anyplace else. The car's rented."

He left me. Halfway back to the empty lot he unbuckled his belt and pulled down his pants and bent over. I fingered the grip of the air pistol, then decided against it. I was mellowing.

10

THE NEIGHBORHOOD had been decent before the city started turning streets with bad reputations into parks and expressways, which was like cutting into a malignant but dormant mole and releasing carcinogens throughout the system. The slide would have begun with occasional B-and-E's and ended with old people crossing the street to avoid knots of cigarette-sucking youths blocking the sidewalk. In a year or so the place would be a park or an expressway and it would be another neighborhood's turn in the box.

For all that, the Jacksons' house showed efforts to slow down the skid. The crabgrass was cut, the old boards repainted recently, and some streetwise flowers grew in boxes under the windows looking like tough kids in bright knit caps. Somebody had painted the house number on the curb, but somebody else had sprayed it over with a word that belonged there. I followed a row of sunken flagstones to the stoop and rapped on the screen door.

I could make out some furniture inside, but the room wasn't lighted and the double-ply screen was set a little off, obscuring details. I didn't figure that was an accident. Floorboards shifted and then a short thick black man came to the screen holding something that looked like a gun.

"Mr. Jackson? I'm Amos Walker, the man who called." I

opened my ID folder and flattened it out against the screen.

He reached up and flipped an invisible hook out of an unseen eye. "Come ahead in."

I opened the door against the pull of an ailing spring and caught it behind me before it slammed. He had stepped back to give me room. He had on a white shirt with an open collar stuffed into colorless slacks and his feet were shod in imitation moccasins with simulated leather stitching. The thing that had looked like a gun was a bar of tarnished lead like they used in Linotype machines, about ten inches long. He saw me looking at it and balanced it on his palm.

"I was a dog-damn good printer before they offsetted me clean out of the business. I got enough of this in the attic to sink the Boblo boat."

"Where's the gun?"

"Hell, the wife won't have one in the house since Davy. Them the ones?"

I held out the crutches. He stuck the lead bar in his hip pocket and took them, fitting them under his own arms. He had a wide mouth and deep creases in his forehead and eyes like shotgun pellets lodged in cracks. And gray hair and a thick neck. So had a lot of older black men, including the one who had helped drive DeVries and me into the lake, if Hank Wakely told the truth.

"A mite tall for Emmaline," said the old man, testing his weight on the aluminum. "She knee-high to a pig knuckle."

"They're adjustable. Just loosen the screws there and there and slide up the bottoms."

He leaned the crutches in a corner. "Take a load off, son. Can I get you something cold? They's all kinds of pop and juice in the icebox. No beer, though. The wife don't hold with spirits. Won't have them in the house."

We were in a living room paneled in woodgrain vinyl with a nylon rug and three chairs and a sofa covered in knobby synthetic. Nothing expensive, but nothing old and worn out either, and all of it very clean. The one quality item was an antique sideboard older than the house, with family pictures on it in brass and silver frames. Several of them featured a more slender, much younger version of Cleveland J. Jackson, wearing a style of clothing not yet designed when he was a youth. The wide mouth was built for smiling. "Davy?" I asked.

"That boy liked having his pitcher took. I did too, his age. You know you got old when you start walking away from cameras. How about that cold one?"

"Thanks, I'm fine. How does Mrs. Jackson stand on tobacco?"

"Won't have it in the house. But she upstairs snoozing." He picked up a candy dish from the end table between the chairs, tipped the peppermints out into another dish containing caramels in plastic wrappers, and set the empty dish down next to my elbow. I lit up and placed the match in the dish. It was close in the room and most of the peppermints were fused together in a bright lump. I asked if Mrs. Jackson had had an accident.

"Slipped in some water at the post office last February and busted her hip." He took a seat in the chair nearest mine, grunted, took the lead bar out of his hip pocket, and laid it on the table. "She gets around with a walker but I don't want her getting used to it. You gots to keep moving, son. That's the secret."

"Any lawyers knock on your door?"

"Like woodpeckers in heat. I should sue the government, let my dead sister's junkie kid Delmer collect when we're in the ground? Anyway, the wife don't like to cause no fuss. You say Richie's out?"

"They sprang him day before yesterday."

"What's it been, ten-twelve years?"

"Twenty. They paroled him."

"Dog-damn. Don't seem twenty. Bet it does to him, though. How's he look?"

"Does it matter?"

"Sure. Him and Davy was some tight. I always thought that

boy was headed for a fall, though. He was just too angry. You don't know what it was like to be black and angry in 'sixty-seven. They was restaurants around here wouldn't serve us. Someone busted in your house with a gun, you called the cops, they might come out before the end of the shift if it wasn't too far and their feet didn't hurt. White folks half your age calling you boy, and them was the friendly ones. It was like that if you lived invisible and didn't talk back. Otherwise they come down on you like a bucket of shit. Davy he went bad, I knew he'd get hisself chewed up; when they called and said he was dead it was like he been that way a long time. But I was scared for Richie. He had a chance to pull hisself out. I see him slapping that ball all over the community court and bringing that hoop down like he mad at it and I think, slow down, Richie. It was like watching your own boy run out into traffic."

"You think he was in on the robbery?"

"Not for the money. Well, some. You see neighbors never even jaywalked all their lives throwing bricks and grabbing anything they can throw their arms around you get to thinking whatever you take ain't half what's owed. It wasn't the money, though. It was the taking."

"His story is he never even knew the robbery was going down. He started the fire just to start the fire. He thinks he was set up."

"Not by Davy."

"Not by Davy. Have you ever seen this man?" I showed him the printout photograph, pointing at Alfred Hendriks.

"I seen him somewheres. On TV, I think."

"Anywhere else? Twenty years ago, maybe, and much younger?"

"Son, my mother died fifteen years ago. I don't hardly remember what *she* looked like."

"Just a stab." I put away the printout. "Where were you Wednesday afternoon, Mr. Jackson?"

"Over at the A 'n' P. I do the shopping Wednesdays."

"Anyone see you?"

"What happened Wednesday?" he asked.

"Someone tried to stop DeVries on the road outside Marquette. I was there. So was someone else, and the description he gave of the man behind it could fit you."

"Be a tough fit. I never been that far north. I ain't drove a car in eight years. You see anything in my driveway besides what the neighbor's dog left there?"

"It wasn't much of a description. It just occurred to me someone might blame DeVries for your son's death."

"*I* do."

This was a new voice. I looked at the top of the uncarpeted staircase by the front door, where an old black woman in a floor-length yellow nightgown trimmed with lace stood supporting herself on the railing. Her hair was white and sleep-tangled and her face had the startled look that faces sometimes take on when their owners can't get over the fact that they've become old. She was trembling fit to shake the whole second story.

"Woman, what you doing up without your walker?" Jackson braced his hands on the arms of his chair.

"Richie killed our Davy," she said.

I put out my cigarette in the candy dish. I felt as if I'd been caught smoking behind the barn.

"I can understand your thinking he's responsible, Mrs. Jackson."

"Responsible? He killed him. Killed him."

Jackson made a little noise that took my attention off his wife. His eyes were shut tight, making a cracked mud sculpture of his face. Only his knuckles turning yellow on the chair arms showed life.

"Tell him, Cleveland."

He opened his eyes slowly. I swore I could hear the lids grating like old shutters. Then he breathed, and it really was like watching a statue become animated, the dead cells blinking on like tiny lights. "It wasn't nothing." He rubbed his palms up and down the arms of the chair. "Something that big lieutenant said."

"What lieutenant?" I asked.

"The one that come to talk to us after Davy got killed. What was his name, Emmaline?"

"Orlander. Lieutenant Floyd Orlander." It sounded like a catechism.

"Orlander, that was it. He said the cops didn't shoot Davy and neither did the 'Guards. The bullet they took out of him at the autopsy didn't belong to any of their guns. Orlander thought one of the other robbers shot him."

"DeVries."

"Maybe. The stickup was like right around the corner and them 'Guards didn't have their eyes on Richie the whole time, what with their attention being split between them. Davy was backshot behind the building running away."

"Why kill one of your own partners?"

"He wanted it all," said Mrs. Jackson. "Greed, that's one of the sins."

"Nobody ever said it was him done it, woman. He didn't have no gun when they picked him up."

"He threw it in the fire."

"Somebody else got the money," I said. "He never left the arson scene."

Jackson said, "Orlander thought Richie and the others worked it out before the robbery. Davy was kind of loud, especially when he drank. They shut him up and sweetened their own pile to boot. Only Richie got grabbed before he could take his split."

"Sounds like Orlander had it in for him."

"Them sportswriters was starting to notice Richie. Some white folks just can't stand watching a brother pick hisself up. I can't say if Orlander was like that. His partner was. He had this rat-face sergeant who would of looked right fine decked out in a sheet and dunce cap. I don't remember his name. Emmaline?"

She shook her head. Her face was shining. The strain of holding herself up was getting to her.

"Mean man," Jackson said. "Wouldn't sit down in my house. Like he was afraid he get something on his pants. It was like I never left Mississippi."

"I read up on the case. I never saw anything about Davy being shot by one of his own."

"Hot time. Maybe they didn't want to stir nothing up."

"Makes sense. They'd never have made a case like that stick anyway, without the weapon." I rose. "Thanks, Mr. and Mrs. Jackson. You didn't have anything to do with what happened up north. I had to ask."

"I would of if I could," she said. "I'm just sorry they didn't kill him."

"Woman, you don't mean that. Killing's a bigger sin than greed."

"I'd burn in hell happy."

He pushed himself out of his chair, caught his balance, and went up to help her back to bed, using the railing all the way. I waited. I wanted to ask if "redstick ranger" meant anything to him. It took me five minutes to realize he wasn't coming back down. Outside, the fresh air washed over me like a spray of clean water.

11

I HADN'T EATEN since Grayling. I ordered off the dinner menu in a seafood place on Grand, made easy work of a bass served in horseradish, and mounted a partially successful expedition for clams in the chowder. Thus sustained I penetrated enemy territory, the granite columns at 1300 Beaubien, Detroit Police Headquarters.

One of the better-looking cops in the Criminal Investigation Division was showing some leg on the edge of Sergeant Cranmer's desk in Robbery, reading items from a hot sheet in her hand over the telephone. She had her brown hair pinned back to beat the heat and a couple of buttons undone on a gray silk blouse to raise the temperature of everyone else in the squad room. Her skirt was matador red and just a little less than knee-length when she was sitting, dangling a silver sandal off her right foot. She answered to Lieutenant Mary Ann Thaler.

"Demoted?" I asked when she had hung up.

"Cranmer's out sick. I'm adding his job to the three others I've been doing since Easter." She adjusted her tortoiseshell rims. "Is there something wrong with your neck, or are you working on your Cary Grant?"

"Honorable injury. I've been out diving for the *Edmund Fitzgerald*. Alderdyce around? He isn't in his office."

"Turn around, Mr. Detective," she said.

I'd walked right past him. He had his broad back to me at the copying machine by the door, coatless, with his salmon-colored shirt pasted to his skin in patches and the curved grip of his department .38 hooking his right kidney. I flipped Lieutenant Thaler a salute and left her.

John Alderdyce jumped a foot when I used his name. He turned his dark hacked-out face on me. "Why don't you use a cattle prod?" he snapped. "I haven't killed a man since supper last night. My average is slipping."

"Next time I'll whistle. What put you on the stick?"

"The heat. The crime statistics. Double shifts. Everybody calls in sick when the sun comes out. Having rank means you get to keep everyone else's job for them. If you're really lucky you'll make commissioner and die before you're fifty. How the hell are you?"

"My neck hurts. But I'm working. Can we talk in your office? Soon as you're through making copies of your hand."

The machine had kicked out four sheets while his left palm was resting on the glass. He swore and turned it off. "Doing khaki work now, for chrissake. Next they'll have me scrubbing toilets. Let's make it quick."

I held the door while he drummed the copies together and tipped them into a tattered interoffice envelope. On the way out he glimpsed Mary Ann Thaler, making another call at the sergeant's desk. "You ought to spring for dinner sometime," he told me. "You two might wind up married and raising little sleuths in West Bloomfield."

"I never date cops. Just when you're ready to pop the question over candles they decide to bust the violinist for disturbing the peace. They're as romantic as a soft-nosed slug." I fell into step beside him in the hallway.

"Suit yourself. I bet she's warm and smells like pink soap. I bet she wears shortie p.j.'s."

"Under or over the shoulder holster?"

"Look who's romantic."

"How's Marian?"

"Edgy as hell. Too early to tell if we belong back together. The kids are great. Most of their friends have parents with different zip codes."

In Homicide he dumped the envelope on the desk of a young plainclothesman in a T-shirt and seersucker coat. "Where were you when I needed these done?" Alderdyce demanded. "Mail them out to the precincts. Maybe we'll have an arrest for Christmas."

The officer pulled out the top sheet. Alderdyce's hand had photographed darker than it was. "I thought these guys went out when Prohibition came in."

Alderdyce snatched it away and crumpled it. "Buy a necktie. This is a police station, not a mission."

"Yes, sir, Lieutenant."

"Don't yessir me, boy. I'm not your grampa."

"Yes, sir. I mean yes. I mean no."

"Kids dress like bums. Can't tell who's doing the booking and who's doing the getting booked." In his office he slapshot the crumpled paper into the wastebasket, then used the vanity mirror on the wall to straighten his necktie. He turned down and buttoned his cuffs and took his coat off the hanger. It fit him like new skin. Good tailoring was one of his vices. "What's your beef?"

"I need a line on an old case. It goes back to the riots."

"We were in high school then. Which case?"

"An arson and a robbery on Brady. A building was set on fire and an armored car tapped for two hundred thousand."

"Richard DeVries."

I kicked the door shut. The sound of typing in the squad room drifted in over the top of the glass partitions. "That came out quick."

"Somewhere in this mess is a Telex from the State Department of Corrections with a list of the cons getting sprung this month." He waved a hand at the pile of folders and envelopes on his desk. "We get it with the gas bill. I try to stay on top of it. He's in town?"

"Seeing his parole officer today. First order of business is

I'm informing you I'm looking into his arrest. Just in case you've got objections to a civilian rooting around in an old police matter."

"By the book. My, my."

"I use it when I can. Second, assuming there are no objections—"

"A big assume."

"—is I'd like to talk with the detective in charge of the investigation. I'm told his name is Floyd Orlander."

"Before my time."

"Dead?"

"Retired. Accepted with the chief's regrets, I hear, and three hip-hip-hoorays and a Hail Mary from the chain of command in between. Legends are hard to work with. You remember the shoot-out in Judge Lorenzo's courtroom?"

"Defense attorney pulled a piece on the witness on the stand and got turned into macramé by the cops in the gallery."

"*And* by the witness on the stand, who happened to be Lieutenant Floyd Orlander. The judge kept his own .45 auto strapped to his ribs under his robes and got down and crawled for the door to his chambers. What you didn't hear was that after the incident, the shooting team found a line of bullet holes four to twelve inches above the floor in the oak paneling behind the bench, or that the slugs they dug out of the wood belonged to Orlander's seven-point-six-five off-duty be-the-first-kid-on-your-block-to-own-one Beretta. The lawyer who started the whole thing got chopped down standing six feet away. The only target anywhere near the floor was the famous four-footed judge."

I rubbed my neck. He went on.

"The thing might've gone further if every cop in the department didn't hate Let-em-go Lorenzo's guts and if Orlander's record on the range wasn't so good. He hadn't really been trying to hit the little bastard, you see. Anyway Orlander took early retirement with encouragement, Lorenzo left the bench for private practice, and I hear he hasn't taken a crap since that day."

"Do it in Detroit," I said.

"Things are better now. At least we stopped shooting at each other." He picked up a fat folder and started thumbing through its contents. "Orlander was living in Romulus last I heard. If you still want to talk to him I can get his address from Personnel."

"I'd appreciate it. Also the name of the sergeant who sided him on the DeVries case if you know it."

"DeVries the client?"

I nodded.

"What's he want, the money?"

That struck too close. I said, "He claims he wasn't part of the robbery. He wants me to find out who was."

"You mean he wants you to locate them so he can bleed them. The statute ran out a long time ago on the heist, but there's that murder still laying there like a dog turd waiting for someone to step in it. DeVries took the drop and he thinks he's owed."

"If that's what he wants and it turns out he's telling the truth about the job, maybe he is."

"Funny, there's nothing on the books about which thief gets title to the booty. So it *is* the money."

"I said *if*. I look for missing people and insurance frauds. Shaking people down requires a whole different set of skills. All I'm after is the straight dope."

He flipped the folder back onto the pile. "The state house is full of innocents. This one waited a long time to find someone who bought his story."

"The thought crossed my mind. Somebody wants him stopped, but that could mean anything. Your enemies don't all dry up and blow away just because they can you up for twenty years. But the P.I. business is rotten with grifters he wouldn't have to lie to for their help in an extortion. He picked me."

"Not my toy soldier. I hope. Ask Orlander who his partner was. What do I look like, the department historian?"

He found a letterhead in a drawer and wrote me out an

authorization for Orlander's address and telephone number from Personnel. I folded it lengthwise and put it in my breast pocket, sucked my cheek for a moment, then held up a hand and left his office. In the hallway outside Homicide I ran into Mary Ann Thaler. She glanced up above my hairline.

"He must be getting better," she said. "It doesn't look as badly chewed as the others."

"What's got him on end? He was getting along just fine after the burnout."

"The inspectors' list is coming out today. He's up."

"What are his chances?"

"None and less. Last winter hurt him. It isn't supposed to, but when you take unscheduled leave to work out a problem it goes into your jacket. Everyone knows it. And the shrinks wonder why there are so many borderline cases in harness. They're afraid to climb out."

I leaned a shoulder against the wall. "I'd ask you to hang an eye out for him if it wasn't all a cop can do to hang one out for himself."

"Thanks for not asking. It's out anyway. I'd still be sorting out pink, yellow, and white forms if not for John."

"How's *your* head?"

"Case steel. But then it's not my job to shovel dead children out of alleys. I don't know how he stood it as long as he did."

"Wheaties."

She had a dimple. "What are you working on?"

"A case the cops closed when you were in pinafores. You wouldn't remember it."

"Never wore them. I was into treehouses and bib overalls. Try me."

"Ever hear the term 'redstick ranger'?"

"Not as often as I read it when I was in Records. The Arson Squad used it all the time."

I stopped leaning. "What's it mean?"

"Firemen's slang. Redstick ranger, that's the hot dog that scrambles up the ladder to save the pretty young widow's cat just before the roof collapses. Cops call it the John Wayne Syndrome, but there isn't an officer with Arson wouldn't rather be wearing a raincoat and riding a truck. Where'd you come across it?"

"Up north."

"Well, you heard it from an old hand. The new breed doesn't use it. Flashy heroics went out with the red helmets."

"Lieutenant, what would you do if I kissed you right on the mouth?"

She paused. Her eyes were robin's-egg blue behind the glasses. "If you were very good at it, I might not cripple you until it was over."

I took her hand instead. Alone in the elevator on the way down I sniffed my palm. It smelled like pink soap.

12

THERE WAS NO ANSWER at Floyd Orlander's number in Romulus. I hung up the pay telephone on the ground floor of 1300, got into the Renault parked in the blue zone, and sat there listening to my sweat break the surface while I thought about what to do next. A uniform driving a blue-and-white made that decision for me when he pulled alongside and gave me one of those cop looks. I started up and left the space.

Marianne Motors kept its administrative offices on two floors of the National Bank Building, five sides and twenty-two stories of gray stone overlooking Cadillac Square. I used a city lot and rode an elevator trimmed in brass to the seventeenth. I hoped the ride would give me time to think of a question to ask Alfred Hendriks that he hadn't answered that morning, but they don't make elevators that slow.

The doors shuttled open and I stepped out just in time to throw my arms around two hundred hurtling pounds.

The man's momentum would have carried me back into the car if the doors hadn't closed. I slammed up against them, jarring loose my grip, and he went down on one knee, then sprang back up, pivoted away from me, and scooped a short-barreled .32 revolver out of a flap holster. I gave him the edge of my hand where his neck met his shoulder. The gun thumped the carpet.

He whirled on me. I reached under my coat and he took two steps backward. His gun arm hung limp at his side. He had on a gray uniform and a cap with a shiny visor.

Behind him, Richard DeVries had another man in uniform lying on his back in the reception area with a size fifteen shoe on his chest. A revolver like the one on the floor dangled upside-down by its trigger guard off the ex-convict's index finger. The other man's holster was empty.

"Richie," I said.

It took him a second to respond. He didn't look at the gun in my hand. He was wearing the suit I had first seen him in, wrinkled now after its soaking and a worse fit than it had been to begin with. The guard on the floor had a black bruise down the side of his face and the uniform of the one I had disarmed was hanging on by a button and one epaulet. DeVries's tie was crooked.

"I axed them to take me to see Hendriks. I got this for an answer." He waggled the gun on the end of his finger. It looked like a charm off a bracelet.

I moved into the room, holding out my free hand. I covered the guard standing by the elevator. "That's a parole violation, Richie. I'll take it."

He made a graceful little movement and the grip was in his hand with the barrel pointed at me. I stopped.

"Nobody's called me Richie since I went in."

"That's what Davy's father called you. I talked to the Jacksons today. He doesn't hate you for what happened to Davy. The mother's a different story." Keep him talking.

"She never did like me."

"Call the police."

This was the guard I'd hit. Out of the corner of my right eye I saw a stack of platinum hair and two eyes showing over the top of a doughnut-shaped reception desk to my right. She wasn't going to move or call anyone. "Someone probably heard the noise and called them already," I told DeVries. "If they find you with that gun you'll go back to finish out your sentence. That's if they don't come off the elevator shooting."

"Man, I don't like being muscled around. I had enough of that."

"Getting killed is worse." I was watching his big finger on the trigger of the .32. I wondered if when it moved I would have time to empty the .38 into him before he shot me. It would take at least that.

"The parole cop told me nobody was waiting to give me nothing on the outside. He didn't say I couldn't axe for nothing." He dangled the gun again and held it out.

While I was stepping forward, a man came through a door on the other side of the reception desk and took it. I covered him. Without taking his eyes off me he rotated the revolver one-handed, dumping the cartridges out onto the carpet, and laid it on the desk. Then he walked past me, picked up the gun the vertical guard had dropped, unloaded it the same way, and returned it to its owner, who was starting to get back the use of his hand and arm. The whole thing took less time than it takes to describe. I might have dreamed it.

"I'm the security chief here. Please let him up."

DeVries glanced down at his foot on the horizontal guard's chest, grunted, and removed it. The other guard came over and gave his partner a hand up.

"They played partners on us, Mr. Piero," the second guard said.

"I saw the last part of it. Get out."

He gaped. "You mean, out?"

"Out of the room. Although out of the building has occurred to me. You might want to move before I give it more thought."

"What about this guy?" The man from the floor spoke out of the good side of his face.

Under the security chief's scrutiny I remembered the gun and holstered it under my coat.

"Take the stairs," he said.

When they had gone through the fire door, one helping the other, the chief turned to the blonde still hunkered behind the desk. "Take a break, Christine. I'll watch the phones."

She stood, looked at DeVries and me, tugged down the hem of her charcoal jacket, and slid out of the doughnut. I pressed the button for the elevator.

Mr. Piero waited for the doors to close on her. He was a small narrow party with white hair and a black pencil moustache. In a blue suit and black knitted tie on a white shirt he looked like a dashboard Cesar Romero.

"No police," he said. "Doesn't do to have them come wailing up to the office with guns and bullhorns. It makes the investors nervous."

"That why you play it safe behind the door?" I asked.

It rocked him like moonlight on flat water. "Who are you?"

"Name's DeVries," the big man broke in. "Hendriks knows me. I seen him on TV this morning."

I said, "They got TV in the Alamo?"

"I'm lucky I got a toilet. I seen it in a bar."

"Bars are hard on paroles." I handed my ID folder to Piero. "I'm representing Mr. DeVries. Sometimes he forgets. I'd like a minute of Mr. Hendriks' time if he didn't bail out when the ceiling fell in."

"I didn't start nothing."

"What's your business with Mr. Hendriks?"

"My client thinks he knows him. I want to ask him if that's true."

Piero returned the folder. "References?"

I gave him a couple of names and numbers. He used the telephone on the reception desk. While he was talking I asked DeVries what happened.

"Woman gave me the stall. I lost it I guess. I ain't used to dealing with them. She had a button under the desk."

"Next time they'll come in with howitzers. You'd better let me drive."

The security chief cradled the receiver. "You check out. I suppose I owe you something for talking your client out of chewing up my men."

"You need new men," I said.

"You take what's available when you're starting out. Hendriks isn't here. The Detroit offices are just a blind to pacify the mayor. Mr. Marianne and the other executives put in three or four hours a week here and spend the rest of their time at the downriver plant."

I said, "Hendriks was here when I called this morning."

"Christine probably rerouted the call. Unless they recognize your name the secretaries are programmed to say they're unavailable. You'd be surprised how many crank calls a fledgling automaker gets. Every backyard crackpot thinks he's solved perpetual motion."

"How do I get into the plant?"

"The big man stays home, right?"

DeVries opened his mouth. I nudged his ankle with a toe. It was like kicking a goal post. "I work solo. Today was just a coincidence."

Piero thought about it. "Use my name. If I take an angry call from downriver you didn't get it from me."

"Thanks."

"Save it. We needed the field test. There are bugs to be worked out; two in particular."

"Don't be too tough on them. The state just pulled the cork on my client after twenty years. He's eager."

"I'd hate to see him excited."

On the sidewalk in front of the bank building I asked DeVries how much play there was in his parole officer.

"Some. He got me a job behind the bottle counter at Kroger's starting Monday. I gets to quit if they whips me."

"Good. I'm thirsty."

We took a back table in the Pontchartrain bar. No one was at the piano and we shared the place with a pair of businessmen on the stools and a bald bartender in a red jacket. He brought us two beers and ghosted off. It was as cool as a mineshaft in there.

"It's him okay." DeVries inhaled half the contents of his glass and set it down. "He had this way of grinning in some other direction when he was talking, like he was laughing at you. I seen it again this morning. He's the one set me up to fire that place."

"Wonder what happened to the blonde?"

"Blowed away on a cloud of psychedelic shit, probably. Wasn't her behind the desk up there. Too young."

"I got Hendriks on the telephone this morning. He says he never heard of you."

"I bet that knocked you flat on your ass."

"He says he was studying in England at the time of the riots. It's something that can be checked."

"Check it?"

"I will. Point is he had an answer for everything."

"Nobody that didn't do nothing has an answer for everything."

I dissected that, then nodded. "It bothered me too. Also he got your name wrong and I didn't like that. It was like he had his lines down cold."

"Squeeze the son of a bitch."

"Couple of other things to run out first. I've got a line on the cop who arrested you and I found out what 'redstick ranger' means."

"That's what Hank Wakely said the dude said when they was fixing to stop us on the road."

"Firemen's jargon. Did Hendriks or whoever he was have anything to do with the fire department in your time?"

"Search me. Be funny, though, wouldn't it?"

"Hysterical. That's the trouble with the detective business. The answers ask their own questions."

"What'd the cop say?"

"I haven't been able to get him yet. I figure he'll have more to contribute about the case than I can get from either downtown or the newspapers. Once they've got a suspect in custody they don't bother reporting all the loose ends. But they remember them. I hope."

"Wrong tree," he said. "Hendriks' the one we want to work on. He's got the money."

I drank some beer. "You're paying me to do the digging. Whatever I churn up won't help you if you break somebody's neck. Didn't prison teach you anything besides license plates?"

"I know. I just seen him on TV and couldn't think of nothing else. Guess I'm glad you come in when you did."

"You need to blow it off."

"What I need's a woman. Saltpeter's wearing off."

I gave him five twenties. "I cashed your check this morning. Look at their teeth first. If they don't take care of them they're just as careless other places. How long's it been since you played ball?"

"Gave it up nine years ago. Wasn't no point. It was like playing with kids and it only made me think what I missed out on."

"You can only sing that song so long."

"I sung it till I don't feel it no more. Hell, I'd be retired now anyway. Just another jock selling subscriptions to *Sports Illustrated*."

"Take yourself over to the Y and shoot a few hundred baskets. Even if it doesn't make you feel better, you'll be too tired to think about taking away people's guns and baseball bats."

"I'm too dark for the Y. They can't see me in them dim lights."

"That's changed. Not as fast as the world, but then we're all running to catch up. Why should you be any different?"

"Maybe I'll do it."

"Just watch your head on the hoops." I started to leave money for the beers. He held up a palm the size of a skillet and laid down a five-spot.

"Beer's went up." He stood. "Where'd you hear that about teeth?"

"The army."

"Someone told it to me my first week in slam. Think they's anything to it?"

"Nothing else I heard in the army was, except keep your butt down and never volunteer. But it's a comfort."

13

NEARING Romulus a DC-8 bellying into Detroit Metropolitan Airport dragged its shadow over the Renault, engines shrieking. The slipstream tugged the little car toward the expressway median and the vibration loosened screws in the dash and popped open the glove compartment. When I parked and got out I was surprised not to find skid marks on the roof.

Floyd Orlander, late of the Detroit Police Department, lived in a well-kept tract built bang at the end of a runway, separated from the airport grounds by a thousand feet of cyclone fence and several miles of community optimism. The first time I rang the bell another jet taking off straight over the house swallowed every sound in the neighborhood. No one answered the second time either, although it was in comparative silence. I wondered if the entire household was deaf. I tried knocking.

A minute later the door opened on a gray-haired woman built for comfort in a green print dress and rhinestone glasses with blue lenses, who showed me a nice set of false teeth and said, "Did you ring before? Everyone's out back."

"I tried calling earlier, but no one answered," I said. "Is this the Orlander residence?"

"I'm Mrs. Orlander. If you're from the city, we're not selling. We like it here, noise and all."

"I'm not from the city. My name's Walker. I'd like to talk to Mr. Orlander about an old police case he worked on."

"Land, he's been retired twelve years. It *must* be old."

"Is he at home?"

She put her fingers in her ears. It looked like a stall. I asked the question again, raising my voice. Then a jet I hadn't even heard winding up shattered the sound barrier directly overhead. The ka-*thump* boxed my ears and rattled crockery in the house.

"Land, that one was low," she said, taking her fingers out. "There's an ordinance against it, but we'll all be dead by the time they hear about it from the FAA. Are you all right, young man?"

I was reading her lips. "How did you know it was coming?"

"I'd explain, but you'd have to have lived here ten years to understand. Follow me, please."

There were books and a cabinet TV in the living room and glass cabinets full of knickknacks and china in the dining room and built-in appliances in the kitchen. Everything was spaced out and lashed down as tightly as aboard ship. The walls were bare of pictures.

"I bet taxes are low hereabouts," I said.

"Not low enough. But lower than other places." She stepped through the screen door in back and held it for me.

The backyard bunted up against the cyclone fence with white pickets on either side. On the square of lawn, a yellow-headed boy and girl of about four were digging holes in a sandbox and throwing the sand out onto the grass. They were twins, dressed identically in red shorts and Smurf T-shirts and barefoot. A heavy big man sat watching them in a canvas deck chair with a glass in his hand. He, too, was barefoot and wore a shirt with parrots on it and khaki shorts and one of those wide-brimmed straw hats with a green plastic eyeshade that gave his face a bilious cast. The face was wide and square and so were his hands and feet. A pitcher of ice and brown liquid stood at his elbow on a pedestal table under a striped umbrella.

"Children, the grass," said Mrs. Orlander.

"Hell with the grass," the man said. "They're my grandkids. What about that beer?"

"Drink your tea. You know what the doctor said."

"Not as good as you do, goddamn it."

The girl stopped digging. "Grampa said G.D."

"Watch your language, Floyd."

"Yes, Dottie."

"This is Mr. Walker. He wants to talk to you about something you worked on."

He started, took off his hat, and looked up at me. The brim had blocked his view. His hair had been red, but had faded to a rinsed-out pink, and was cropped so short he would have looked bald from a distance. He had faded blue eyes and blotched skin and one of those faces that came either with age or from both ends of a lot of beer bottles. He wasn't that old. After a long look he hung the hat on the arm of his chair and drained his glass.

"You're since my time. Most of you are, I guess. Changing mayors put a lot of good men back out on the street."

"I'm not with the department." I gave him one of my cards. "You worked the DeVries arson case, right?"

"You mean the robbery." He read the card and floated it in a puddle of iced tea on the table.

"That's what I wanted to talk about. He may be innocent."

There was a chaise longue on the other side of the table. Mrs. Orlander took a *Ladies' Home Journal* off the flowered cushion, stretched out, and began turning pages. Orlander refilled his glass from the pitcher. "He after a new trial?"

"He's out."

"Then what's the point?"

I played it straight up. "He thinks he knows who pulled off the robbery. If he's right he wants the money."

"That's fair. If he was innocent, which he ain't."

"If he isn't it will come out. I don't work so well with whitewash. My thinking is you could tell me lots about the robbery that isn't on record. At the very least it might turn Davy Jackson's killer."

"Who told you about that?"

"Jackson's parents. You don't think DeVries killed him or you'd have charged him with first-degree murder at the time."

"Not charging him and not thinking he did it don't even go to the same school."

"Do you think he did it?"

"No."

"Why not?"

He poured tea into his mouth and swallowed it. "Throwing up smoke to cover a heist is an important job. The guy you give it to can't be bothered with pulling off a hit besides. The rest of it was planned too tight. They wouldn't make that mistake. Two guys hit the truck, Jackson and one other. The money wasn't on Jackson so his buddy capped him during the fade and took off with it. DeVries going down meant he didn't have to split with nobody."

"Wouldn't he be worried about DeVries talking?"

"At that particular time a black perp would of went to the chair before he'd give up another black to the white man's po-lice." He whined the last word like Willie Best.

"Thin."

"You had to be there. You had to see it. Nothing I ever heard or read told it like it was. We had to tell our kids they couldn't play with their black friends. Had to tell them it wasn't the kids we were worried about. It was their parents."

"The robbers wore stocking masks and gloves. How do you know the one that got away was black?"

"Salt and pepper? Not that week."

A jet canted in for a landing over the fence, making conversation impossible for a minute. The boy and girl went on digging in the sand and never looked up.

"When did you close the case?" I asked when the roar had faded.

"It was still open last I knew. But the snitches didn't know nothing and the money never turned up and we figured it got laundered someplace, Mexico or someplace. You can only spend so much time on a thing, and we had a city to put back together. Did a rotten job of it too."

"What about a driver? They wouldn't have left the getaway car empty with all hell breaking loose."

"Not so much as a treadmark. Investigating conditions weren't ideal. Flak jackets and auto-rifles, quick and dirty, get in and out with your ass and whatever you can pick up running."

"The driver might have been a woman," I said. "The man DeVries suspects hung out with a hippie blonde."

"Age of Aquarius. Peace and love. Shit."

"Floyd." Mrs. Orlander didn't look up from her magazine.

"Yes, Dottie."

"Who tipped them the armored car would be there?"

"If you got a look at the security in those outfits you'd bury your money in a Mason jar. We couldn't turn an inside man."

"Swell."

"Wish I could remember more," he said, "but not too bad. DeVries was guilty as hell and we won't count Jackson. Five hundred was a good average in my day."

"How's your partner's memory?"

"Barney Drake? I heard he blew a vein in his head ten-twelve years ago. His daughter stuck him in a home in California or someplace. I bet they wash him every day and dress him up just like he was folks. Couldn't happen to a nicer guy. I never worked with anyone so miserable in my life."

"Why work with him at all?"

He spread the thumb and forefinger of his right hand and pointed at the web of flesh between them. "See that scar? Well, maybe you can't so good anymore. Back in 'sixty-two this snitch we was questioning kind of hard behind the old Demosthenes Bar pulled a .45 and stuck it in Barney's stomach and squeezed off. The punk just never carried, we weren't ready for it. There wasn't time to do anything but jam my hand into the action.

After that we sent the sorry snitch to Receiving to get his jaw wired. I saved Barney's cookies that night."

"Wouldn't that make him loyal to you instead of the other way around?"

"Hell no, it made him even more miserable to be with. But you give a man back his life, you just naturally want to hang around and make sure he doesn't throw it away. I guess he's grateful out there in the Piss-Your-Pants Home for the Terminally Fucked in Pasadena or wherever it is. Sorry, Dottie."

"You do the explaining when we send these children home swearing like muleskinners."

He didn't hear her. He was looking at the twins, and his thoughts were as clear as the welts on his face. I said, "If they're raised right they won't stick you in a place like that."

"Five minutes alone with my department piece, that's all I'll ever ask them for."

He put on his hat. It was a dismissal, but I wasn't ready to leave the spot. The sun felt good on my stiff neck. "City looking to expand the airport?"

"Three years now. I'm the one standing in front of it. I bought this place out of my pension, cash on the barrelhead. First place we ever owned. They'll meet my price or 'doze us both under."

"What's your price?"

"Sixty-five."

"You might get it. In Detroit they'd just invoke eminent domain and roll right over you."

"It's why I left. That it?"

I hesitated. "I'm curious about that shoot-out in Judge Lorenzo's court. It's not my business."

"Was I really trying to hit him?"

"That's the question."

"That little pimp. You know what he's doing now? Handling palimony suits for celebrity fags. I should of took aim."

"I appreciate your time," I said.

"Yeah, yeah. Good-bye."

Mrs. Orlander started to get up, but I said I knew the way out. She showed me her dentures. Whatever she'd overheard was nothing on what she'd been hearing for decades. As I turned toward the house, a wrestling match started up in the sandbox. Orlander said if it didn't stop right now he'd twist some heads off. The boy laughed.

14

It was the damnedest case, and knowing where to find the man I had been paid to look for was no help. It was like one of those game shows where they give you the answer and you have to come up with the question. I took the Edsel Ford eastbound into Detroit, eating cool air coming in through the windows and listening to the not-so-distant sound of Richard DeVries's twenty-year fuse burning low. It sounded just like a big black jet waiting its turn at the runway in Floyd Orlander's backyard.

Exiting the expressway, I found myself pointed south and kept going. That way lay knowledge. Most of what little I knew about the case had revealed itself while I was moving in that direction. It was a deal more tidy than sacrificing farm animals.

Downriver is a mystical name to most Detroiters, as the New World was to Europeans in the sixteenth century; a place where dragons drank the blood of mariners and pretty women sat in their underwear on rocks, plucking at lyres and waiting for ships to sail too close. Geographically it refers to a collection of bedroom communities strung out south of the city on the U.S. side of the international border, factory towns with dirty air and clean streets protected by lamps and the cyclops eye of the Neighborhood Watch. Some of the communities have French names to remind their neighbor to the north of the explorers who brought the world to the bend in the river that the Indians called the Crooked Way. But it's a wasted effort, because the city is barely aware of its satellites, and everything it doesn't understand it calls downriver.

Civilized gray smoke was leaning from the stacks of the old tractor plant–turned high tech automotive center when I swung through the opening in the chainlink fence. No guard appeared, so I rolled on until I found a space in the dozens of rows of parked vehicles with security stickers on their windshields and got out. The pavement was spongy in the late-afternoon heat and made little smacking sounds when I lifted my feet.

A red-painted fire door bore the legend AUTHORIZED PERSONNEL ONLY in yellow stencil. I pulled it open. Inside, a guard in a gray uniform looked up from the sandwich he was eating behind a library table. A fan with a white plastic housing blew hard-boiled egg odor at me.

"Security badge," he said, spitting bits of egg-white. He was a hard-looking number with graying hair and black eyebrows and a neck like a pork butt. His revolver rode high on his hip with its black rubber grip showing above the table.

I let him see my ID. "Mr. Piero in the Detroit office said to use his name."

"Okay."

"Okay?"

" He gives out his name like I give out hundred-dollar bills. Offices or plant?"

"Offices."

He reached into a corrugated box full of colored Lucite tags on the table and held out a blue one. "Hang that on your pocket and take the elevator down the hall. No detours."

It was stamped with a large white numeral twelve. I clipped it to my handkerchief pocket and followed a narrow hallway covered in painted corkboard to a single elevator. There were no buttons for individual floors inside, just UP and DOWN.

When the doors opened to let me out I made room for a brunette in a peach-colored business suit, who glanced at my tag.

"I used to be a thirteen," I said.

She was turning that over when the doors sealed us off from each other. Anyway it beat finding myself in the middle of a brawl.

It was one of those fast-food offices with three women behind a reception counter and rows of waist-high partitions opposite it with desks between them and men and women working like ants at the desks. I asked for Alfred Hendriks.

"When is your appointment?" The woman who responded was at the other end of the counter from the one I'd addressed. She had silver-rinsed hair and rimless glasses and looked over her shoulder at me from a cabinet where she was filing something. I recognized her quality-controlled voice from the telephone that morning. I said I didn't have an appointment and told her my name.

She turned her head away. "I'm sorry, Mr. Hendriks is out."

"Would he be in if I said I'm from Stutch Petrochemicals?"

"Are you?"

"No. I tried it before. It can't work twice. When will he be in?"

"He didn't say. You can wait if you like."

I took a seat and flipped through a glossy copy of something called *Modern Aerodynamics*. It had a cartoon page but the jargon was out of my reach. I laid it aside and lit a cigarette.

I had been there ten minutes when a woman entered from another hallway and stopped before the counter. She was tall and slender and had on a suit that looked as if it had been designed for a whole different kind of business from those I'd been looking at. It was satin, for one thing, and a shade of blue you don't usually see in offices this side of Las Vegas. Her hair was shoulder-length and deep auburn—it would be red in sunlight—her complexion fair, and she had high cheekbones accentuated by hollows and Mongol eyes helped along with a breath of mascara at the corners. They didn't need help.

"Is my husband in?" Her voice hung somewhere around the middle register and reminded me for some reason of magnolias and Georgian columns. I'd never been to Georgia and didn't know either of them from asparagus.

"Go right in, Mrs. Marianne," said the receptionist with the glasses. "He's expecting you."

She walked past me, heels snicking, and around the counter, where a hallway swallowed her up. The place was lousy with hallways. I smelled a spring night for several minutes after I lost sight of her.

I smoked another cigarette and listened to the room. A woman called the *Free Press* to add something to a full-page advertisement she'd placed earlier for tomorrow's edition. A man complained to someone on the telephone that his middle initial was missing from a nameplate he'd ordered. Two guys laid bets over the partition separating them on that night's game with New York. The woman called back the *Free Press* to cancel the advertisement. It was a going office.

The redhead in the blue suit came out of the hallway behind the counter and left the way she'd come. She hadn't learned to walk the way she did watching Aunt Pittipat.

I got up and leaned on the counter by the woman with the glasses. "That Timothy Marianne's wife?"

"Yes."

"She looks like a model."

"She was." She folded her arms atop her workspace. If she had on make-up behind the granny lenses it was strictly basic. She was younger than she tried to appear. "They met at the auto show when he was with Ford. He took her off the hood of a brand new Thunderbird. I thought everyone knew that story. It was in *People* and everything."

"I guess I was wasting my time with *Billy Budd* that week. Do you need those?"

She touched the glasses. "Only to see with. Why?"

"You ought to try contact lenses. Green ones. And shampoo that tinsel out of your hair. What are you really, twenty, twenty-two?"

"Twenty-five. And you're out of bounds."

"Just restless. Mr. Hendriks get in?"

"You didn't see him, did you?"

"I figured there was a back way. You know, like Al Capone had."

"Who?"

"He was an Italian saint. Forget him. Might Mr. Marianne be free?"

"When is your appointment?" She'd turned on the deep freeze.

"We did that already. Tell him it's about his general manager, Alfred Hendriks. And an old robbery-murder."

The room got quiet, or maybe it just seemed that way because all three of the receptionists were looking at me. After a moment, Specs lifted the receiver off her intercom and flipped a switch.

15

"WHAT YOU SAID out there was textbook character assassination," said Timothy Marianne. "If Al doesn't sue it sure won't be because his lawyer told him he had a weak case."

I said, "My assets include a bottle of Scotch and one of those kitchen knives with a fifty-year guarantee. He can have the Scotch but I need the knife. I might want to cut my throat someday."

He made a noise halfway between a grunt and a chuckle. We were sitting in his office, which wasn't nearly as big as you'd expect it to be, especially in a building constructed from his own plans. He had a good view of the river and of Fighting Island behind his desk, but except for the antiques and a hardwood floor you could skate on, the room might have belonged to any corporate vice president in town. His big tufted chair was tipped back as far as it would go and he had one of his Thom McAns cocked up on a corner of the desk. It shared the gold leather top with a pen set, a telephone intercom, and a fiberglass model of the Stiletto the size and approximate shape of a bedpan.

"I learned something of the private investigation business when my first wife was divorcing me," he said. "Even the sleaziest of them hang out with lawyers too much to think they can get away with slandering a big gun in front of witnesses. What've you got?"

"A client who says Hendriks buffaloed him into providing cover for an armored car robbery in 1967. And something Hendriks told me when I spoke to him on the telephone this morning, which I'll go into later. Just now I'd like to discuss how he came to be with you."

"Shouldn't you ask him that?"

"I would if he didn't hide under his desk every time I try to talk to him. He's got that in-a-meeting and out-to-lunch line down cold."

"He's busy. We all are." He rolled the Stiletto model forward and back two inches with his toe. He was an angular six feet, slumped almost horizontal in a blue suit that looked as if it had fallen off a truck and he had picked it up and put it on and come straight there. No matter how good his tailor, the careless way he sat and moved would have any suit looking just like it in half an hour. His shoulders were high and narrow, his neck long, his face not as big as it seemed at first because I had been seeing it in newspapers and on television for a couple of years. It was long, tan, and rugged and his brows were darker than his hair, which was clipped short around the thin spots and left long where it was full to play down the retreat. I liked him, I don't know why. Maybe it was the suit.

"You mentioned murder," he said.

"One of the robbers was killed. The cops think he was shot by a partner."

"You think the partner was Al Hendriks?"

"What I think isn't part of the package. My client thinks Hendriks set him up to take the fall. If he's right, Hendriks got away clean with two hundred thousand cash. How much has he got invested in Marianne Motors?"

"Not two hundred thousand to start, although his holdings are worth twenty times that now. He was among my first backers when I left Ford to start my own firm. I took him with me out of the accounting pool there. Al's the best man with numbers I've ever seen. If he wanted to steal he could have stolen far more without ever leaving his desk."

"He wasn't an accountant yet when the armored car job went down. About when did he start working at Ford?"

"I don't know. I'd been aware of him for some time when he asked to join the team. He'd run figures for me sometimes as a favor. It was both our jobs if the brass found out. That was eight long years ago. If I'd known how long it would take . . ." He played with the model car some more.

"None of the stolen bills ever turned up, according to the cops," I said. "It takes time to launder that much dirty money. Years sometimes, and then you only get a few cents on the dollar. Meanwhile he had to live. When the cash did come through he couldn't spend it all right away. Your venture might have come along just at harvest time."

"I shouldn't be talking to you."

"Better you talk to me than I talk to the press. Old Man Stutch might get nervous and withdraw his investment."

"The Commodore's too busy concentrating on breathing to worry about money. The man is one hundred years old. But his grandsons are very, very conservative. You don't strike me as the type who goes crying to the press."

"I'm not. It was a bad bluff. But I'm fresh out of open doors, and I think you're just as curious about this as I am."

"You said something Al told you this morning made you suspicious. What was it?"

I uncrossed my legs and recrossed them the other way. "The man my client claims set him up was a student at Wayne State at the time of the stickup. Hendriks admitted he went to Wayne State, but he said he was studying in England on an exchange program during the race riots, which is when the thing took place."

"I know he went to Cambridge."

"Not then. I called Wayne State. Their records say he was carrying a full course load right here in Detroit that July."

"A mistake."

"Maybe. I want to hear him say it."

After a space he took his foot off the desk and got his intercom working. "Denise, when Mr. Hendriks comes in, would you ask him in here? He is? Yes, now." He hung up. "He's in his office."

The room got quiet. Then the man himself came in. He was wearing his dark hair shorter these days and it had started to gray, but his even features and trim build and the Cupid's-bow mouth could still stampede the distaff side of any singles bar in town. His dark suit and paisley necktie lay on him like cloth of gold. When he saw me sitting on the customer's side of the desk his stride slowed, but he kept coming and stopped in the middle of the room. He had never seen me before.

"Al, this is Amos Walker," Marianne said. "He wants to ask you a question. I'm sure you can satisfy him and then he can leave and we can go back to work."

"Walker." He pulled up the crease on his pants and sat in the chair facing mine. He had a dandy's taste in shoes, alligator with gold ornaments on the straps. He recognized the name from that morning. When I told him what I'd told Marianne he crossed his legs.

"I admire your deviousness," he said. "You could make it in the business world. Not far, but you might survive the office intrigue. Universities don't open student files to anyone who asks. Certainly not in the time since we spoke."

"I never even called them."

"I didn't think so. Anything else, Tim?"

"I guess not."

Hendriks rose and looked down at me. "I ought to take you to court. You'd be bareass in the street by Thanksgiving."

"Nice shoes," I said. "Know where I can get a pair like them for thirty bucks?"

"Stupid. Your client's got a stupid detective."

He went out. Marianne propped his foot on the desk, stuck

his hands in his pockets, and hoisted his eyebrows. "What was that about? You didn't strike me as a crank."

"I didn't expect him to break down and confess. Maybe I hoped he'd cook up some kind of excuse, but not too hard. Mainly I wanted to see how he'd take it."

"Pretty calm, I thought."

"So did I. If he'd shown just a little indignation I might be closing the file on him right now."

"You'll continue?"

"I'm like a bad cold that way."

"Are you always this sure of yourself?"

"I'm not sure now. If I were, this job would be a lot closer to finished. I'm being paid to find the ones who committed the robbery."

"You could lose your shirt. Al doesn't make empty threats. It's one of the reasons I made him general manager."

"The day I get a summons with his name on it and mine, I'll know I've got the wrong man."

"Explain."

"It would force me to prove he's guilty. Only an innocent man would risk it."

"You've got a hell of a lot to learn about the law," he said. "Just when you think you've got a handle on it, it changes color and scoots out from under you. Why do you think it took me eight years to get this far?"

"It's far."

"The higher I go the scareder I get. At first I was afraid I'd never have the money. Now that I have it I'm afraid someone will take it away. Never make a pretty woman your wife."

I couldn't tell if he was talking about the auto business or Mrs. Marianne. I got up. "I'll let you get back to work."

He nudged the model car with his toe. It rolled six inches and stopped at the edge of the desk. "My security chief isn't working out. There might be an opening there soon."

"I met him. Firing him would be a mistake. I wish you hadn't said that. It puts you on the dark side of the list."

"I can't have you running around raising suspicions, even unfounded ones. This is a superstitious industry. One bad rumor and investors take to the hills." He pushed the car back the other way. "Don't make me destroy you, Walker. I'm just starting to like you."

The guard downstairs had finished his sandwich and was reading a paperback with a naked woman and a scar-faced cowboy on the cover. He collected my tag and deposited it in the box without looking up.

"Mr. Hendriks asked me to put something in his car," I said. "I forget what it looks like."

He turned the page. "What am I, a car hop?"

I didn't push it. Outside, the skyline was clawing at the sun. I took off my coat, loosened my tie, picked a direction, and started walking along the front of the huge building. It wouldn't be parked where the general population left its cars.

My shirt was soaked through when I found the executive lot, two rows of diagonal spaces behind the building on the far end. It would have been closer if I'd gone the other way. But the exercise had loosened the muscles in my neck. Most of the cars, including the one parked in front of a sign with Marianne's name on it, were Stilettos. The one in Hendriks' space was a blue Porsche. It must have been a topic of some lively conversation upstairs.

I looked around. The lot had no guard. I inspected the underside of the canopy over the executives' entrance and stepped away to scan the roof, but there was no surveillance camera either. Mr. Piero was wasted on the dummy offices in Detroit. I walked around behind the Porsche, unholstered the Smith & Wesson, and shielding the movement with my body, smashed the right taillight lens with the butt. I scooped up all the shards from the pavement, wrapped them in my handkerchief, and put them in my left side pocket. Then I walked back the short way to get my car.

There were some unoccupied spaces opposite the Porsche.

I pulled into one that was starting to come into shadow and killed the engine. I cranked down the window on the passenger's side for cross draft and sat back and wanted a cigarette but didn't light one. The sun hung lower and lower in my rearview window and then dropped below the edge.

16

IT WAS NEARLY DARK OUT when Alfred Hendriks left the building, moving in that executive's stride I had seen in Marianne's office, unlocked the Porsche, and got in behind the wheel. The taillights sprang on, one of them white where the bulb was exposed, and the car shot backward out of the space and swung around and pounced forward, passing the Renault where I sat slumped below the headrest. I had to hustle to start the engine and get out behind him; I'd been expecting some noise when he started the Porsche. He was halfway to Jefferson by the time I rounded the building, but I needn't have worried. That white taillight stuck out like a cauliflower ear.

The shift had changed half an hour earlier, but traffic was still heavy. I kept him in sight easily until Detroit, where it cleared a little and he picked up the pace. The Renault had to think about it before kicking in when I punched the accelerator. I almost lost him when he turned onto Woodward, but I spotted the taillight at the last second and cut somebody off taking the turn, getting a chirp of brakes and an angry horn in my right ear. I closed to within half a block of him on Woodward. There the lights were against him.

The rules of detection are pretty specific on what to do when the bird won't flush. Following him until he does is long and boring and pays off about a third of the time, but up to a point it beats giving up. Just where that point is depends on the detective. Any way you play it you have hemorrhoids in your future.

For forty-five minutes we toured the city and its northern suburbs—it was full dark now and the lamps were lit—and then we skinned off into the side streets of Birmingham, a place where the alleys shine and the muggers are well above average. Cars were scarce. I gave him several blocks. At the top of a hill on a street lined with trees and low brick walls, the taillight winked and his headlamp beams raked a concrete post at the end of a driveway. I glided past, turned off my lamps, and coasted to a stop against the curb two houses down.

The moon was standing on edge. I got out with the flash from the glove compartment and walked back and checked the number on the concrete post, inserting my body between the light and the house. It occupied two levels, flat-roofed, horizontal, looking like a deck of cards with the top half cocked to the side. Low hedges bordered both levels at windowsill height.

The front door opened, spilling light onto the driveway at the far end. I trotted back to the Renault and climbed in. Two doors slammed, then the Porsche backed down the driveway and into the street. Light from a gaslamp on the lawn splashed on a woman in the passenger's seat and then the car slid out from under it, powering back the way it had come. I didn't get a long enough look to see if I could recognize her. I U-turned and followed.

He lost me at the second light. When he slowed for the yellow I did too, and then he hit the gas and shot across the intersection. I stopped on the red to avoid broadsiding a delivery van. By the time I got across, cheating by a couple of seconds, the white taillight had vanished.

I drove around a couple of blocks, then headed back to Woodward and took it down to my office. I called Lee Horst, an information broker who never goes home. We haggled a while, then I gave him the address in Birmingham and asked him for a name. After a minute or so of computer time he came back on.

"You need new clothes if you're going to move in this company," he said in his high soft voice. "Dressing the way you do you could be picked up for prowling in Timothy Marianne's neighborhood."

I thanked him and said I'd send him a check in the morning. I sat there chewing my lip for a while, then closed the office and went home. I'm not Lee Horst.

It was none of my business. Hendriks probably had a perfectly legitimate reason for driving off with the boss's wife. You get thoughts in this work that make you ashamed of your calling.

It had been a long day. I was too hungry to skip supper and too tired to talk to a waitress. I tracked down two minute steaks that were starting to curl in the refrigerator and grilled them for fifteen seconds on each side, apprehended some okra that had been hiding in a can in the cupboard, and released the works into my custody. Detecting is a hard habit to break, even at home. I interrogated a bottle of beer and turned on the TV to watch a pair of cops in unstructured jackets mow down some crooks and an innocent bystander or two with automatic weapons, in stereo yet; but not on my set. The telephone rang while I was changing channels.

"Anything?" It was my client.

"Where'd you get this number?" I asked.

"They's three more books than when I went in. I thought you was exaggerating about the telephone companies. I axed you did you get anything."

"I had a talk with the cop who arrested you. Also Hendriks, in person this time. Marianne was there too."

"So?"

"So nothing. Hendriks still says he was in England. The difference now is I'm sure he's lying."

"*I* knew that."

"You're not conducting this investigation."

"So what now?"

"Now I go to bed. You should too. You aren't used to staying up this late."

He paused. "How come you never answer a question the first time I axe it?"

"What?"

"Hey, I thought you at least was friendly."

"Sorry. It hasn't been one of my more productive days. I may have an angle on Hendriks. Maybe not, but it's worth looking at. Meanwhile you might want to stay close to your room this weekend. I don't want you spooking him. Besides, whoever made that try up north might be looking for you here."

"That don't scare me."

"Your brains in your lap wouldn't scare you. It's your parole I'm worried about. The board doesn't take to ex-cons with high profiles even if the attention isn't their fault."

"What's your problem? You been paid."

I said, "That wasn't friendly at all."

"Yeah. Okay. Call a guy, okay? This waiting shit's worse than slam."

"You try shooting baskets like I said?"

"I started to, but I didn't get that far. Listen, what you said about checking their teeth?"

"Yeah."

"It ain't true."

I said I'd call. He said okay again and broke the connection.

My neck was almost back to normal, but now my head ached. I washed down two aspirins with Scotch straight from the bottle and went to bed. Lying there I thought about prison.

Time is the real punishment, not any of the several things that can happen to you inside. Sadistic guards aren't the problem they are in movies. They exist, but given shift rotation and the high burnout factor, the hell they represent is short-term. Shower-room rapes aren't any more common than the alley kind, and anyone who went to public school knows how to conduct himself during the bullying in the yard. The longer you're in the less frightening the prospect of sharing another inmate's bunk, all things being relative. The storied Hole is extinct. Modern administrators know it's unnecessary. They've got isolation, and the old dark-cell with nothing but an unsanitary hole in a bare floor is no worse and maybe even a little better than being left alone in medium-gray light for an indefinite period with nothing to do, no books to read and nobody to talk to. Outside isolation, the routine doesn't change: up at six, twenty minutes to shave, shower, dress, and eat breakfast, work till eleven, thirty minutes in the yard, work till four, twenty minutes for supper, an hour in the TV room if you haven't killed an inmate or sassed a guard lately, lights out at nine. It keeps you from thinking, so that's not punishment. The worst of it is day on day in an institution and time passing outside. Darkness is abolished. There is always light coming in from somewhere, and like a space traveler marooned on a planet with two suns you close your eyes and pretend you're surrounded by night. Then you open them to that bland light and you know you'll never make it. Or you're afraid you will. It's the one thing in life that's worse than you picture. I didn't even want to think about how it was when you were innocent.

I wondered what was taking place between Alfred Hendriks and Timothy Marianne's wife and if it had anything to do with anything.

It seems I slept. At some point I stopped thinking about prison and was in it. I had on starched denims and shoes corrugated inside from the rubbing of many feet. Someone big and hairy laid an arm across my shoulders in the library—a library whose books carried no mention of crime or violence or sex, rows of *North American Birds*, anglers' guides, and Laura Ingalls Wilder—and told me I was his girlfriend tonight. I ducked the arm and then was glad to find myself suddenly in my own bed in darkness. Only something was wrong with that, because my bedroom is never dark. There's a streetlamp outside the window. Then I smelled cigar smoke.

He was sitting in front of the window, the solid dark bulk of him standing out a little from the night. The orange eye of his cigar hovered around his thighs, then came up, etching a glowing trail, and brightened as he pulled at it, highlighting a city block of face and light hair and beard. Then it subsided. Gray smoke caught its light, turning in the still air.

"You sleep hard." He sounded cheerful.

"You work quiet." I sat up, not too quickly. "My wallet's there on the bureau. You don't want the watch. Not worth the trip to the pawnshop."

"I'm not a burglar."

"I was afraid you wouldn't be. Okay if I turn on the light? When I get the hell beat out of me I like to see it." I keep the Smith & Wesson on the lamp table at night.

"I'm not muscle either."

"Listen, it's okay, so long as you don't find me attractive. I just went through that."

"Not hardly. You must lead an interesting life."

"More all the time." I waited.

"I knocked. No one answered, so I came in."

"The guy that sold me the lock said it was burglarproof."

"No such thing. I was a locksmith's apprentice. There are just so many kinds and I've knocked them all down and put them back together. Combination's the best, but who wants to live in a bank vault?" He puffed. His eyes were set back under a round brow. "Get dressed. We're going somewhere."

"Casual, or shirt and shoes?"

"Doesn't matter. The Commodore isn't picky."

17

I TURNED ON THE LIGHT. To hell with permission. The gun wasn't there.

"Over here," he said. "On the windowsill. You ought to keep it under your pillow."

"Not in this weather. They rust when you sweat on them." I looked at him. He was a healthy thirtyish in a gray double-breasted with tight black leather gloves on his hands. His face was round and smooth and babyish but for the ginger-colored beard. His hair was lighter, curly, and starting to recede. He had Irish eyes. His boots were black vinyl with zippers inside the ankles and he wore his pants outside them. As far as I could tell he went a little under six feet and something over two hundred, some of it fat but not enough. I said, "I know someone who could take you."

"Wouldn't surprise me. I'm not tough." He forked the cigar between gleaming black fingers and ground it out in one of my ashtrays in his other hand. "I don't mean to rush you, but the old man isn't going to live forever."

"He already has. If we're talking about Commodore Stutch."

"There's another?"

I got up and dug a pair of slacks and a sportshirt out of the bureau. I didn't see myself getting back to sleep that night anyway. The alarm clock read eleven after two. "He's awake at this hour?"

"It's his best one. He fades out around four, but he does more in those two hours than anyone you ever heard of does in eight. I watched him bail out a country once."

"Must've been something to see." I tucked in the shirt.

"Not really. Just the old man making a couple of calls, until you thought about what he was doing. It beat hell out of the limousine rental business."

"That what you did before?"

"Yeah. His regular guy didn't show up at the airport one time and I was there hustling fares. He hired me on the way to his place and used the cellular phone to fire his old guy. The limo was new, so he bought that too. That was, what, six years ago."

I tied my shoes. "You must like the work."

"The hours stink, but it pays great. He doesn't get out much anymore. Mostly I run errands."

"Like putting the snatch on PI's."

"It isn't a snatch. I almost forgot." He pulled an envelope out of his jacket and tossed it on the bed. The springs swayed. "For your time."

I picked it up and counted the new bills inside. "My time's not worth this much."

"Call it a tip."

I held out one bill—Grant's one of my favorite presidents—and flipped the rest into his lap. "Buy yourself some better cigars. I'll talk to the man first."

"Six years," he said, looking inside the flap. "Nobody's ever handed back one of the old man's envelopes without an audience to appreciate it."

"Maybe they were afraid you'd forget to tell him."

"Your house. I guess you can call anybody a crook you want to in it." He stood and put away the package. "Ready?"

"Do I get to ride up front?"

"Sure. Be nice having someone to talk to for a change."

He loved to talk. I learned he'd given up locksmithing because his fingers were too big, driven a cab for a couple of years, then went to work for the limousine company and was saving up for a reconditioned stretch Lincoln of his own when the Commodore came along and offered him twice what he could have made freelancing. Now he was driving a gray Cadillac with cream leather seats and a fuzzbuster and CD player built into the dash. His taste ran toward Julie Andrews and the Original Ink Spots.

"What was that about finding you attractive?" he asked. He didn't miss a green light the whole way.

"Just a dream I had. You ever do time?"

"Uh-uh. You?"

"Just the soft kind."

"I'd crack up," he said. "I've got to move. It's another reason I left the shop."

"What do they call you, Irish?"

"Gerald. And I'm Swiss on both sides."

The Grosse Pointe house was on Lake Shore Drive, of course, with a view of St. Clair shining like polished shale under the same narrow moon I had seen in Birmingham earlier that night. He swung through the open gate, wound through a quarter-mile of lawn, and stopped in front of a round white portico attached to all the brick east of Wisconsin, where he unlocked my door from a button on his side of the car.

"Go right in, they're expecting you. The old man doesn't like leaving the car outside in this damp air. He's cheap about some things."

I had my choice of two doors, either of which would have let in Moby Dick on a platter. I chose the one on the right. The big front hall echoed when I drew the door shut behind me. A gold-bordered rug big enough to carpet all the walls, floors, and ceilings in my house looked puny in the center of a tesselated floor an acre across. Other than that the room was bare, lit gloomily by the fanlight over the door. I had been standing there the better part of a minute when a heavy dark-suited bald man separated himself from the shadows and came my way, being careful to walk around the rug. I wondered if that was a house rule.

"Mr. Walker? I'm Hector Stutch, the Commodore's grandson." He took my hand in a doughy palm.

I got it back as quickly as I could without offending him. "I've seen your picture, Mr. Stutch. You run Stutch Petrochemicals."

"I'm the president and board chairman, yes. Does our generation really run anything?"

He had at least a generation on me, but I didn't say anything. He arranged his face into a businesslike mode. It was as doughy as his hand. "I wonder if I might speak with you before you see Grandfather."

"The Commodore is ready for Mr. Walker."

I hadn't seen or heard this one coming. He was my age, dark and Arabic-looking, in a white coat and pants and white shoes with rubber soles, which explained his silent approach. The outfit looked medical, but a tailor had been at it. He didn't dump it into any community hamper at the end of the day.

"Yes." All the business went out of the soft face. It was like hoisting a white flag. "This is Raf, Grandfather's nurse." He spelled the name. "He'll take you to him. I'd be grateful if you'd see me before you leave."

"Aren't you coming along?"

"He hasn't been invited," said Raf.

Hector glared. "I'm capable of telling Mr. Walker that."

"The study is this way."

I accompanied Raf down a passage illuminated by fluorescent tubes mounted over portraits best left dark. "What was all that?"

"The Commodore seldom confides in his grandsons."

"That's your privilege, huh?"

"A man his age has no secrets from his nurse." He rapped on a heavy maple door and opened it for me.

The room was nearly as large as the entrance hall. The rug was identical and the walls, paneled in baroque carvings, towered into darkness above a dome of green light on a massive old desk at the rear. Behind it, tall drapes covered a Cinemascope window to within a foot of the center. Squarely between them sat a thin very old man. His ears turned out, what hair he had was very pale and very fine, and his skull was plain under the skin of his face. Only his head was visible in the eerie green light, resembling in its disembodied absolute stillness the pendulum of a stopped clock. He looked dead.

The door clicked behind me and I realized I was alone with him. I started forward.

"Stay there," he snapped. "I need a magnifying lens to read a newspaper, but I can count the strokes of a hummingbird at a hundred yards."

I stopped. "That must be a hot betting item at picnics."

"Levity in the young is unseemly. Repellent in the old."

"I fall somewhere in the middle."

"Shut up and learn."

His voice was thin but far from weak. It had a New England crack in it you don't hear much anymore, even in New England. I shut up.

"Your name is Amos Walker, no middle initial," he said. "You're thirty-six years old. You fought in Vietnam and Cambodia, not without distinction, re-upped and transferred to the military police after you shipped home, left there after three years, and received your private investigator's license while employed with Dale A. Leopold, deceased, at Apollo Investigations. You're divorced—irreconcilable differences—live alone, drink rather too much but you're not an alcoholic, and smoke Winstons. The application you filed for a MasterCard last month has been turned down. Right so far?"

"I don't know about the application. I'm still waiting for word."

"Trust me. You were dropped from the Detroit Police Academy just before graduation for assault and battery of a fellow cadet, a congressman's son. Reason given was he made a homosexual advance on you in the shower. What was it really?"

"I didn't like his towel."

"Bah. What's your interest in Alfred Hendriks?"

"I give up, what?"

The head moved a fraction of an inch. "I've paid you well for this information."

"You paid me fifty bucks for pulling me out of a nice warm nightmare and dropping me in this mausoleum. Ask Gerald for the rest."

"You gave it back?"

"My house has been hit twice in a few days. I didn't want it lying around."

"Sit down. Please."

He had to twist his mouth to get the word out. It had been cooped up in there a long time. The chair nearest his desk was a big chocolate leather overstuffed, as heavy as a tractor wheel. I sank into it, and when I found bottom we were still far enough apart to fly pigeons. At that angle he was wearing a metallic gray suit and a striped necktie snugged up painfully tight for three in the morning. Loose skin hung over the collar in speckled garlands.

"Go ahead and smoke," he said. "I never did but I always liked the sting of it. Henry didn't. He was the very last to install ashtrays in his cars. Stubborn bastard."

It took me a moment to realize he was talking about Henry Ford. I lit up, using my cupped hand for an ashtray. His office had nothing on Henry's cars. Raf would probably have seen to that.

He was looking at me. His eyes were large and very much alive in the skull face. "Returned the money. You're past your era. I started this business on a handshake. Not the petrochemicals business, the other one. That was how we did things then. Not like now. If I paid in taxes what I'm paying lawyers to keep me from having to pay taxes, I'd be ahead of the game. If I could spit, which I haven't had the energy to do since I was ninety, I couldn't do it without hitting a calfskin briefcase. That's the only leather you'll find in the industry these days, the lawyers' briefcases. Have you smelled a new car lately, Walker?"

"Cheap shoes."

"Worse. A new car should smell of leather and varnished wood. Well, it's one of the reasons I got out. The business didn't smell the same. It wasn't just the plastic, it was the smell of the people I found myself doing business with. Japs and gangsters. Arabs now, like my nurse. You met Raf?"

"He doesn't think much of your grandson."

"Which one, Hector? Hector's competent. He won't gamble, though, and that's how I built this company. The first one too. It's probably my fault. He's scared of me. His father wasn't, but I raised him myself. My son wouldn't have anything to do with the business. I wish his sons had half his guts, but if they did they wouldn't be here. I'd give up the reins if I wasn't convinced they're what's keeping me alive. I'm fond of living, obviously."

"You're my first centenarian," I said.

"What I am is a freak. But I won't be spoken to as one. I'm wandering, where was I? Yes, the Japs. I never liked doing business with them. Not that I'm one of these wimps screaming for trade restrictions. The Big Three have been rolling fat for decades, forgot what it's like to compete. Peerless, Hudson, Studebaker, Durant, Edison, Packard, Rickenbacker—bet you never knew Captain Eddie tried his hand at automaking; lost his shirt, too—two dozen more, they're all gone now. American Motors is anybody's whore. It'll do the survivors good to sweat a little. That has something to do with why I told Hector to sign seven hundred and fifty million over to Marianne."

"I wondered about that."

"He hasn't a chance in hell," the Commodore said. "I told Kaiser the same thing, but he wouldn't listen and GM and Ford ground him up like flour. I made the investment under certain conditions. When Marianne folds, Stutch Petrochemicals gets the plant and equipment and whatever material he has in stock. I'll sell it to one of the others, turn any profit back into the company, and apply any loss against taxes. There are loopholes in the new code you could drive a truck through."

"What if he doesn't fold?"

"Then I'll be significantly richer than I already am."

I pinched out my cigarette, dropped the butt into a pocket, and wiped the ashes off my hand with my handkerchief. Said nothing.

"No doubt you're wondering why I'm telling you all this," he said. "It isn't because I'm a garrulous old man."

"My guess is since you know so much about me you also know I'm curious to a fault. You're trading."

"You're smart. It's too bad your mouth is smarter, but you'll grow out of it. I've given Marianne a year to fail. That would be the time frame under normal circumstances. Naturally, if you know something about him or his general manager that could speed up the clock I'd want to hear it. There are gears to set in motion."

"Who's your plant in Marianne's office, one of the receptionists?"

"You haven't paid to see my whole hand," he said.

"Tell Raf to go sterilize something first."

"Raf."

A section of baroque paneling to the right of the window slid back. The nurse's white outfit looked green in the lamplight.

"That'll be all. Come back at bedtime. No, use the door. Leave the panel open so Mr. Walker can see inside."

The Arab crossed the room as quietly as running water and went out. I waited for the click. Then: "Any others, or does he hang outside the window?"

The old man moved his head negatively. "Once in a big while, like tonight, I make a direct contact without going through my grandsons. Since nobody deals in handshakes anymore I prefer to have a witness present. But a man behaves differently when a third party is in the room. How did you know he was there?"

"He just looked to me like the kind that sneaks around."

"I don't like him either. He has a reliable memory for conversations and having him around forestalls my heirs from placing me in a home. Once you've survived everything else you have to protect yourself from your family." Skin twitched over his skull. "You have my word no one is listening, electronically or otherwise."

I believed him. I told him most of it. I left out my client's name and Alfred Hendriks' moonlight drive with Marianne's wife. It ran long even without them. Toward the end he was still listening closely, but his eyes were less alive. It was coming up on four o'clock.

"I can get that information from Cambridge and Wayne State," he said. His speech was slowing. "In return you'll come to me with whatever you learn. I'll decide whether to go to the authorities with it and when."

This time I shook my head. "I haven't got as far as the authorities in my thinking. If it looks like it's for them, that's where I'll go. But I'll let you know before it goes public. That will give you time to pull some levers."

"My father did a little horse trading. He enjoyed the haggling. I never did. I'd name a figure, the other party would name a figure, and we'd decide on one or the other or call it quits. Well and good. You won't mind if I give you the information through Raf?"

"I'd prefer Gerald."

"My driver? Why?"

"He likes his job too much to be running his own game. Also he's Swiss. Maybe some of the neutrality rubbed off on him."

He sat back. It was the first time he'd moved more than just his head. "Pleasure doing business with you, Mr. Walker." He lifted his right hand from under the desk and held it out.

I got up and went over and took it. His grip was surprisingly frail. The bones of his wrist were obvious and brittle-looking under the spotted skin. The metallic suit was big on his shriveled frame. The brain in his skull was the only strong thing about him, and it was tiring.

"Hector will be hovering around out front," he said. His thin old voice had lost most of its crack. "Every time I meet with someone privately he thinks I'm conspiring to unseat him from the board. Reassure him, but don't tell him anything."

I said I'd take care of it. He withdrew his hand and closed his eyes. I waited to see if he was breathing. Then I left.

18

HECTOR STUTCH WAS WAITING for me in the big hall. He might have been standing there all this time. Raf was nowhere in sight, which given his liking for cramped dark places with peepholes didn't mean he wasn't with us. A Caesarean birth, probably, still searching for the womb.

"How did you like the Commodore?" Hector asked.

"I liked him fine," I said. "I get along with most of the older landmarks around town."

"I overheard when he told Gerald to pick you up. That's how I knew your name. You were in there quite a while."

"I got a history lesson. When the first tire blew, he held the jack. I guess you know everyone around thinks he's no longer actively involved in the business."

"His idea. What business are *you* in?"

He'd been eyeing my slacks and slip-ons and green shirt with a golf club on the pocket. "I'm the pro at Metro Beach. Your grandfather was having problems with his slice."

He found a scowl. "No call to be rude. I have a family at home. I don't hang around here this late to be treated like an idiot child."

"Sorry, Mr. Stutch. It's just as late for me and I've got a headache. The Commodore likes his business private. Your name didn't come up, if it means anything."

"Of course not. I don't live on Grandfather's good opinion." But his expression had come around a hundred and eighty. He made me think of Pillsbury for some reason. "He's just —difficult. I worry about him, the hours he keeps."

"I don't think he'll endow any cat hospitals or anything. His faculties are the last ones you have to worry about. Is Gerald handy, or do I walk from here?"

"He's waiting out front with the car. That's standard at this time when Grandfather has someone in. At this hour— "

"He fades out. I saw."

"I suppose so. Well, as long as it didn't have anything to do with the company."

I went on looking at him. His bald head glittered in the fanlight.

"Well," he said, "good night."

It was morning, but the point wasn't worth arguing. "Good night, Mr. Stutch."

Gerald was behind the wheel of the Caddy, listening to "My Echo, My Shadow, and Me." I got in beside him. He was grinning in his beard.

"Pip, isn't he?"

My visitor was hesitant.

It was past nine. I'd slept two hours after Gerald dropped me off and awakened with my head and neck feeling fine and my eyes like two flesh wounds. I had been deducing behind the desk in my office with my feet on the calendar pad and my mouth wide open when the buzzer went off, telling me someone had just opened the door to the reception room. I waited for the knock. It didn't come and I decided that someone had looked into the wrong office and gone on down the hall. It was Saturday anyway and I was only there because the Concorde to Paris was full up. Then he came in.

He didn't open the connecting door wide enough, bumped into it, and slid in around the edge. Opening it further would have been a commitment he wasn't ready to make. That kind of reluctance is old stuff in my line. In this case I figured he'd probably be a lot less tentative without the gun.

It was a piece of junk with plastic side-grips and that learn-gunsmithing-at-home bluing that comes off on your hands when the humidity's high. It was more black than blue and the gun itself was squat and ugly and probably lethal from both ends. The man holding it was black too. His hair was gray and he was spreading in middle age under a navy blue suit that was as cheap as Timothy Marianne's looked. This one wore his without irony. He wasn't wearing a tie and his shirt was wrinkled. His face was just a face. He had a thick neck.

"Hands up."

I raised them. He handled the gun in that sloppy way they do in movies and it didn't seem worth the chance of his hitting the ceiling instead of me. Under the desk I worked the middle drawer open with my knee. The Smith & Wesson was inside, giving my kidney a break.

"Wrong mark," I said. "The safe's full of my dirty laundry."

"This isn't a robbery."

I'd been through this before. If I was still asleep I was dreaming of strangers now. I said, "I gave up guessing. I stink at it."

"Where's your client?"

"Which one?"

His face wore a skin of sweat. The gun was shaking. I hate it when they shake. "DeVries. Where's he staying?"

"No DeVrieses today. Sure you got the right building?" The drawer was open now. The Smith was two feet from my hands and turned the wrong way. I wasn't asleep.

"Don't be funny. I got a friend in Lansing. He ran your plate. I know you're not hiding him at your place because I watched it all day yesterday. Tell me where he is or I'll shoot you. I mean it."

"I know that. What do I look like, a redstick ranger?"

It surprised him. His brain didn't work that fast anyway.

He was still turning it over when I threw the telephone at him. He tried to catch it.

I didn't expect that. Most people try to dodge. It told me something about him, that however slowly his brain might function his reflexes were better than good. But in trying to catch it he forgot about the gun and I lunged across the desk and slapped it out of his hand. I had my revolver on him before his hit the rug.

I kicked my chair back and stood up the rest of the way. "Put the telephone where it belongs. That squawking goes right up my back."

After a moment he stooped over and lifted it in two hands and put it back together on the desk. I came around, covering him, and picked up his gun. It was a .32, made in West Germany. Stickum from the pawnbroker's label still clung to the frame. "Ever fire this thing?"

"No." He was rubbing his hand, which had bent back on itself when I'd knocked the gun out of it. "I bought it six months ago. There's no place to shoot it in Detroit."

"You're lucky. At least I left you with a hand. Who are you?"

"George St. Charles."

He didn't say it as if it meant anything, which it didn't. "Let's see your wallet," I said. "Toss it on the desk."

He went on rubbing his hand. I gave him one of those gun looks. He said, "You won't shoot me."

"Mister, that's what they're for. The wall."

He went over and leaned on his palms. I kicked his feet apart, put his gun in my coat pocket, and covered him with mine while I patted him down. I kept going after I found the wallet. No hideouts. I backed away.

"Sit down."

He straightened awkwardly and found his way to the customer's chair, where he sat working the sprained hand. I put away the Smith and went through the worn wallet. George St. Charles was the name on his driver's license, which had him living in Cleveland. I found a Social Security card under the same name and an insurance card from the Detroit Firemen's Fund Association, the last dog-eared and dirty. One hundred and forty-three dollars cash. I tossed him the wallet. He was quicker this time and caught it.

"Travel money," I said. "You don't look like the kind that carries that much all the time. Where are you staying?"

"Red Roof Inn by Inkster. I drove up from Ohio. My wife thinks I'm at a retired firefighters' convention in Cincinnati."

"The DFFA card explains the lingo. You should've been more careful talking to the Wakelys." I cocked a hip up on the corner of the desk. "What's your gripe with DeVries?"

He said nothing. The wallet lay forgotten in his lap and he was looking at my left ear. I took out his gun and laid it on the calendar pad.

"You should stick to driving. You're better behind the wheel than on the range. My guess is you had charge of the fire truck. You working alone or with Hendriks?"

"I don't know who that is."

"I believe you. If he outsourced the job he'd get someone who knew a weapon from a doorstop. So we're back to a gripe. What was Davy Jackson to you?"

"I don't know who that is either."

I leaned back across the desk and broke out the office bottle and two ounce glasses. I filled both and held one out. He took his attention off my ear, identified the item, and curled his fingers around it. He held it there.

I waved mine around the office. "This is strike two. Strike one was when you and Hank tried to stop us up north. I'd bunt."

"Are you turning me in?"

"*There's* a thought."

"Shit." He bent his arm then and drank. Made a face and lowered the glass. "I was with the department thirteen years, the last four with Engine Twenty-One. Know where that is?"

I shook my head.

"Well, I don't know where it is now, but back then we specialized in mattress fires and blowed furnaces. That tell you anything?"

"You weren't with Grosse Pointe."

"Not on the same planet. If a rickety old place went up in town, chances were it was in our wheelhouse. Sherman, Antietam, Mt. Elliott—"

"Twelfth Street."

"Especially Twelfth. Especially in July 'sixty-seven. That March my sister's boy joined the company. He put in for it. Wanted to learn from his old uncle, see. He was twenty. Henry Waters, ever hear the name?"

I drank. "If I did it would be twenty years ago, right?"

"Right. Henry he loved the work. Got his uniform tailored, waxed his helmet for parades. First one down the pole when the bell rang, first one up the ladder when somebody screamed. He was good, too. Even when he was off duty, if you smelled smoke you knowed Henry was there in the middle of it, getting his suit tore and his face all smudged. Well, I guess I don't need to tell you what's a redstick ranger. Wasn't just showing off for whitey, though. He wanted to be a good fireman."

He emptied his glass and stuck it out. I refilled it. He drank off half.

"Sunday night," he said, "first Sunday of the trouble, we made a run to a dry cleaner's on Clairmount. Arson. Place was totally engaged when we got there. Owner had SOUL painted on all the windows in big white letters, but that didn't mean anything after the first day. They tried blocking us off—"

"Who did?"

"The people. The fucking brothers and sisters that lived on the street. Didn't matter what color you were or that all you wanted to do was keep the whole fucking city from burning down, if you had on a uniform you were the Man. They linked hands when they heard the siren, formed a human chain. I was driving—you were right about that—and I geared down and crawled till somebody lost his nerve or his grip and broke. Then they started throwing shit, bricks and busted paving and shit. It was the ugliest thing I ever seen, and I helped pull people out of fires burned all over with their flesh coming off in my hands.

"We got to the place. Henry was on top of the truck before it stopped. He grabbed point on the hose and rode the ladder to the roof. A brick hit him in the leg on the way up and he almost fell, but he hung on with the nozzle under one arm and got his footing and climbed up a couple more rungs, I guess to get out of throwing range. He never seen the power line. He took forty-eight hundred volts, the coroner said."

I took a hit from the bottle. The alcohol splashed loudly in the silence. "You promised your sister you'd look after Henry?"

"I sure stunk at it."

"How'd she take it?"

"How you think? She blamed me. She got over it, though."

"But you didn't."

"Maybe if she didn't I would've. I don't know."

"That when you quit?"

"No, I hung on for a year. They were getting set to fire me so I left. My driving went to hell. Didn't care if I got there on time or not. They frown on that. I took the wife and moved out. I'm a certified mechanic in Cleveland."

"Can you hot-wire a car?"

"Gets easier every time they add a new anti-theft feature. I watch TV. I know you never use your own car when you go to kill someone. I never thought doing it would cost so much, though. You seen how much I got left." He finished his drink and turned the glass upside-down on the desk. "I got a friend in Lansing, like I said. He let me know when DeVries was getting out."

"He didn't set the fire that got Henry killed. That was another building."

"I know that. What am I going to do, track down the brother or sister that throwed that brick?"

A symbol. A large black headline-draped symbol, Richard DeVries. I wondered how many George St. Charleses there were in Detroit, in the world. I wondered how many other victims' survivors were still looking to collect on forgotten debts. Suddenly I got mad. It might have been the whisky on an empty stomach. I slid off the desk. The room tilted, then returned to center. "Let's go. My car's down the block."

His face got tired. "You're turning me in?"

"No. Here." I held out his gun.

He stared at it. "Where we going?"

"You asked to see my client."

After a long time he accepted the gun.

19

THE ALAMO HOTEL looked worse by day. Dirty sunlight canting in through the front window threw the neon letters across the old rug and an older man snoring in the elephant's-foot chair. He had on a stained shapeless sportcoat over a dirty undershirt and his ankles were bare above deck shoes worn through at the toes. The hole in his gray stubble had one tooth in it.

In that light the man propping his chin on his hand behind the counter looked less like Vincent Price and more like a long stagnant drink of water with shoeblack on his hair. He was wearing the same shawl collar and brown wing tips, but he had shaved recently. Tufts of bloodstained toilet paper clung to his chin like dandelions gone to seed. His runny eyes took in St. Charles and me with a look that said nothing could surprise or repulse him.

"Double's forty bucks. Up front."

I said, "Where's Hank Aaron?"

Recognition sank in like rancid butter melting. He took his chin out of his hand. A piece of toilet paper fluttered like a moth to the counter. "Home," he said. "With four cracked ribs and a pink slip. I got a scattergun back here."

"I remember. Mr. DeVries in? We want to talk to him."

He relaxed visibly. "Eighteen. Upstairs—"

"End of the hall. I remember that too."

The tight staircase smelled of dust and worse. We kept our hands off the walls. At the top St. Charles hesitated. I looked back at him and he caught up. He had his hand on the gun in his side pocket. We stopped before eighteen and I laid my knuckles against the scaly wood.

"Yeah." The big man's voice was muffled on the other side.

"Walker," I said. "I brought someone with me."

The door opened a crack. A brown eye looked down at us from near the top.

"Who's he?"

"George St. Charles. You wouldn't know him."

"What's in his pocket?"

"The ugliest gun you ever saw. I told him to keep it out of sight or get slapped with an anti-blight citation."

"What's he fixing to do with it?"

"Shoot you, what else? Open the door."

The command was just weird enough, or else he was used to obeying orders from men who sounded like they expected him to. Anyway he opened the door. Standing there he blocked whatever light was in the room. He was wearing stiff new clothes from a Big and Tall shop, but the buttons were strained on the plaid flannel shirt and the twill pants rode dangerously low on his hips.

"Stay away from the stomach and lower torso," I told St. Charles. "Takes too long; he might get medical help. The heart's too easy to miss. Bullets glance off the skull sometimes. The groin's best at close range. There's a major artery there and it'll all be over in a few minutes. Make the first one count."

DeVries didn't move. Neither did St. Charles for several seconds. Then he took the gun out of his pocket.

He wasn't shaking now. Somehow that seemed worse than when he was. I bent my fingers under the hem of my coat. If I'd gauged him wrong I'd have to be quick. The Police Special was all the way behind my hip.

"Shit." He thrust the German weapon across his body, turning the butt up.

I took it. I breathed for the first time in a while. "Go home,"

I said. "Nineteen sixty-seven's over finally. Happy New Year."

He turned exhausted features on me. "How'd you know?"

"You're no killer. Twenty years ago you might've been. Henry's a long time dead."

"I hope you're not waiting for thanks."

"You can get a cab on Jefferson."

He walked down the hall and descended the stairs. We listened to the lobby door slam.

"What the hell was that?" DeVries demanded.

"Not a redstick ranger," I said. "He wasn't lying to the Wakelys about that."

"That was him? No shit. What's his problem?"

"Nothing to do with you. Can we go in, or have you got a woman in there?"

He started a little, then moved aside. "Make it quick. I'm going out."

The room had a chair, a bed, and yellow-painted walls. A braided oval rug had started to take on the contours of the boards beneath. The window looked out on a block wall. The toilet he'd said he was lucky to have was down the hall, the telephone mounted next to the door. He shared them with the floor, and maybe with the rest of the building. He left the hall door open and hung a leg over the footboard of the bed.

I pointed my chin at the door. "House rule?"

"Hot in here, man. Window's stuck shut."

"Headed anywhere in particular, or just restless?"

"Thought I'd take your advice, shoot some hoops. You my parole cop now?"

"You act wired."

"Yeah. You think I'd be used to sitting around. It's harder when nobody's making you. Would you of let that dude shoot me?"

"If he were ever going to he'd have done it up north when we came out of the lake. One siren wouldn't have stopped him. You didn't look too worried."

"I never seen the dude in my life. I didn't know what was what."

I told him what was what. He ran a hand over his short beard.

"I thought I was the only one still fighting that fight," he said.

"Some wounds take more stitches to close."

"I was a stupid kid. I got no trouble admitting that now. But I didn't start out to hurt no one. Especially not a brother."

"He knew that. Finally." I twirled the chair and straddled the seat. The legs swayed under my weight. I figured DeVries had never sat in it. "We could be getting a break from high up. Leland Stutch has offered to find out some things in return for whatever we scratch up on our end."

"Who's Leland Stutch?"

"You never heard of the Commodore?"

"Him. Hell, ain't he dead by now?"

"Not hardly."

"What's his angle?"

"He spent an hour explaining it. The point is he's got drag."

"Can he get the money out of Hendriks, you figure?"

"If he wanted to he could draw a check on the household account. What he's going to do is help us prove Hendriks was here at the time of the robbery. Don't say you know that. The cops don't."

"What's the cops got to do with anything? Man in jail can't give me what I got coming."

"He can if he wants to stay *out* of jail."

He grinned slowly and leaned back against the headboard, lacing his hands behind his shaved head. The box springs groaned. "Thought you said you was honest."

"There's honest and honest. Gouging stolen money from thieves was good enough for Errol Flynn."

"You ain't wearing green."

"Even Errol would put on gray in Detroit."

"You believe me about not robbing that armored car?"

"It's nothing I could take to court. Yet. But yeah. If there's a way to make Hendriks square up with you we'll do it. But if he hit that car and killed Davy Jackson he's going down for it either way."

"I ain't paying for eithers."

"Call a plumber. They guarantee their work."

Something started beeping. DeVries was off the bed and halfway to the door when he realized what direction the noise was coming from. He hung back. I unclipped the paging device from inside my coat and turned it off. "You got a date for basketball or what?"

"Lady called," he said. "She's calling me back. It ain't worth talking about."

"I guess not." I watched him starting to pace. "You letting me do this like we agreed?"

"Yeah, yeah. Shit. You as nosy as one of them guards. I'm getting my ashes hauled is all."

"You do pretty good for a guy just out of the joint."

"Coach always said I was a self-starter."

I decided I was wired too. It was getting so you couldn't count on two hours' sleep doing the trick. I rose and turned the chair back the other way. "I've got a message. Okay if I use the horn?"

"Don't tie it up."

The hallway had been repainted recently, judging by how few numbers had been scratched on the wall beside the telephone. A film of grime was forming already. I bonged two dimes into the slot and dialed my service. The mouthpiece smelled of bad breath.

"One call, Mr. Walker," said the sugary voice. "She left a number to call back. A Mrs. Marianne."

20

THE EARLY HOT SPELL was in its third day. Ralph Lauren halter tops and alligator sandals were out in Birmingham, in convertibles and on bicycles and walking dogs on the sidewalks. I was starting to feel less strung out as I turned in between the concrete posts and ground to a halt before an open garage with a Stiletto and a maroon Turbo Saab parked inside. The driveway looked strange without Alfred Hendriks' Porsche sitting in it.

In broad daylight the house looked less like a cut deck of cards and more like the place where James Mason lived above Mt. Rushmore in *North by Northwest.* Decks and balconies ringed both levels and cedar siding blended with tall evergreens planted in the yard. Sprinklers swished there, part of an underground system.

She answered the door herself in a gold silk blouse and the tight black pants we used to call toreadors when cornfed blondes wore them and nothing else in magazines. They had gold stitching down the sides. Her feet were bare in open-toed pumps. "Mr. Walker? My God, twelve o'clock on the button. I'm Edith Marianne. Thanks for making the time."

She laid a slim cool hand in mine and applied some pressure, making eye contact the whole time. Hers were gray and tilted like a cat's. Her complexion was fair, almost pale, and her chin was a shade too large for the rest of her features but perfectly round. It gave her face an aggressive cast. I'd been right about her hair turning red in sunlight.

"It's such a beautiful day I thought we'd have lunch outdoors. I hope you don't have hay fever or anything like that."

"If I did I'd lie."

She made polite laughter and led me through a living room done in eggshell and cream and light. Artists' charcoal renderings of the Stiletto hung everywhere in mats and frames. We went up three steps and between sliding glass doors onto a redwood deck, where Timothy Marianne got up from his seat at a wicker table to shake my hand.

"Good to see you again, Walker. We're breaking in a new cook this weekend. You can take your chances with the rest of us."

He had on a thin white cardigan with blue piping over a blue sportshirt and brushed jeans. The outfit ran around five hundred dollars and looked as if he had been wrestling in it. I said, "I've eaten in places where they served antidotes for dessert. I can take it."

From our ice cream chairs we had a view of hills and trees and suburban communities as far north as Iroquois Heights. At that distance the Heights looked well-ordered and clean, which they were to a point. A Hispanic woman with thick ankles and her hair in a bun came out of the house carrying a tray and set a tall glass containing pieces of fruit in front of each of us. We unfolded our napkins and dug in with long-handled spoons.

"I get more business done here than in the office," Marianne said. "Edith says it's because I'm more charming when I'm relaxed, but I think it's her. My life took a steep upward swing when I met her." He reached across the table to squeeze her hand. She smiled.

"I heard it was at the auto show."

He gave her back the hand. "That story. I don't know where it got started. It's true she used to model for one of the agencies that handle the exhibits, but actually we met at a party following the dedication ceremony for the General Motors plant in Hamtramck. The Big Three were all represented, and I was still connected with Ford as an independent consultant. She was with some old wheezer from the Chrysler advertising department."

"Public relations," she corrected. "He was a sweet man. I reminded him of his granddaughter." There were definitely magnolias in her speech. One of those delta accents.

"Anyway it took me a year to sweep her off her feet. I was going through a divorce at the time. Ever been in love, Walker?"

"Once. I was going through a marriage at the time."

"The right wife is more than a companion. She knows your head better than you do. Every time I bounced something off her when I was building the business, she echoed the same doubts I had but was unwilling to admit. If I'd met her sooner I'm convinced it wouldn't have taken eight years."

"More like eighteen," she said.

He laughed. Then he wasn't laughing. "So that's why I asked Edith to invite you to lunch."

"I was wondering about that."

"At first I wanted Al Hendriks here too, but he's busy in the Detroit office today. Now I'm glad. I sensed a hostility between you yesterday that didn't have anything to do with this mess you're investigating."

I finished my fruit. So far the cooking was okay.

Mrs. Marianne said, "Al's abrasive but honest. I can see that quality in people. I see it in you." She smiled. "If he did something wrong in the past, which Tim and I don't believe for one minute he did, it should have no bearing on his present position as general manager of Marianne Motors. It can only hurt a company that promises to employ over six hundred thousand people during the next five years."

"My client was framed for armed robbery. He did twenty years."

"He was an arsonist."

I looked at Marianne. His face had gotten stony, but free enterprise glittered in his eye. "I have contacts on the police," he said. "They looked up the case. Your man set a building on fire. Hardly an innocent."

The cook collected our glasses and dealt out wooden bowls of lettuce and tomato slices without dressing. I waited until she withdrew.

"You don't do twenty years for a botched arson in an uninhabited building when everyone else is doing it and getting out in two. They hooked him for robbery armed resulting in the death of an accomplice. He didn't do it."

"Why?" Marianne demanded. "Because you're representing him?"

"Actually it's the other way around."

He started to say something. His wife touched his arm. Her eyes were on me. "What does Mr. DeVries want? To clear his name?"

"He doesn't think it's worth clearing. He wants cash."

"How much?"

"Two hundred thousand. That's the amount that was stolen."

Mrs. Marianne touched her husband's arm again, although he didn't look as if he wanted to say anything this time. "Does it have to come from Al?"

"He didn't say." I crunched lettuce.

"What do you think?"

"I think he'd take it from anyone who offered it and be satisfied. To the point of not doing anything against Hendriks anyway."

Marianne shoved aside his salad untouched. "Say I give him the two hundred thousand. I'm not saying I will. What's my guarantee he won't come back for more?"

"Call the cops if he does. If you don't believe his story you've got nothing to lose. This isn't blackmail. That takes evidence and we don't have it. The money works out to a living wage over two decades. He thinks it's owed."

"Tim, pay the two dollars."

He looked at her, then at me. I folded a tomato slice with my fork. I've never found a delicate way to get one into my mouth short of cutting.

"I'd have to have something in writing," he said. "An agreement not to go public."

"Nonsense, Tim. What would you do with it if he reneged, take it to court? Think of it as a nuisance settlement and enter it under public relations."

After a moment he put his palms on the table. "I'll get my checkbook."

"While you're at it," I said, "make one out to Mr. and Mrs. Cleveland J. Jackson for a million."

"Who the hell are they?"

"The parents of the young man who was killed. If twenty lost years are worth two hundred grand I figure a son's life runs to a million at least."

"You said DeVries would be satisfied."

"We're not talking about satisfying DeVries now. We're talking about satisfying me."

He stood. "I was going to apologize for threatening you yesterday. The thing took me by surprise and I was worried about a company I spent eight years developing and my entire life dreaming about. I'm not feeling sorry now. In fact—"

The cook came out empty-handed. "Telephone, mister."

"Who is it?" he snapped.

"Onderson, he say. He say he waiting, where you?"

"Anderson. Damn it, I forgot. I promised to conduct him personally through the downriver plant."

"Have somebody else do it," said his wife.

"I can't. I promised. He's the biggest dealer in the Southwest." He looked at me. "We're not through."

"Go play tour guide. I'll talk to Mr. Walker."

He hovered. She said, "Twenty percent of Marianne stock is in my name. I'm not going to sell out the company."

"No deals without my approval."

"You're the chairman. Run along now, shoo."

He went out, trailing the cook. A minute later we heard

the Stiletto's exhaust booming down the driveway. His wife smiled at me. "My rival's a sports car," she said.

"He's an idiot."

"Those things he said—he isn't that way, really. He's a gentle man with dreams."

"I didn't say I didn't like him."

She leaned her chin on her hand. She looked almost Oriental except for the hair. "I'm thirstier than I am hungry, how about you?"

"I'm caught up on my fruit and roughage quota this week," I said.

She summoned the cook. "Elda, we won't be dining after all. Take the afternoon off."

"Roast is almost ready." She wiped muscular hands on her apron.

"I'll put it in the refrigerator. Mr. Marianne and I will have it for dinner."

When she'd gone, banging the front door behind her, we went into the living room. Mrs. Marianne walked a little in front. She had a trim waist and slim hips, slightly rounded. Trailing behind I smelled a spring night.

"What should I pour?" She mounted a platform behind the bar.

"Anything over ice is okay."

She got the ice out of a pygmy refrigerator, filled two barrel glasses, squirted soda in one, and poured from a Stolichnaya bottle. I was sitting in an ivory-upholstered rocker when she brought the drinks over. "The sofa's more comfortable."

It looked it, six feet of white crushed leather with yellow claw feet. I switched seats and accepted the glass that didn't contain soda. She curled up on the cushion next to mine, slipping off her shoes and tucking her feet under her. This close I could see fine lines at the corners of her eyes and mouth. They looked better than the amount of make-up it would have taken to cover them completely.

"Were you a police officer?" The last *r* almost wasn't there. We were pretty far down the Mississippi now.

"I took the oath."

"And?"

"It didn't take me." The imported vodka had a bite. It wasn't a polite Saturday afternoon drink by any standards.

"You said you were married once."

"Not enough."

"Tim changed my stand on marriage. My sister had a bad common-law relationship. She died in an accident soon after it ended. I always thought she planned it."

"I'm sorry."

"She was an early casualty of the sexual revolution. You remember how it was."

"I was majoring in sociology. I missed Woodstock."

"You don't look like you've missed much since." She was pretty close now. The Scotch I'd had that morning and the vodka I was having and her dewy perfume were lifting me out of myself. I was treading fog.

"Do you really own a fifth of Marianne Motors?" I asked.

"Tax precaution. Tim has my proxy." She was studying my face. "Did you break your nose once?"

"Twice. It helps hold up my dark glasses."

"I'm glad you didn't have it fixed. It saves you from being pretty. I had my fill of pretty men in the modeling business."

"I bet you did."

"I wasn't born the day I met Tim."

"You said."

She watched me over the rim of her glass. "Do more women hire you than men, or is it the other way around?"

"Women had the edge when I started. Now it averages out about equal. Wives and mothers ducking out on their families to get themselves fulfilled. The husbands come in."

"The women—the ones who hire you and the ones you find—I imagine they're desperate. A Casanova could make out like a rabbit in your profession."

I drank. "I should warn you I don't seduce so well on melon balls and lettuce."

"I bet you do."

She climbed into my lap, all hungry lips and busy hands and her thigh pressing my groin. I fought, not hard enough to spill my drink. Her lips tasted of strawberry gloss and Stolichnaya.

When we came apart she said, "Do you have something to ask me?"

"Yes."

"Ask."

"Where did you and Alfred Hendriks go last night?"

She stiffened and drew back. Rattled the ice in her glass. "Well. Aren't we the good little detective."

"The good randy little detective. I believe in telling someone when she's done a good job. But I work Saturdays. Does your husband know?"

"Why, are you thinking of telling him?"

"So I'm right. You and Hendriks are fooling around."

She laughed. It was a tinkly kind of laugh, straight off the levee. "I bet that works most of the time. But not in this case, because we aren't. I'm faithful to Tim."

"You felt faithful."

"What I did here was for him. You're an attractive man, so is Al. I already said that doesn't affect me. Even if I didn't love Tim, if I were some kind of leech, do you think I'd jeopardize a goldmine to play nice with the help?"

"I don't know what you'd do, Mrs. Marianne. I just met you. So far I've been fed and liquored and almost ravished by the mistress of the plantation. Laying out the one million two would be a lot less trouble. I'd like to know what makes me worth it."

"Go ahead, tell my husband. He'll laugh in your face, just before he has you hauled before a judge."

"There's nothing to tell. One automobile ride isn't grounds for anything, and by now you've already started on your story. Besides, I don't work that way. All I did was ask where you two went. You gave me the rest."

She swung a bare foot back and forth off the edge of

the sofa. "If you're waiting for me to walk you to the door, forget it."

"I'll find it. I'm a detective." I set my glass on the carpet and got up. "Thanks for lunch. I'll recommend this place to all my overweight friends."

"You don't have any friends. Only clients."

"And not enough of them. It's none of my business now, but I think your roast is burning."

She didn't move. "What will DeVries say when you tell him you turned down two hundred thousand dollars?"

"He might fire me. I've been fired before. If I gave you a list of some of the people who have canned me you'd be impressed. We don't always agree on what they hired me to do."

"You keep saying you're a detective. What are you really?"

"Protoplasm in an eighty-nine-dollar suit, plus tax. But it's my suit. Enjoy your weekend, Mrs. Marianne."

Driving away from there I could still smell her perfume. I opened the windows and smoked a cigarette to flush out my sinuses. I had sweated a little in spite of the air conditioning in the house, and by the time I parked in the lot near my building I had a chill. The heat in the stairwell warmed me.

There was no good reason to be there except the homing instinct. I'd reached another dead end and had nothing to do upstairs but check for customers. As it happened I had one waiting.

21

IT WAS A BLUE SINGLE-BREASTED today, with a matching cap and visor planted on the back of his head as if to halt the retreat of the curly hair. If I knew my chauffeur's etiquette, it meant he was driving blue today instead of the gray Cadillac. When I entered the waiting room he rose lazily from the upholstered bench, grinning in his beard.

"You're more important than I had figured," he said. "The old man almost never works this time of day." He handed me a gray cardboard folder sealed with shiny black tape.

"Do I tip you or what?"

"You could if you want your arm broken. I left all that when I went to work for the Commodore. You get any sleep? You look awful."

"It's my love life."

"Man, I hope she's worth it." He pulled the cap forward. "Anything back?"

"Tell him thanks and I'll be in touch."

When he'd gone I picked up my mail, unlocked the inner office, and put the mail on the desk without looking at it. I slit the tape with a letter opener I never used and spread out the folder's contents. Personnel at Wayne State and the University of Michigan had worked fast to get student transcripts printed out and hand-delivered to the mansion in Grosse

Pointe, and Cambridge had worked just as fast to cable information across the Atlantic to a terminal at Stutch Petrochemicals. There would be scholarships involved, maybe a college or two. Here and there someone had penned clarifying comments in the margins in a faint but steady hand that had to be the Commodore's. It had all been supervised by someone who either didn't know or refused to acknowledge that in the computer age nothing has to go anywhere without collecting dust and disinterest on several desks in between.

After twenty minutes I swiveled away and looked out the window at the roof of the tax office next door, where a half-naked workman burned brown to the waist was spreading tar. What I'd found out looked the same when I was watching him as when I was reading it in print and the old man's spidery script.

A scholarship had come through for Alfred Hendriks, a freshman studying at Wayne State, to enroll in the Cambridge School of Economics beginning in April 1967. He didn't register for classes until that fall, pleading delay due to a death in the family. Mail and messages until then were to be forwarded to an apartment address on Detroit's Twelfth Street in care of a Frances Souwaine. She would be a skinny blonde hippie-type, although there was no mention of that in the folder. Whether she was or not, it put Hendriks where Richard DeVries said he was at the time of the riots in July.

The other item of interest, included only because the Commodore was thorough and got everything, was a copy of an application for a student loan from the University of Michigan, where Hendriks had taken his accounting degree in 1970. Under PAST EMPLOYMENT Hendriks had listed several positions, including a part-time bookkeeping job at a quick-print shop on Brady.

It wasn't court evidence. All it meant was that Hendriks had planned and conducted the robbery for which DeVries had gone to prison. He had finessed DeVries into bombing a building as cover and had shot Davy Jackson, his own accomplice, in the act of fleeing the scene. But not where the statue of the lady with the blindfold was concerned. She had to have it in her lap.

I slid all the papers back inside the folder, resealed it with the tape, and locked it in the safe with my shirts and underwear. Then I closed the office and fired up the rented Renault and took off for the National Bank Building, where according to Marianne, Hendriks was working overtime on a Saturday. On the way I unholstered the Smith & Wesson and checked the cylinder. The chambered cartridges glinted golden in the sun. Maybe he'd confess and I'd arrest him, just like on TV.

The lobby was nearly deserted, as was the street out front. Lake St. Clair would be jammed with tanning bodies and bright sails. Hendriks and I seemed to be the only ones on company time that afternoon. I punched the button for the express elevator and waited. None of the others stopped at the Marianne offices. I tried twice more. It was out of order. I took the local to the next closest floor and climbed the stairs the rest of the way. Stairwells reveal the true nature of a building. This one was as bleak as a banker's compassion.

The fire door let me into an anonymous hallway lined with locked doors without identifying signs. Light from a window at the end streamed unbroken down a square tunnel smelling of Mop 'n' Glo, silent but for an echoing noise somewhere on that floor. At first I thought it was a truck on the expressway. More trundle than rumble, it sounded like a bored child rolling a supermarket cart back and forth, over and over across an uneven floor. I stood listening to it for several seconds before I could tell which direction it was coming from. Then I turned and started that way along the corridor, following my own gray shadow.

No one appeared for the hall's entire length. My footsteps clapped back on themselves from the walls. They were the only footsteps on that floor.

A door stood ajar a third of the way down. I pushed it

open farther and looked at a computer terminal on a steel desk with a swivel chair turned at a right angle. The screen was blank but for the word HOLD flashing on and off in emerald green in its center. A manual the size of a monk's Bible lay closed on top of the terminal. I withdrew my head. The noise, louder now, seemed to have taken on a distinct rhythm, like a conga line. For no reason that I could put words to I reached back and closed my hand around the butt of the revolver in its holster.

The hall cornered around at the end, where I started down another just as long, the gun out now. The noise was louder yet. At midpoint another short passage divided the inner wall to my right. This was the reception area, where DeVries had trashed two guards yesterday. The noise was there. An arm was there too, on the floor and sticking out from the wall in a dark coatsleeve.

I kept to that wall as I approached it. A head of dark hair sprinkled with gray lay on the arm. Both protruded from inside the express elevator car, where the doors kept trying to close, encountered the arm, and shunted back open to try again. The trundling was hypnotic.

I put the gun in both hands, stepped away from the wall, and executed a policeman's turn, covering the interior of the car. It was full of dead man and air conditioning. The walls were paneled in smoked glass, starred in three places at the rear where something the size of my finger had struck it. The carpet was stained dark. Part of the stain overlapped into the hallway. The edge smeared when I touched it with a toe.

I didn't look for a pulse. When the doors were open, Alfred Hendriks' one visible eye looked past my shoulder, admiring a view I hoped not to see for a long time. He hadn't been planning on it himself as late as yesterday. It made you think about tomorrow.

Not for long, though. I put away the gun and stepped inside to search those pockets I could reach without disturbing the body. You never know what might show up in a lab these days. His wallet held cab fare and enough cards in plastic windows to clear up the deficit, at least until the bills came. I put it back and took out a leather folder containing the keys to his Porsche and a couple of others. That I pocketed. The contact my hands made with his skin told me he'd begun to cool but not yet to stiffen.

That was as much as his body could tell me. I couldn't be any more thorough without getting blood on my hands and clothes. ("Kind of sloppy with the spaghetti sauce there, Walker. You won't mind if Forensics has a look at your tie.") I left him, not paying much attention now to how much noise I was making. Whoever had done the shooting was as long gone as the smell of spent powder.

Hendriks' name was lettered in gold on a frosted panel in the front corridor. The first key I tried unlocked the door. More cold-blooded design had gone into this office than into Marianne's downriver: From deep red pile to hand-rubbed walnut to thick unread first editions on built-in shelves the place was rigged for power. Even the window was bigger, although not nearly as large as the one in Commodore Stutch's study in Grosse Pointe. The chairs were covered in maroon leather and an Impressionist painting of a locomotive charging through a misty night hung in a heavy gilt frame on one wall. The artist had left it unsigned, but the odds said he was French and dead.

I lifted a corner of the painting, looked at bare paneling behind it, and let it back down. I inspected the carpeting around the desk but there were no breaks or seams where a floor safe might have been installed. The desk was tidy, with no papers or folders left on top. Even the calendar was bare of notations. A neat man, Hendriks. Or a careful one. The drawers were locked. I selected the smallest key on the ring, inserted it in the slot in the top drawer, and turned it. Somewhere inside, a bar slid out of a track, releasing all the drawers.

I wasted time on pencils and stationery until I reached the second drawer on the right side. There a basket rack had been mounted to hold half a dozen computer disks upright in paper sleeves. Each pocket except two was labeled in neat felt-tip capitals on strips of masking tape; current and projected expenditures and profits and monthly business correspondence were all assigned to their proper pockets, each sleeve marked accordingly to keep them from getting mixed up. The remaining two pockets were blank. One of them was empty. I drew the disk out of the other. The sleeve was blank as well. I put them in my coat pocket.

More desk stuff in the other drawers, all good quality but boring. I lifted things from the top and looked under them. Nothing, not even some respectable dust. Where the disk was that belonged in the last pocket bothered me. Then I realized what else was missing from the office, and then I remembered. I touched everything I'd touched a second time, this time with a handkerchief to remove prints, and left the room.

The doors were still trying to close when I passed the elevator alcove. I didn't know how to stop them short of moving the body, and anyway Hendriks didn't seem to mind. Around the corner I found the door still open to the room containing the computer terminal. Inside I found something else, a blank paper sleeve with nothing in it on the desk next to the machine.

HOLD was still flashing onscreen. I sat down and studied the keyboard. That didn't tell me anything so I hoisted down the manual from atop the terminal and did some homework. After ten minutes I put it back and punched the key marked ACCESS. If what I'd read made sense and HOLD meant the file was still open, I was already past Security.

The screen went blank and stayed that way for a second. I was starting to think I'd erased the disk in the machine when it began to print out. From left to right the bright green characters darted across in three neat vertical rows headed INVESTOR, AMT INVEST, and DATE, line after line, striping the screen faster than the human hand could type or the human eye could follow. When it finished, the screen was full, with the little green blip that had towed out the data flashing on and off at the end of the last line, awaiting further instructions.

I didn't have any for it even if I knew how to enter them. I was looking into a universe beyond my tight little orbit of thugs and grifters, bad-check artists and runaway daughters. There were too many abbreviations and acronyms in the left-hand row, too many digits in the middle. I had once held a thousand-dollar bill and another time I had peeked inside a briefcase containing several hundred thousand in neat bills bricked and banded. Millions were abstract numbers in a newspaper article with a Washington dateline. Glimmering there onscreen, all those zeroes presented black holes for a man to fall into and never find bottom. They were like dead men's eyes. Hendriks' had been the last to see them, just before he had toppled in.

I shook off their spell and looked for the key that would eject the disk. I didn't think the disk in my pocket would tell me much more than this one. Someone who spoke the language might. At length the machine kicked it out through a slot in the side and I put it in its sleeve and slid the slim package into my other side pocket. I flipped off the power switch and wiped my prints off the keyboard with my handkerchief. Then I got up and turned toward the doorway, where the guard DeVries had put on the floor yesterday was crouching with his gun pointed at my heart.

22

"WHAT HAPPENED to your face? He do that?"

"No, the big black guy gave me that yesterday. I told you about it."

"Tell me again."

The guard sighed and told it. DeVries and I had jumped him and his partner from behind. They had a lively time of it, but they were getting the upper hand when Mr. Piero, their boss, came in and broke it up. They were for turning us in there and then but Mr. Piero said it was bad public relations. "Ask me, bad public relations is them two on the loose and Mr. Hendriks laying there cold as a carp," he said.

"Tell me again how you found him."

"I finished my rounds on the other floor and pushed for the elevator. It wasn't working so I came up the stairs to check it out and that's when I seen him laying there. I hear footsteps then. There's no place to duck except the elevator and I'm in there when this guy walks past. My gun's out but he just keeps walking. I figure he's making his getaway, only he isn't, because when I get back out in the hall I hear him in there working the computer. That's where I got the drop on him. That's his gun."

His listener, a chubby towhead I recognized from headquarters called Sergeant Toynbee, looked at my revolver on the doughnut-shaped reception desk. "You handle it?"

"Well, I had to take it off him, didn't I?"

"Check it out."

His partner, who was standing closer, picked it up, swung out the cylinder, and held it up to the light to inspect the inside of the barrel. He was a black plainclothesman with delicate features and eyelashes as long as a woman's.

"Clean." He flipped the cylinder back into place. "A little dust."

Toynbee nodded. He called the black officer Banks; Duane when he wasn't introducing him. The sergeant went over and rested one large ham on the desk and looked at me smoking a Winston on the settee. The guard who had disarmed me and called the cops was sitting inside the doughnut. One side of his face was still bruised and swollen from the run-in with DeVries. Banks was just standing around slapping my gun against his thigh, and the two uniforms who had answered the radio call hovered over the man lying in the elevator, their thumbs hooked in their belts. Someone had found a way to keep the doors open. Hendriks was still dead.

"What'd you do with the piece you used on him?" Toynbee asked me.

"I ate it."

"It'll turn up. If it doesn't we'll still make the case. We hardly ever get the time to tie up all the loose ends anyway."

"The case won't be yours to make after Alderdyce gets here."

"Who says he's coming?"

"The guy on the floor. Corporate chiefs are too big for a sergeant's lap. Also I'd be on my way downtown in cuffs by now if you weren't expecting him."

He picked up the leather key folder I had taken off Hendriks' body. The guard had put it on the desk next to the gun. "Yours?"

"Yeah."

"It's got the initials A.H. inside."

"It belonged to Adolf Hitler. I bought it in a Nazi supply store in Dearborn."

He picked up the ring containing the keys to the Renault and my house and office. "What about these?"

"I'm a collector."

He looked at Banks. "You pat him down good?"

"He wasn't stealing office furniture, if that's what you mean."

In fact he and the guard had both missed the flat computer disks in the saddle pockets of my coat. I dumped some ash on the carpet and rubbed it in with my toe. "What the hell, frisk me again. I'm a three-times-a-day man."

"What were you doing with the computer?" Toynbee asked.

"Saving the world from space invaders."

"We got us a comic, Duane. Regular Chevy Chase."

"Makes you miss the guys that exercise their right to remain silent," Banks said.

Others arrived, including a kid photographer and a Vietnamese medical examiner who hummed while he worked. John Alderdyce came last, in a cocoa poplin suit and a brown tie with gold stripes on a tan shirt. He watched the M.E. fussing over Hendriks' fingernails.

"Shot?"

"Once in the stomach and once in the thigh." The Vietnamese sat back on his heels and stripped off his surgical gloves. "Thigh shot did it, from the amount of blood. Hit the femoral. Wouldn't have taken more than twenty minutes after he went into deep shock."

"Time?"

He shrugged. "Today. When I know what he had for breakfast and when, I'll pin it down."

Alderdyce made the rounds of the uniforms and plainclothesmen, interviewing each separately in murmurs like a stage director. Finally he came to the guard at the reception desk. "Where's your Mr. Fierro?" he asked.

"Piero. Vermont. His vacation started today. Otherwise

you'd be talking to him instead of me. If it wasn't bad public relations."

"Describe the black man you had trouble with here yesterday."

He gave a fair description of DeVries, adding four or five inches to his height. It was a natural error. Alderdyce said, "Okay, thanks. Did the detectives get your address and phone number?"

"Yeah."

"Go home then."

"I got four hours left on this shift."

"Spend them on the other floor. Nobody's going to walk away with the place while we're here."

The guard got up and headed for the stairs. Alderdyce spent a few more minutes with Toynbee and Banks, then sent them back to 1300 to write up their report. Toynbee hesitated. "What about this guy?"

"He didn't kill anyone today."

"He was heeled."

"So's three-quarters of the local population. If you want to bust someone, get out a reader on Richard DeVries." He spelled the last name. "Have Lansing wire his mug and prints and ask them who's handling his parole. He's fresh out of Marquette."

Toynbee wrote it down in his notebook and turned to go. "Oh, congratulations, Lieutenant."

"Thanks."

I got rid of my cigarette and looked up at Alderdyce. "Inspectors' list come out?"

"I'm on it. As soon as seven inspectors die or retire I get to move up a notch. Or if they add seven new precincts. What happened?"

"I found him. Then the guard found me."

"How'd you know he'd be here?"

"Marianne told me he was working."

His brow puckered. "Lieutenant Thaler?"

"Not her, the other one. Timothy Marianne. I had lunch with him today, sort of."

"Busy weekend."

"About par. I found a corpse and almost got laid."

"When's the last time you saw your client?"

"This morning."

"What's his beef with Hendriks?"

"Not here."

He glanced around. The morgue team had arrived and a man in a plaid sportcoat and green tie was dusting the control panel for prints. "There a room somewhere?"

I nodded toward the leather key folder on the reception desk. "One of those probably fits Hendriks' office door."

"Probably?"

"The guard came before I could check it out."

"Uh-huh. Let's do." He picked up the folder.

I stood and fell into step beside him. "What about my gun? Banks took it with him."

"You know how that works."

"Last time nobody cleaned it for six weeks."

"You still got that unregistered Luger?"

"What unregistered Luger?"

"Just keep it out of my sight. The commissioner's watching me." He found the right door and let us into the dead man's office.

"This is warrant country," I said. "What's the commissioner say about violating the Bill of Rights?"

"The Constitution's been suspended in Detroit, didn't you hear? We got TV cameras on street corners and in public rest rooms. Traffic's out conducting unlawful searches for drunk drivers." He trailed his fingers over the desk's glossy surface. "This guy did all right for himself. Too bad he croaked."

"To think it all started with two hundred grand in stolen bills."

He stuck his hands in his pants pockets and waited. Either

consciously or unconsciously, he had maneuvered to have the desk between us.

"DeVries saw a picture of Hendriks in stir," I said. "He recognized him as the college kid who put him up to firing that building. Some of the serial numbers from the armored car job were on record, so Hendriks kept his profile down for a few years, first while the money was being laundered and then to avoid drawing attention to himself. He even took out a student loan from the U of M to tide him over. He went to work in the accounting department at Ford and eventually invested what he'd stolen in Marianne Motors."

"All this on a picture?"

"Hendriks told me he was in England when the riots and the robbery took place. Except the records say he didn't go there until the following fall. Meanwhile he was living where DeVries met him, in an apartment on Twelfth Street with a blonde named Frances Souwaine. She may have been an accomplice, or maybe not. The point is he lied."

"So he lied. So far I wouldn't tie up a man to question him if he were alive."

"I think you would. You've got instincts same as me. But try this. According to his loan application at Michigan he was working part-time at a place called Merc-U-Print on Brady during the summer of 1967."

"Brady's where they hit the car," he said.

"It was there to transport cash from businesses threatened by the riots to the bank. Someone working in one of the stores—especially a bookkeeper, which is what Hendriks was—would know the car would be there at that time. It gave him time to plan the robbery and set DeVries up for the fall."

"Why kill Jackson?"

"Maybe they fell out. Maybe Hendriks wanted Jackson's cut. The heist had gone down, they were running away, and his services were no longer needed. The other possibility is that with Jackson dead and identified at the scene, DeVries stood a better chance of taking the frame. He and Jackson were known to be friends. It would blow some of the heat off whoever else was involved."

"Too risky. Hendriks couldn't know DeVries wouldn't put it together and talk."

"Maybe. He'd seen how drunk and disoriented DeVries could get on at least one occasion. By getting him drunk again he might fog the details just enough. Or not. He needed the fire as a diversion and arsonists were escaping arrest all over the place. DeVries not being able to tell the cops anything might have been just a lucky fall."

Alderdyce started looking in drawers. I'd left the desk unlocked. "You're overlooking the most likely scenario. DeVries was in on the plan from the start. I don't buy him being as dumb as you say."

"Your way he was dumb enough to choose eighteen to thirty over the deal the cops offered him for talking. You can't have it both ways."

"You can't, but I can. You'd have to be black in the middle of a rebellion and be asked to trust a white police department." He paused over the drawer containing the rack not quite full of computer disks. "You sure you weren't in here?"

"I won't say it wasn't on my list."

"What were you doing in the computer room?"

"Frisking the place. The door was open."

"Find anything?"

"Not a thing."

"Machine on or off when you got to it?"

"Off."

"Funny, I felt it on my way in. It felt warm."

"You didn't feel it."

He slid a thumb over the rack. Then he closed the drawer. "You're right, I didn't. Anyway I hope your client enjoyed his little vacation. He's going back for life. Not that I blame him for killing Hendriks. If I did two dimes without pay I'd figure I had something coming."

"He didn't kill him."

"Who did?"

"Someone he trusted. You don't sneak up on a person in that hall."

"DeVries could've been waiting when Hendriks stepped out of the elevator. Or he could've marched him there at gunpoint and drilled him as he was stepping inside."

I didn't have an answer for that. It was one of the reasons I wasn't on the force.

23

THE BANK BUILDING LOBBY was quiet, obsequiously so. I might have been in a cathedral on Martin Luther's birthday. When I slotted a quarter into the telephone, the rattle echoed.

"Yes."

How Raf got so much Arabic intonation into so short a word was a mystery. I said, "Walker. The Commodore included this number in some stuff he sent me today. Can you take him a message?"

"He's sleeping."

"I think he'll want you to wake him up for this one."

The roast I hadn't eaten at the Mariannes' had come back to haunt me. Maybe it had to do with Alfred Hendriks being dead meat, but I had to have some. After Raf and I finished talking I bought a sack of burgers at a White Castle and ate them in the car. I didn't feel like fit company for people.

I turned on the radio, heard some music, and listened to the news. Hendriks wasn't on it. By the next report he would be; Detroit is a reporters' town. I turned it off and ate and thought. Mostly I ate.

I went back with John Alderdyce further than anybody. In that time I had given up trying to trace the workings of his mind. There was no telling which way he'd have run with a piece of evidence like Edith Marianne's nighttime ride with

Hendriks. It suggested a couple of simple explanations. Cops like their murders simple, and the murderers usually oblige, theirs being the one crime almost always perpetrated by amateurs. But you dug your hole plenty deep when you expected Alderdyce to think like most cops. What went on in the Commodore's century-old skull was one for the archaeologists. So I sat on the information. I felt like one of those birds that squat in strange nests and never know if they're hatching another bird or a snake.

That line of thinking was about as nourishing as the burgers. I hit the ignition, then had to sit back and wait for the battery to recharge itself before starting the Renault. Finally it turned over and caught and I took Woodward down to Jefferson.

I didn't stop at the Alamo. A gray four-door Chrysler without chrome was parked on that side of the street with two men in the front seat. They had their coats on and the windows up. The temperature was in the high eighties and they were sitting in the sun, but you can only turn down some two-way radios so low and they wouldn't want the noise leaking out. It told me two things: DeVries wasn't in, and we don't pay our police near enough. Not being in a position to change either situation I doubled back into town, parked behind a truck unloading mammoth rolls of newsprint onto a dock on Lafayette, and went into the *News* building. There the female security guard called upstairs and told me Barry Stackpole was out playing racquetball at the Detroit Athletic Club.

Before the glaziers and steelworkers won the architectural wars, Albert Kahn left his thumbprints all over downtown in the form of Italian Renaissance arcades and Greek pilasters. The DAC combines both in a seven-story candy box just off the Grand Circle on Madison. I used the defunct county star in my ID folder to bluff my way past the silver-haired gent at the front desk and went to the courts. A ball exploded off the wall next to my ear when I opened the door.

"Idiot! Tired of your head?" Barry caught the ball on the

fly and smashed it against the concrete wall on the other side.

It was no way to greet an old war buddy, but then we hadn't spoken much over the past year or so, and when we had it dealt with our respective businesses. We'd gone from friends to two guys who knew each other; never mind why. I said, "I thought exercise was good for your health."

"Bullshit. It keeps you from assaulting people." He caromed the ball off the floor and wall and backhanded it when it returned. He was wearing a green-and-white Michigan State basketball jersey plastered to his cylindrical torso and gray sweatpants that covered his artificial leg. Sweat had slicked and darkened his hair, streamlining his head like a seal's.

"They told me racquetball was a two-man sport."

"My opponents say I'm too aggressive. I don't see it." He slapped the wall three times in almost the same spot, leaving marks like grouped revolver shots. Finally he bounced the ball off the floor near his feet and stood dribbling it with the short racquet. "What's the headline?"

" 'Auto Executive Murdered.' "

"No good. Passive voice. Give me a lead."

" 'Police found Alfred Hendriks, general manager of Marianne Motors, shot to death in the elevator of the corporation's headquarters in the National Bank Building.' "

"Too busy. And you left out when."

"About two hours ago."

"As a journalist you're hell for sleuthing. Who and how come?"

"Why I'm here," I said. "Off the blotter?"

"If I get to put it on later."

"I need an accountant."

"Tap the lottery?"

"Hendriks kept some kind of ledger on floppy disks that he locked up in his desk unmarked. I need someone who can read it. New Math ruined me for life."

"So get an accountant. What am I, the Yellow Pages?"

"An accountant who can keep his mouth shut is what I

need. You write about organized crime. You must meet them all the time."

"The ones I know are too good at it. They don't even talk to me."

"My client's on the hook for murder. I doubt he did it. If Hendriks was fooling around with company funds it opens up other avenues."

He went on dribbling.

"The Commodore's involved," I said.

He stopped. "Old Man Stutch?"

"How many Commodores do you know?"

"I interviewed him ten years ago. He was getting set to buy Atlantic City before the Mob took up residence. The deal went sour. If he killed anyone it would be straight up in the middle of Cadillac Square at high noon."

"That's the way I read him. Anyway he's got three quarters of a billion dollars tied up in Marianne. Hendriks was juggling millions. This is no alley mugging."

He studied the ball. "Amos?"

I waited.

"Hell with it. Not important. Exclusive?"

"Yeah."

He tossed the ball in the air and slammed it off the door frame. "I'll get back to you."

I left. In the old days we'd have struck the bargain on a case of Scotch. When you lose a friend, the price goes up on everything.

In the office time hung like a willow branch. After washing my face and neck in the water closet I turned on the antique fan and watched a twist of cigarette cellophane hop and slither across the floor. That was good for a minute and a half and then it hung up in a corner. I retrieved it and threw it at the wastebasket. Getting it unstuck from the static charge in my fingers was good for another thirty seconds.

I went through the mail I hadn't looked at earlier. I wrote

out checks for a second and a final notice and put them in envelopes and addressed and stamped them, filed the invoices, slit open the junk just for exercise, and threw it after the cellophane. I dumped the ashtray and stared at the telephone and wondered why no one had need of a private investigator on weekends. It rang.

"Walker?"

"Speaking."

"Floyd Orlander, remember me?"

"I remember, Lieutenant."

"Forget that shit. I been retired longer than I held the rank. Listen, I was wondering—"

The rest of it was drowned out by a roaring on his end. He was calling from his home at the end of the runway. When the noise died I asked him to repeat it.

"I was wondering how you were coming with that DeVries thing. I been thinking about it ever since you were here."

"Is there something you didn't tell me?"

"I gave you what I had. What it is, I been thinking about that miserable partner I had, what a bigoted son of a bitch he was, and how things were after the riots. I mean between black and white. I was a straight cop. I don't like what I been thinking."

"You think maybe you and Sergeant Drake railroaded DeVries into prison?"

"I don't mean we made anything up, twisted things around to make him look guilty. Maybe we didn't look as hard as we would of if things were different, that's all I'm saying. I still think he did it. I'm just wondering if that's why we made the case."

"Have you been discussing this with your wife, Mr. Orlander?"

"Yeah, but what's she got to do with anything? I'm saying what I'm saying."

"Thanks for saying it."

"I'm not using you for a priest. If you need help I'm offering it. Maybe it's time this thing went by the numbers."

"I hope you still feel that way after you watch tonight's news." I gave him the official version.

"Think he did it?" he said after a moment.

"No."

"You got faith."

"The evidence of things unseen."

"Just the kind the D.A. loves. Anyway the offer holds."

"Thanks, Mr. Orlander. At the moment I'm stuck in neutral myself."

"Maybe now I can look at my grandkids and see my grandkids."

I cradled the receiver and left my hand on it. Cops. Just when you've got the plant classified as a noxious weed it sends up a blossom.

Quitting time came and went. I stayed. The longer I sat there the less respect I had for my brains. When I left, whenever it was, Barry would call right after; it was some kind of law. The telephone rang. It was John Alderdyce.

"Hear from your client?"

I sat back. "That means you haven't."

"His parole cop told us where he's staying. I wonder why he hasn't shown."

"I didn't tip him."

"How's he know we're looking for him if he didn't cap Hendriks?"

"Hell, John, I was by the Alamo. You can smell cop from Belle Isle."

I heard a bureaucratic buzzing in the background. He was at 1300. Finally he said, "Listen, I ran your Frances Souwaine through the computer. She's dead."

"Dead how?"

"Wrapped her Corvair around an Edison pole on Hastings in 1968. If it didn't happen, though, some pimp would've got her or she'd have tripped out someday and lost the way back. Couple of busts for solicitation on her sheet and ninety days in DeHoCo for possession of LSD. Whatever happened to LSD?"

"Where's Timothy Leary?"

"Doing a road show with G. Gordon Liddy last I heard. We're old."

"John, has it occurred to you that everyone involved in that armored car robbery is dead?"

"All but one," he said. "You know the drill: you hear from your client, I hear from you. He can't hide. All he's got to do is stand up. He's a parolee wanted for questioning in a murder case and he's considered armed. I don't have to tell you what that means."

"You'd think it would've changed in twenty years."

"In court, yeah. The street's still the street." The line clicked and hummed.

I gave it another ten minutes, then locked up. It was what I had a service for. Then I had to run back from the stairs and fumble with the keys and spear the receiver on the fourth ring. It was Barry, instructing me to meet him at his place in Harper Woods at ten o'clock, and to bring the disks.

24

IF ANY EVIDENCE WAS NEEDED to prove that the Mafia had lost its teeth, Barry Stackpole's address would do.

After a bomb had blown off his leg and two fingers, Barry had written his column on a portable typewriter all over the city for years. His address had included some thirty apartments and motels and, for one two-week period, my living room. He never unpacked his suitcase the whole time and used a Luger for a paperweight. Rumor had it the local capos had hung a fifty-thousand-dollar tag around his neck.

But for the past three years he had been living like ordinary folks in a rented brick house in Harper Woods. With half of the organization facing federal indictments and the other half more worried about the new tax code than the Code Siciliano, the fate of one reporter had lost all priority. Never mind that that reporter's investigations had brought about the public outcry for an end to gang rule and the evidence that had brought that end in sight. The damage was done, and mere survival had made revenge too expensive to consider.

Barry's problem was he had been too successful. With the war won, or at least fought to a bloody draw, his ammunition was no longer needed, and his readers had found new interests at the same rate at which the enemy had lost its interest in him. His syndicated column had been losing newspapers for months. A major publisher, after a flurry of early excitement, had decided not to accept a book he had written about his experiences as a correspondent in Southeast Asia, and it had since been rejected by half a dozen others. This sudden drop from a peak that had included an interview on *Nightline* and a bylined cover story in *Time* had soured him and damaged his personal and business relationships. Yet he continued to write about and gather proof against the bosses, underbosses, street soldiers, shooters, bought judges, bent cops, drug runners, and pimps, in the end the only people toward whom his attitude had not changed, and whom he and a few others knew were down but not dead, defeated but not destroyed. He had become head cheerleader in a game everyone thought was over.

Barry opened the door before I could ring the bell. He had on a denim shirt tail-out over a pair of patched jeans, his working clothes. "Get in here before somebody sees you."

He hadn't done anything to the living room since my last visit except change the magazines on the coffee table. At that time he'd been living with a model and there had been the odd *Vogue* and *Ms.* among the copies of *American Rifleman*, *Soldier of Fortune*, and the *Harvard Lampoon*. We went into his office, where he had added a word processor and a short round man in a white shirt and brown corduroy trousers. The light was off and the short round man's face was bilious in the glow of the electronic screen, reminding me of Commodore Stutch under the influence of his green-shaded lamp. It was the only thing about him that reminded me of the Commodore. He had blue jowls, a full head of glossy black hair, and great brown eyes that swiveled like casters in their sockets. He swiveled them from me to Barry. "Was he followed?"

"I circled a couple of blocks to make sure I wasn't," I said. "It's standard procedure after I've been talking with cops."

"You didn't tell me the police were involved," he said quickly. So far he'd spoken only to Barry.

"They don't know about you." Barry looked at me. "A ten-year-old gambling ring in New Orleans is looking for new management because of this gentleman's testimony before a federal grand jury. The Justice Department gave him a new identity and relocated him here. One condition of his cooperation tonight is I can't tell you what that identity is or who he was before he assumed it."

"How is it you know?"

"I was on the case six months before the Justice Department."

"He an accountant?"

"Did Rembrandt dabble in oils? On the way here he added up the numbers on all the license plates we passed and divided the total by my address, all in his head."

"It was more of a feat before vanity plates," the short round man admitted.

"How'd you check his answer?"

Barry said, "You bring them?"

I produced the disks. He slid them partly out of their sleeves and replaced them. "They're compatible."

"Let's hope he hasn't demagnetized both of them by carrying them around in his pockets." The short round man accepted them. He hadn't forgiven my challenging his best trick. "If you'll excuse me. I work best when no one's gaping over my shoulder."

Barry and I went into the living room. "Coffee?" he said. "I'm on the wagon. Again."

I said coffee was great. He filled two mugs in the kitchen and brought them out. He slung his Dutch leg over the arm of the sofa. "Shouldn't take long. One thing the Justice Department boys didn't find in his deposition was a mistake in arithmetic."

"He that rabbity all the time?" I took a chair opposite.

"I wouldn't know. This is the first time I've seen him in two years."

"I thought you were friends."

"The man knows the square root of seven."

"Then what's his percentage?"

"Creole shooter named LaPointe found out his route to the courthouse in Baton Rouge from the hotel where the U.S. attorneys had him stashed. I got wind of it and tipped them. Local cops shot LaPointe just as he was drawing a bead."

"It isn't like the Justice Department to move a witness to a place where someone knows him. Especially a reporter."

"It was going to be North Dakota. I had more use for him here."

"Just like that?"

"Cost me a couple of markers." He swallowed some coffee. "Tell me about Hendriks."

I fed him the whole thing, starting at Marquette and ending at the National Bank Building. I included Edith Marianne's auto ride with Hendriks and her hospitality to me at her house that afternoon. Barry didn't take notes, but I wasn't fooled. His memory for names and facts was at least as good as the short round man's memory for figures. I could hear the word processor bleeping in the next room.

"DeVries the kind to turn himself in?" Barry asked.

"Would you?"

"He's bigger than anything on the police range. You'll have to work fast if you don't want a dead client."

"What I'm doing."

He raised his voice. "How's it coming?"

"I'm not boiling fish," said the man in the office. "Give me a few minutes."

"Artists," Barry said.

I asked him how things were at the *News.*

"I'm about ten papers away from being called into the managing editor's office for a little talk in those concerned tones he's famous for. There's a lady gossip columnist who's been eyeing my space a long time. I know she's a lady because I haven't caught her drooling yet."

"You could try writing about something else."

"I could write doggerel about the British Royal Family or compare restaurants in the area, as if there were more than three worth trusting your stomach to. Probably land myself a five-minute spot on one of the local TV stations."

"You don't have to go that far."

"How far is far?" He put his fiberglass foot on the floor and set his mug on the coffee table. "There's a mobbie out on the Coast who's into a White House aide so deep that when his shorts ride up the guy grunts in Washington. Last month men working for the mobbie kicked down the door of an apartment in Hollywood, made the three teenagers inside kneel on the floor, and shot each of them in the back of the head, one by one. It was the wrong apartment. The one they wanted was two doors down, where some Chicanos were dealing cocaine without the Good Housekeeping seal of approval. *This* month, the White House aide published the results of his study of the long-term effects of pornography on the white-collar class. What should I write about, who serves the best breadsticks in town?"

"Write about why you write about what you write about."

"It's too much like whining."

"Why tell me?"

"You I can whine to."

The short round man came out of the office and handed me both disks. "I'd like to meet the man who kept these," he said.

"He's dead."

"Too bad. There's something about a man stealing millions that makes you want to see him get away with it, whereas you wouldn't if it were a few dollars or an item of no particular value."

"He was stealing?" I asked.

"Not precisely stealing. Flimflamming is more accurate, also a bit roguish and rather romantic. Simply put, your man allowed other corporations and individuals to buy approximately two hundred eighty percent of his corporation's stock."

Barry said, "You're saying he sold the same horse several times?"

"It's considerably more complex than that. It involved blind accounts, a double-entry system of bookkeeping, and a rather original method of electronic transference that automatically erased all record of the transactions and effectively rendered the money nonexistent insofar as the corporation was concerned. But yes, that's the basic concept."

"In other words, if not for these two disks there would've been no way of finding out what he was up to," I said.

"Not until it came time to pay off on the investments. By then your man would have had some five hundred million dollars socked away in numbered accounts in Andorra. The numbers are listed on the second disk."

"Andorra?"

"A small autonomous state located between France and Spain. The secret of its autonomy lies in its banking system. Most people are unaware that Swiss accounts are subject to lien and seizure by the Zurich government under certain extreme conditions. Andorran accounts are not. I established some close contacts there on behalf of my last employer."

"How'd you get access?" Barry asked. "Our man wouldn't let just anyone tap into that kind of information."

He swiveled his eyes floorward modestly. "I have a system. It's a kind of skeleton key and I'm not prepared to share it."

"Five hundred million," I said.

"Give or take ten million. Those are projections based on the trends indicated."

Barry said, "I'm small time. Guys I write about whack each other for thousands."

"He wasn't above dealing in thousands," said the short round man. "And he wasn't above dealing with the people you write about."

We waited, watching him. He glowed. I had him tagged then. People who turn state's evidence usually do it for basic reasons. Getting center spot is one of the top five.

"CerbCorp," he said. "Maybe you recognize the name."

I said, "It was one of the investors listed. I never heard of it."

"I have." Barry drank and made a face that said his coffee had grown cold. "The Cerberus Corporation is parent company for the Miskoupolis brothers' restaurant chain."

"I thought they were all dead," I said. "Or in jail."

"Nicholas died a long time ago. Aristotle last year. Sherman's alive and free pending appeal on a conviction for suborning to commit perjury. I interviewed a witness to the deal."

"Sherman?"

Barry grinned. "The old lady had to get in one shot. Anyway Sherm has no plans to die this century, if what he spends on cosmetics and desiccated monkey balls means anything."

"How much did CerbCorp have tied up?" I asked the short round man.

"Six hundred fifty thousand."

I looked at Barry. "Would he kill over that?"

"He's killed over a hell of a lot less."

25

ALFRED HENDRIKS MADE THE LEAD in the Sunday *Free Press*. I didn't and neither did Richard DeVries, although Alderdyce told the reporter he had a suspect. Timothy Marianne was unavailable for comment, but a Ford vice president had complimentary things to say about the former accountant based on ten minutes with his personnel file, and Hector Stutch submitted a prepared statement to the effect that the tragedy would have no influence on Stutch Petrochemicals' deal with Marianne Motors. I wondered if the Commodore had dictated it or written it out in his frail but unwavering hand. In any case, whatever resemblance it bore to any telephone calls he had made between two and four that morning would be slight. I turned to *Doonesbury* for the lowdown, but the strip's concern that day was the President.

I had left Barry's place shortly before eleven-thirty and been in bed by midnight. The morning news on television had few details to add. Neither account looked or sounded like what I'd seen or heard in the National Bank Building. There never is much resemblance.

I made a local call. After breakfast and ablutions I put on slacks and a knitted shirt and a cotton jacket. Cooler temperatures were predicted. Outside I took off the jacket and flung it into the back seat; the weather was as hot as it had been right along.

The Argo chain, encompassing some forty restaurants throughout the Midwest, offered Greek fare in homogenized fashion to middle-income diners who would probably never see Athens. Appropriately, the anchor of the chain was in Trappers' Alley, a vertical conglomeration of boutiques, eateries, and craft shops under one roof in Detroit's historic Greektown, which is to Hellenic culture what Disney World is to the military-industrial complex. It's nearly as easy to get lost in as the Renaissance Center, and Lord help the diners and browsers the day someone yells fire.

The busboys were setting up for lunch when I entered and told a large, dark-eyed waitress in ceremonial dress that I was meeting Sherman Miskoupolis. She nodded once and plowed a path through gold coats to a high booth at the rear, where a small man in a sharp suit rose and clamped my hand in a grip that had had some practice.

"Good morning!" He had one of those booming Mediterranean voices that usually go to small men. "What will you eat? You're my guest."

"Thanks, I had breakfast."

"What, toast and coffee? Daphne, baklava and espresso for Mr. Walker. I'll have the usual."

The waitress turned. I touched her arm. I went on looking at the boss. "Nobody's going to yell *opah* and set anything on fire, are they?"

"Many of our customers expect it. But in your case we'll resist the pyrotechnics."

I let Daphne go and we sat down. He had a thick brown mug of what was presumably espresso in front of him. Sherman Miskoupolis dressed young for his age, in a severely tapered jacket with flared lapels and bright orange tie with green fleurs-de-lis. But then he was a young-looking sixty-two. His face was small and boyishly smooth and his chestnut hair, teased into classical curls, grew too far down on his forehead for a man at his time of life. It was a good lift but the transplant surgeon had gotten carried away. The dye job was expert.

"You said something over the phone about this Hendriks tragedy," he said. "Terrible thing."

"Murder's a crime, not a tragedy. The press gets them mixed up often." I sat back while the waitress set a mug and a saucer containing a sticky-looking sweet in front of me. She left, saying she'd be back with Miskoupolis' order. "Hendriks' records show the Cerberus Corporation had a substantial investment in Marianne Motors. I'd like to talk to you about it."

"Hadn't you better talk to my broker? Managing the chain takes most of my time. He tells me what looks good and I send him a check."

"Is he connected?"

I got the stone face. "I don't know what you mean."

"I'm tired of being coy, Mr. Miskoupolis. The person I represent will be charged with Hendriks' murder if the police don't shoot him first. I've been dunked in the lake and threatened with guns and lawsuits and almost seduced. I ran out of this month's allotment of tact sometime yesterday."

"I can respect that. One of my earliest memories is of my oldest brother Nicholas eating breakfast in our father's home in Mistra with a shotgun leaning against the table. We were fishermen. One of our neighbors claimed someone had cut his nets."

"Nicholas?"

"What did it matter? In those days when you had a grievance against a man you took on his whole family. Nothing changed when we came here. After the Italians dumped Nicholas behind the Grecian Gardens, women in black lit candles for their dead husbands all over the east side for a month."

The atmosphere in the booth had changed. We sat in silence while Daphne put a plate in front of Miskoupolis and freshened our espressos from a glass carafe, then withdrew. Miskoupolis' meal looked like thistle pods floating in skim milk. Whatever it was it didn't look good enough to be anything less than healthy.

I said, "Hendriks kept a set of books nobody else knew about. According to them he sold the same shares in Marianne almost three times over. Which makes CerbCorp's six-hundred-fifty-thousand-dollar investment essentially worthless. Does that come as a surprise?"

"If I said it doesn't, I killed him. Is that how you see it?"

"Not at all. You'd have someone do it for you. No one in your family has carried a gun since you muscled into the restaurant business."

He lifted his spoon and shipped some skim milk. "If either Nicholas or Aristotle were alive and you suggested that, you wouldn't be."

"Ouzo under the bridge. You didn't answer my question."

"I began to suspect it. In the restaurant business you develop an eye for the patron who is planning to climb out the bathroom window and beat the check. My lawyer was preparing to call for an audit when this thing happened."

"I'd be disappointed if he wasn't. That's what I'd have mine do if I were rigging a murder I didn't want to do time for."

"Your information is out of date. I merely represent a corporation. The stockholders share the loss. Even if I wanted revenge—which would be counterproductive financially, as it wouldn't recover what was lost—it would have to be for a great deal more than my minority share of an amount that wasn't much to begin with."

"Every second hood I meet these days says he's into legitimate profit and loss," I said. "I have trouble buying it."

"I'm not selling it. Only drastic circumstances call for drastic action. As long as the person who did the fleecing remains alive there's a chance he'll repay. I'm not saying it wouldn't be good business to make an example of him afterwards. But only afterwards. Murder as an option is useless once it's exercised."

"Are you always this candid, Mr. Miskoupolis?"

"You strike me as a man who appreciates candor. Of course, I'm only speaking hypothetically."

"Of course. What decided you to invest in Marianne?"

"It was a board decision. We thought there was a market

for a sports car in that class. Now that the energy sham has ended, the country wants to get back out on the highway and laugh at the limit. It was worth a gamble. The money wasn't that big, as I said."

"Did you approach Hendriks or did he approach you?"

"I can't recall. What difference does it make?"

It was the first time he'd shown impatience. I felt a tingling. Maybe it was the espresso.

"It was your decision, wasn't it?" I said. "Not the board's."

"Yes."

"Where did you know Hendriks from before?"

"I didn't." He spooned a thistle pod into his mouth and chewed it silently.

"One of your brothers, then. Or one of their people. Say twenty years ago, before the restaurant business. When laundering stolen money was a family staple."

He went on eating.

Bingo.

26

The lunch crowd had started to wander in. A speaker mounted over the kitchen door crackled, whooshed, and released one of those Aegean tunes that sound like violinists tuning up on a hot griddle. Sherman Miskoupolis finished his meal and set aside his plate. I hadn't touched my baklava.

"I spent some time last night with someone who knows enough about you to write your family biography," I said. "You were a long time finding your specialty. A little gambling, a lot of loansharking, some drugs, even a legitimate fishing and charter service back home in Greece. Generally speaking, when a family operation like yours has foreign interests, sooner or later they're used to lay off goods and cash too hot to handle in the States. Who put Hendriks on to you twenty years ago?"

"Suppose you tell me."

"Doesn't matter. He had a live-in hippie girlfriend who probably had drug connections. One affiliate talks to another and pretty soon young Hendriks is here in Greektown eating moussaka with Nicholas or Aristotle or their kid brother Sherman. Maybe he talked to you before the robbery, but you wouldn't have struck the deal until afterwards when he'd proved himself. He was just a squirt after all. But he delivered, and the money went to Greece and got converted into—what is it over there, sesterces?"

"Drachmas."

"—drachmas, and then returned and reconverted into dollars, with everyone taking his cut down the line. The amount left would still be substantial, but hardly enough to keep an ambitious young bandit in tropical splendor for the rest of his life. The process had already taken so long he had to take out a student loan to live on.

"So he banks the squeaky new money and goes to work for Ford for nine or ten years—maybe knickknacking the accounts to feed his larcenous soul, or maybe he'd learned patience—until Timothy Marianne comes along with an investment prospect he can't refuse. Bang, he's in on the ground floor of Marianne Motors, and bang again, a few years later he gets made general manager. It's a desperado's dream."

The waitress came and refilled my cup. Miskoupolis put a hand over his and said nothing. She left.

"I think you approached him," I said. "Maybe even CerbCorp's shares in Marianne stock were a gift to keep you from tipping the authorities to that old armored car job. The statute ran out a long time ago on the robbery, but Davy Jackson's death makes it murder and that just stays there like atomic waste. This is a longshot, but maybe your demand for a cut is what started him laying off shares already owned by someone else. Maybe not. Try this: After dealing you in at gunpoint, Hendriks gets to thinking about it and realizes there's no way you can make good on your blackmail threat without implicating yourself as an accessory after the fact. So he deals you right back out. Maybe that's what he was doing yesterday with his computerized ledger when your mechanic marched him to that elevator and fed him two slugs."

He laughed then, one of those roaring Greek-fisherman laughs that stopped every other conversation in the room. It didn't have the hollow note I would have liked. It sounded relieved.

"Do you think I'd send a man in to kill him and not retrieve the records of our transaction?" he said, when he stopped laughing. "How long did you spend on this theory?"

"Just the time it took to serve it up. It only came to me five minutes ago."

"I'm glad for you. It means you didn't waste any more of your time than you have of mine. Now unless you intend to eat that, others are waiting for this booth."

I pushed away the saucer. "It didn't look like any contract job I ever saw. There were three holes in the back of the elevator and only two in the victim. Whoever fired the shots missed at least once, more unless both slugs went through Hendriks. I had to see what you did with it."

"Sorry you made the trip."

"I'm not. I can see I was right about his laundering the stolen money through you. You're not the poker player you think you are. Too warm-blooded."

He let that pass. "Look for your killer among the other investors. Start with the one that stood to lose the most."

"That'd be Stutch. That still leaves the problem of the extra holes. The firm would hire better talent."

"Unless someone wanted to make it look like an amateur job," Miskoupolis said. "I suppose that puts me back in the running."

"I can't see you being that cute." I drained my cup. "I don't guess you'd consider telling the police about that twenty-year-old deal. It would corroborate my client's story. They couldn't charge you except for the murder, and that's so many times removed a man with your lawyers could beat it over the telephone."

"I'd have no reason to take that risk. If it were true."

"I had to ask." I got up. "Thanks for seeing me. I still don't like gangsters."

"I'm a restaurateur."

"You make good espresso. Save the baklava for somebody whose sweet tooth kicks in earlier than mine."

"Don't come back."

I got to my favorite Woodward bar a few minutes before noon and stood smoking on the sidewalk among the class of people who stand around Sunday mornings waiting for bars to open. Some of them were dressed better. I consoled myself with the difference between ends and means. When the barkeep threw open the bolts I took the end stool and ordered a Strohs.

The keep had the TV set over the bar turned on with the volume down, warming up for the baseball game. I drank beer and tapped ash into a cheap glass tray and watched a dancing wiener cha-cha with a jar of French's mustard. A laid-off GM worker and a junior high school track coach argued politics at the other end of the bar. When I looked at the screen again my client was on it.

It was an old front-and-profile mug from Jackson, where DeVries had spent the first part of his sentence before getting kicked up to Marquette. He was slimmer and beardless and still had his hair, but it wouldn't make much difference. A Swede who stood six-eight and weighed 280 would be stopped for questioning that day. I told the barkeep to turn up the sound.

". . . believed still at large in the Detroit metropolitan area. Police declined to say why DeVries is a suspect. Hendriks, shown here during a press conference Thursday . . ."

I asked him to change channels. Two stations over they were showing black-and-white footage I hadn't seen in years, of city blocks in flames and people bucket-brigading furniture and TV sets out of smashed shop windows and paratroopers in incongruous camouflage trading automatic fire with unseen snipers on littered streets.

". . . convicted in 1967 of felony murder and conspiracy to commit armed robbery after he set fire to draw attention from . . ."

On the next channel, a black woman reporter was interviewing the security guard who had held me for the police in the Detroit office of Marianne Motors, and whom DeVries had knocked down and stood on the day before that.

". . . busted in here yelling for Mr. Hendriks to show himself. I wanted to call the cops then, but Mr. Piero—that's my boss . . ."

"Okay, put it back."

"There's what comes of turning killers loose." The barkeep returned to the original station, where a young weatherman was calling football signals over Kansas. "I'm with Cecil Fish. Let's get back the death penalty in Michigan."

"Iroquois Heights prosecutors make that same noise every couple of years," I said. "None of them's made governor yet."

"Well, he's got my vote."

"He deserves it."

The keep leaned his big meaty face close enough to tell me he was a better customer there than I was. "What might that mean?"

"It means I need a new favorite bar." I paid for the beer and left.

I had an acquaintance in Security at the Detroit Public Library who let me in the back way when it was closed. I found the drawers containing old issues of the *News* and *Free Press* on microfilm and clamped the ones I wanted into a machine in the reading room. I was getting to know the layout better than the warehouse district and Detroit Police Headquarters. The private eye of the future will wear spectacles with Coke-bottle lenses and carry a rubber thumb in place of a gun. He will talk in computerese and spend good drinking time browsing in the software department at Hudson's. That's if he'll be needed at all, with a portable electronic brain in every household. Of course he will be. People will always need someone to stand in front of bullets and fists aimed at them.

Nineteen sixty-eight blurred past, stopping here and there at pictures of DPW crews cleaning up riot damage and young longhairs in fatigue pants with flags sewn to the seats and soldiers on the line in Vietnam with flowers in the muzzles of their M-16s and Richard Nixon and Hubert Humphrey and Eugene McCarthy campaigning and Bobby Kennedy lying on his back on a hotel floor with surprise and confusion on his face. It made me feel as old as erosion.

It took an hour longer than I'd expected. Even then I

missed it the first time and had to turn back on a hunch. It claimed two inches of the city section between an interview with Mayor Cavanaugh and an illustrated advertisement for Listerine that promised an end to sore throats caused by viruses. "CITY GIRL KILLED IN AUTO MISHAP," read the headline. I digested all it had to offer in ten seconds and turned, unenlightened, to the obituaries.

> SOUWAINE, MARY FRANCES
> Aged 19, died suddenly Monday, Oct. 14. Born May 11, 1949, in Birmingham, Ala., daughter Harold and Mary Katherine (Joiner) Souwaine. They preceded her in death. Moved to Detroit 1967. Attended Wayne State University. Survived by a sister, Edith. No services planned. Donations in lieu of flowers to the National Highway Safety Council.

I read it through twice. Then I put back the microfilms, found some more recent ones in another drawer, and spent another hour with them. They only went back five years, but they made me feel just as old.

The little parking lot on West Grand River was as barren as a proving ground. I crossed the street on foot against no traffic at all and used my key in the front door because the super had locked up and gone home. He had stopped living on the premises after a black revolutionary had cut loose at me with a light assault rifle in the foyer. It's a lonely sort of life but not always dull.

My building was quieter than the library, quieter even than the Detroit office of Marianne Motors with Hendriks dead in the elevator and the doors bumping him like amateur pallbearers trying to carry a coffin through a narrow doorway. The stairwell echoed and the hallway on my floor with its dingy linoleum and impertinent new suspended ceiling might have belonged to an evacuated shelter. I was alone. Even rats don't hang around a place where there is no promise of food.

The busted brokers, dirty-nailed tailors, credit dentists with Mexican degrees, chiropractors, sign painters, orange-haired cosmeticians, electrical contractors, legal experts with malfeasance suits pending, TV repairmen, palmsters, tattoo artists, carpet salesmen, escort pimps, bookies, clowns, geeks, freaks, Sikhs, mercenaries and model agencies, martial-arts instructors with greasy smocks and tattered eastern philosophies, all the floating jetsam from the higher rents downtown, were home living their lives or away trying to forget them. I felt like the last whooping crane.

A shadow fell across me while I was unlocking the door to my outer office. I knew who it was without turning around. I pushed the door open and stood clear to let him inside.

27

I SET THE BOTTLE and a glass on the desk. DeVries ignored the glass, fisted the bottle, and pointed the base at the ceiling. It glugged twice and he pounded it back down and swept a flanneled arm across his mouth. Sweat broke out in studs on his forehead when the heat hit his belly. I turned on the fan and pushed some stale air around.

"Stuff tastes like piss," he said. "You drink it all the time?"

"It loses something without the ceremony." I sat down and put my feet on the scribble pad. "Hot, isn't it? Especially where you are."

"Guy left his office open next door."

"Who let you into the building?"

"Little Jewish guy on his way out. I said I had an appointment with you. He said not to make no holes in the walls. What'd he mean?"

"Insider humor. He recognize you?"

"Didn't act like it."

"If he did he wouldn't do anything about it. Rosekrantz doesn't even mind his own business."

"I wasn't sure you'd show today, but I couldn't stay where I was."

"No Sundays in this work. Drop a load."

He remained standing. "I didn't do it."

I picked up the bottle and shook what was left. "I just watched you."

"Kill Hendriks, I mean. That wasn't mine."

"How'd you find out the cops wanted you for it?"

"Seen them watching the hotel yesterday. They didn't see me. I went down an alley. After that I went—"

"For a walk. Don't tell me where. So far I can beat the harboring rap. Where were you yesterday morning?"

"At the Alamo. You seen me there."

"Before that."

"I was there all morning till you came with that St. George."

"St. Charles. Where'd you go after I left?"

"Mt. Elliott Cemetery. I was meeting somebody."

"Who?"

"A woman."

"The one whose call you were expecting?"

"Yeah. She didn't show."

"Name."

"I don't know. She called before, said she had the money Hendriks owed me and not to tell nobody. She was scared of him finding out. Said she'd call back to set up the meet. She did, after you left."

"Anybody see you there?"

"Some bums. I walked. I waited two hours and then I gave up and went home. That's when I seen the cops sitting outside waiting."

"You should've told me."

"She said not. I didn't want to scare her off."

"You couldn't scare her if you'd walked in with your head under your arm."

"You know who it was?"

"I know someone wanted you someplace where no reliable witnesses could place you at the time Alfred Hendriks was killed. That's twice in twenty years you've had a frame hung on you the same way. Didn't Marquette teach you anything?"

"They got some bad dudes inside," he said. "I thought they got them all."

"They don't make that much barbed wire."

He sat down then. He was wearing the clothes I'd seen him in the day before. "So what'd you find out?"

"The good news is I found someone who can pin Hendriks to the robbery."

He watched me and said nothing. That's the trouble with good news–bad news jokes; they depend too much on who's listening. I gave up. "He won't come forward. He'd only implicate himself. But I know who killed Hendriks. If I work it right I can get you clear of that."

"What about the money?"

"The money's gone. Forget the money. If I had the money right now I'd use that fan to blow it out the window and watch the traffic back up. The trouble with you, besides being too damn big, is you think because they dressed you up like a citizen and let you through the gate you're out of prison. You're not, as long as you keep worrying about what you've got coming to you."

"So what do we do now?"

"I'm going to go talk to Hendriks' killer. You're going to turn yourself in if you don't want to wind up dead on a sidewalk because you didn't hear a cop tell you to throw up your hands the first time."

"You going to turn me in if I don't?"

"You bet. I'll hit you on the head with this desk and wrap you in the rug like Cleopatra and carry you there under one arm. Let the cops do their own job if you won't."

"Well, I won't."

"I never thought you would. Sit tight." I picked up the telephone.

"Who you calling?"

I was dialing. "Relax. Does this look like nine-one-one?"

"What's nine-one-one?"

"*Sí?*" A woman's voice.

"Elda?" I said.

"*Sí.*"

"This is Mr. Walker. I almost had lunch there yesterday."

"*Sí.*"

"Is either Mr. or Mrs. Marianne at home?"

"No."

At least it was a change. "Where's Mr. Marianne?"

"He say downriver."

"What's he doing at the plant on a Sunday?"

"Meeting, he say. About *Señor* Hendriks."

"What about Mrs. Marianne?"

"Exercise. She run."

This was getting to be like pulling boxcars. "When do you expect her back?"

"*No sé.*"

"Can you take a message?"

"*Sí.*" Paper rustled.

"Tell her I know who killed Hendriks. I'm going to see her husband about it now."

I made sure she had it, then depressed the plunger. I let it up and dialed again. This call was quicker. I didn't use any names.

"I'm coming along," DeVries said.

"I figured you would. You'll have to scrunch down in the back seat in case we pull up alongside any prowl cars at traffic lights."

"It wouldn't be anything like I ain't been doing since yesterday."

I took the West German revolver George St. Charles had given me out of the drawer and slapped it down in front of him. "If you get caught with this maybe they'll let us be roommates. Use your left hand and keep it away from your face if you have to fire it. My advice is don't. These days the Krauts make better cars than they do guns."

He picked it up and examined it, then stood and stuck it inside his pants, pulling his shirttail out to cover the butt. "Where's yours?"

"Collecting rust in the property room at thirteen hundred. I'll use the Luger." I got up. "You won't mind if we swing west to pick someone up."

"Guy you just called?"

"That's the one."

"Who is he?"

"The cop who arrested you."

He met us at the door, buttoning up a black nylon shirt with white orchids on it. He had on gray flannel trousers and his feet were shod in black high-tops with brass hooks and steel toes. His scalp gleamed through his short bristly pinkish hair, but he looked younger than he had relaxing in the backyard with his wife and grandchildren. The air was charged, as if a big jet had just passed over, or maybe it was the situation. "Come ahead in," he said. "I'm just—" He saw my client looming behind me.

"Floyd Orlander, Richard DeVries," I said. "You might remember each other."

"Lieutenant."

Orlander looked at me. "He still wanted?"

"If he weren't I would've called the cops instead of you."

"If you told me he was in it I would of said no."

"That's why I didn't tell you."

He hadn't moved from the doorway. "In the old days I played nice sometimes with pimps and stickup guys. I had to to get what I was after. Not with pushers or killers, though. Never once. I'm not about to break a perfect record just because I'm retired."

"I got as close as I'm ever likely to get to a confession from Sherman Miskoupolis that his family turned around the money from that armored job for Alfred Hendriks. Hendriks killed Davy Jackson. Not DeVries."

"Sherman Miskoupolis, of the Miskoupolis brothers?"

"I hope there's just the one family. The name's too hard to pronounce."

"I met Ari one time and I helped investigate after they

scraped Nick off the pavement in Greektown. It should of happened to all three of them. Anyway I was talking about the Hendriks kill."

"He didn't do Hendriks either. We're on our way to meet the killer. You coming or not? You said you wanted to see this through."

"Who's the killer?"

"You didn't pay to see that hand."

"Man, I hope you know how lucky you are I mellowed." He made chewing motions with his big jaw. Then he looked up at DeVries. "You got bald."

"You got old," DeVries said.

"Old's better than bald."

"I can put on a hat."

Orlander turned around and walked away from the door, leaving it open. DeVries and I went inside. In the dining room Orlander took a key down from the high top of an antique china cabinet and unlocked a drawer in the base.

"Where's your wife?" I asked.

"I sent her to visit the kids. Said some old friends from the department were coming and the language could get unrefined."

"She buy it?"

"Not for a damn second. But she went." He took a glistening brown leather rig out of the drawer and climbed into it. "Ever wear one of these?" He snapped the bottom of the holster to his belt and adjusted the elastic strap across his back.

"Years ago. Felt like a goiter."

"Still does. But those belt clips are hell on the kidneys. What are you carrying?"

I showed him the Luger. I'd put on my jacket to conceal it.

"Shit. That Fred Flintstone action's what lost them the war. Here's a gun." He lifted the top off a pasteboard box in the drawer and picked up a square black automatic pistol with a checked grip.

"Nine-millimeter," I said. "Lieutenant Alderdyce said you had a smaller Beretta."

"Never heard of him. That seven-sixty-five was too light. Almost got me killed once." He popped the magazine, looked at the cartridges, heeled it back in, and racked one into the chamber. He holstered the weapon. "Dottie wants me to get rid of it on account of the kids. Women teaching kids to be scared of guns is what's got this world in deep shit. What's King Kong carrying? Don't tell me he just wears his shirts sloppy."

I said, "You don't want to see it."

"That bad?"

"Worse."

"That's the trouble with this place. Nobody's got no pride. Where we headed?"

"The Marianne plant."

"How you figure to get past Security?"

"I thought I'd wing it. It's not that great there."

"They see you before?"

"Just once."

"That's plenty. Wait here." He went through the dining room arch.

DeVries stood around looking big and quiet. I asked him how he was doing.

"I got my description on every police radio in three counties and I'm standing in a white cop's house. If I was doing much better I'd be in the gas chamber."

"They don't do that here. Yet. They'd give you a hundred years tops."

"Hell, I'll probably be dead by then."

Orlander came back with a gray felt hat and stuck it out. "Pull this on."

It was too big. I tucked the top half of an ear inside the crown and tugged the brim down over my right eye. Dick Tracy looked back at me from the glass in the china cabinet.

"Nothing changes a face like a hat," Orlander said. "You be the mean one. If we do it right they won't ask to see our shields."

"We look kind of casual for cops."

"How many neckties you see on Sunday? Plainclothes means plain clothes."

"What do we put on DeVries?"

"DeVries stays in the car."

"I don't like splitting up."

"We could have him go in on his hands and knees and tell them we're with the Canine Corps."

"I didn't come this far to sit in no back seat," the big man said.

"It's how it gets done, junior." Orlander pulled a thin green sweater on over the shoulder rig. "Otherwise it gets done without me. Which means it don't get done."

I said, "He's right. They take one look at you and we'll be up to our eyebrows in real cops."

"Our eyebrows," Orlander said. "Your ass."

"We don't need him."

"We need him," I said. "Last time we hit a Marianne office it was just the hired help. This time we're dealing with the first string."

"Ain't nothing changed. It was the Man when I went in and it's still the Man."

Orlander stepped up to him. The top of his head came to DeVries's sternum. "Don't fuck with me, boy."

"Don't call me boy, fuck."

"God bless us every one," I said.

28

IT WAS THE KIND of Sunday afternoon that's wasted on cities, custom-built for chicken and dumplings after church and playing checkers on the front porch. The sun was Crayola yellow in a scrubbed sky with chunky clouds lying on it as motionless as old men in a park. Buildings floated on layers of rippling heat. The skyline was sharp at the edges, as if cut out with a steel punch, and the pavement made sucking sounds as our tires rolled over it.

We took the Edsel Ford east from Romulus and turned south on the John Lodge past the empty haunted skeletons of Wonder Bread and Vernor's, putting more distance between ourselves and chicken and dumplings every block. On West Jefferson the river caught the light in little platinum bursts, reminding me of Lake Superior as seen from Marquette. We drove along entire streets without meeting another car. Short of an air raid, nothing empties a city faster than a nice weekend.

Floyd Orlander rode with his window cranked down and his eyes on the road ahead, flicking them to the side only to note each street sign automatically as we passed it. His brutal profile never stirred. DeVries lay hunched on the floor of the back seat. Every time he moved to relieve a cramped muscle, my seat strained forward. The little Renault labored under the extra weight.

"I don't get this Hendriks at all," Orlander said, when we were stopped for a light in River Rouge. There was no traffic going in either direction. "My old man carried car batteries up and down three flights of stairs for twenty years. I had to get a job to finish high school. If I had an economics scholarship to England I sure wouldn't hit no armored car."

"Bet you would for two hundred large," DeVries said.

"Too much risk. And he couldn't know there was that much. The guards stretched their route that day to cut down on the number of trips."

"It wasn't just the money." The light changed and I crossed the intersection. "Some people are honest because they're honest. Just as many or maybe more never do anything dishonest because they don't get the chance or they're afraid they'll get caught. You're a college kid pulling down a buck and a half an hour doing the books in a print shop and it's fine until the dam bursts. DeVries said it: Everyone around you is breaking the law, smashing and burning and boosting merchandise and the cops are letting it happen for the most part because it's gotten too big for them. Then your boss tells you to tot up the accounts because he's shipping them out tomorrow in a lot with every other business in the neighborhood. It's the money, but not just that. It's a once-in-a-lifetime opportunity and you've got at least twenty-four hours to decide what you'll do with it."

"I never bought that help-a-good-boy-go-bad shit."

"Nobody does. There's no such thing as corrupting a person. There has to be a foothold to begin with. Hendriks was a firecracker waiting to go off, though maybe he never knew it. So was DeVries, only in a different way. One robbed, the other burned. The rules were suspended and the opportunity was there."

"Wasn't the same at all," DeVries said. "I was drunk and black."

Orlander said, "Bullshit. Your kind gets a boil on your ass, it's because you're black."

"You ever been?"

"No. I got a boil just the same."

"Don't it give you a headache?"

"Fellas." I passed a line of bicyclists in helmets pedaling along the shoulder. "Hendriks was drunk too, in his way. People who work with money love it. They'll say it's figures they love, but take away the dollar sign and they lose interest in a fat hurry. But it's the sixties and love and peace are supposed to be more important. You've got a hippie girlfriend who believes it, or pretends to, and anybody who's been force-fed that wall-poster philosophy along with the usual hallucinogens is a ready tool. Maybe you tell her you'll give the money to some cult group or a Democrat.

"Davy Jackson you handle a little differently. He's drunk almost as often as he's black, and a big heist under those circumstances is just another way of Getting His. He's like DeVries that way."

"Reason enough for DeVries to be in on it," Orlander said.

"Go to hell."

"Not near enough," I said. "He's got a shot at professional basketball and he's engaged to be married. If the first doesn't change your perspective, the second sure does. I've seen you with your grandchildren and I know you know what I'm talking about. But he's drunk and black too, so him you take in partway and don't tell him the rest. You play him the way you play the girlfriend and Jackson, only with different pieces. Hendriks was the only one in the game with all the pieces. In a little over a year, two of the others were dead and the third was in prison. Hendriks quit winners."

"Until yesterday," said Orlander.

"That's the trouble with winning. There's always a challenger."

The gate was open, the employee parking lot filled. There are no Sundays in the automobile industry either. I steered around the building and parked in the little lot off the executive entrance. Timothy Marianne's Stiletto was there, with a plate reading TIMTOP. There was no sign of Mrs. Marianne's car.

"How many on the desk?" Orlander asked.

"Just one in front," I said. "Back here I don't know. I didn't go in this door."

"I'll talk. You snarl every little." He opened his door.

DeVries winched himself up onto the back seat, filling the rearview mirror. "What do I do, sit here and play the radio?"

"Slide down if any other cars show up," I said. "Wait for whoever it is to get inside, then lay on the horn."

"Who you expecting?"

"A good-looking redhead driving a maroon Turbo Saab."

"What the hell's a Turbo Sob?"

"You'll know it when you see it." I put a foot on the pavement.

"I ain't sitting here all day counting license plates."

"Give us twenty minutes. Otherwise wait for a signal. Then come in hard, but don't kill anyone."

"Twenty minutes is a long time."

"Not compared to twenty years."

The steel fire door looked like the one on the employees' entrance in front. This one was locked. Orlander squashed the button on an intercom mounted next to it.

"Yes?" A masculine, radio-modulated voice. They've developed most of the tinniness out of closed-circuit communication.

"Open up."

"Whom do you represent?"

Orlander looked at me. "Did he say *whom*?"

"Yeah. Let's make him eat it."

"Whom do you represent?" the voice repeated.

"The next forty-eight hours of your life, junior, if you don't open up before we shoot off the lock. That's the standard drop for interfering with a police officer in the performance of his duty."

"You're the police?"

"Man's got a lot of questions," Orlander said.

"Let's throw him in with some fag bikers."

"I don't think we got any."

"We'll arrest some," I said.

"Hang on," said the voice.

A buzzer razzed. Orlander turned the knob and we went inside. The guard was sitting in front of six television screens on a console. He was my age, trim, and tall-looking in a gray uniform with the tie tucked inside his shirt. He wore steel-rimmed aviator's glasses and a revolver in a spring clip on his hip.

"Lookit the soldier suit," I said.

He was staring at Orlander. "You're kind of old for a police officer."

I said, "He got gray watching me bounce cheap rentals off the ceiling."

"Shut up. Where's your boss, junior?"

"The security chief?" He adjusted his glasses. "He's not—"

"I mean the big kahuna. Where is he?"

"Mr. Marianne?"

Orlander looked at me. "He's just as dumb in person."

"He'll smarten up when those bikers start getting friendly."

"Bwana Marianne, junior. The chairman of the board. The head honcho. The high colonic. The jerk that owns this building and your brass buttons. It's about his general manager that got himself dead yesterday. You read about it after the funnies."

"He doesn't read," I said. "He cleans his gun and thinks about Clint Eastwood."

The guard colored. "There's no reason—"

I took a step forward and ran into Orlander's arm. "Tear him up on your own time," he said. "You got your job, junior, we got ours. Just point us his way and we'll be out of your life like last year's calendar."

"He's on the floor, talking to the employees."

"You wouldn't be just telling us that so you can call up to his office and tell him we're coming," Orlander said.

"See for yourself."

Marianne's lanky, loosely clad frame slouched on one of the TV monitors with his hands in his pockets, facing a crowd of coveralled men from a low catwalk over a conveyor. He looked like a man who hadn't slept in a while, but it could have been the black-and-white photography. There was no sound.

"Where might that be, junior?"

"Through there." The guard pointed at a pair of swinging doors with square grilled windows. "You'll need these."

Orlander snatched the yellow Lucite tags off the guard's palm and gave me one. We put them in our pockets.

"They're supposed to be worn on the outside."

"It's okay, junior. We're plainclothesmen."

At the doors I turned around, went back to the console, and pulled the telephone out of the wall. It took two yanks. I handed the frayed end of the cord to the guard. "Charge it to the city."

"What about your badges?" he said.

The doors swung to behind us.

"Fucking ham," said Orlander.

"Don't blame me," I said. "Your good cop is most cops' bad cop."

We were in a corridor done in yellow tile without a window or door on either side. There was another set of swinging doors at the other end with red letters on a white sign reading SAFETY GLASSES BEYOND THIS POINT. Timothy Marianne's voice droned on the other side. We pushed through into the plant proper.

29

THIS SECTION was one of the few remaining from the old tractor plant. Thick mullioned windows the size of garage doors lined the walls from just below the twenty-foot ceiling to within eight feet of the floor. Between them was bare brick, with exposed girders crisscrossing overhead and a freshly poured concrete floor going white in mottled patches. A railed catwalk six feet high circled the walls, stepped ladders on all four sides leading down from them to the floor, where a row of Stiletto chassis stood on a stopped conveyor belt. Space-age robot limbs posed along the belt with their drills, torches, and high-speed sanders pointed ceilingward like weapons at parade rest. In the aisles between the belt and the catwalks, fifty or sixty workers in gray coveralls stood looking up at Timothy Marianne slouched behind the railing.

". . . died while at work for the company he did so much to help build," he was saying. "Why he died isn't our concern. What is our concern is that we continue to work together as we have from the beginning to ensure that the dream he gave his life for becomes fact. It's as much of a monument as Al would care to have, and greater than most."

At his side and a little behind him hovered a large black man in coveralls with his hands on his hips and his head down, listening. He'd be the foreman. Orlander and I had come out onto a catwalk adjoining theirs, angled across from them. Our path was blocked by a white vinyl-covered kitchen chair with steel tubing where the foreman probably sat when the conveyor was moving. Rather than call attention to ourselves by moving it we stayed where we were.

"I know there are rumors among you already that Al was into something that got too big for him," Marianne said. "None of them has any foundation. From the beginning he invested his time and skills and most of his personal finances into this plant and the great mechanism behind it. Put simply, without Al Hendriks there would be no Marianne Motors. I can't stop the speculation, but I won't have him tried and condemned because he had the temerity to be killed in a violent age.

"Many of you are wondering about the future of Marianne Motors. You are its future. Which direction it takes is entirely up to you. As long as you and those who come after you continue to show the dedication and loyalty you have so far, the firm will go on. And now I've kept you from your work long enough."

There was a little silence after he finished. Then someone clapped and someone else took it up and applause crackled through the crowd. It rose when Marianne lifted his right hand in his characteristic wave and died quickly as he turned to leave. At its peak it wouldn't have drawn a second curtain call at the Fischer Theater. At the labor level, pep talks are followed by pink slips too often to get excited about.

Marianne stopped when he saw us. "How did you get past Security?"

"What Security?" Orlander said. "Captain Video in the back room?"

"Who are you?"

Whatever answer he might have made was drowned out when the conveyor started with a report like a pistol shot. Then the robots with drills and sanders and welding torches cut in, sparks splattered, and the air grew sharp with the stench of scorched metal. The foreman had gone down to supervise the startup. I raised my voice. "There someplace we can talk without yelling?"

"Say what you have to say right here. I have a business to put back together."

"I thought the Hendriks kill wasn't no more than pissing in Niagara," Orlander said.

"Who is he?" Marianne asked me.

"A friend. You throw a stirring rally. Things that bad?"

"Unless you're a stockholder I don't see that it's your business."

"I know who killed Hendriks."

"Take off that hat. You don't look the least bit like Harrison Ford."

I'd forgotten I was wearing it. I removed it and tossed it onto the seat of the foreman's chair. It hadn't been needed anyway. Marianne came around the corner and stopped on the other side of the chair. "Who?"

"You should have asked that right away," I said. "I might have believed you didn't know."

"I know, all right. It was your client. You're hiding him, I suppose."

"We're not talking about DeVries and you know it. That bewildered air doesn't cut it anymore. You're too shrewd a businessman not to suspect the real killer."

He put his hands back in his pockets. "Suppose you explain."

"It's all craft. The neglected hair and clothes, the careless posture, the outward appearance of boyish innocence; that whole inverted corporate polish is obvious enough to fool the business world, but cops are used to obvious ploys. They'd see through it the way a kid sees through a professional magician. It's a weapon against nonliteral minds, just like Commodore Stutch's age. You know, all right."

Orlander said, "*I* don't."

"Every case needs a place to start," I said. "After I'd heard enough of DeVries's story to buy it I started on Hendriks. Prison's a little like going blind. The last thing you see before you get cut off stays with you. Years later he recognized Marianne's general manager in a photograph as the Wayne State student who encouraged him to throw that firebomb." I looked at Marianne. "The second time Hendriks stonewalled me, in your office, I followed him to your house and saw him pick up your wife and drive away with her."

He laughed easily. "So I found out they were having an affair and killed him. How Napoleonic."

"I can see she told you about it after I confronted her. I thought she would. It might have been anything or nothing. Extramarital flings among couples at your social level aren't exactly special bulletins. When Hendriks turned up dead the next day, a lazy cop might have made jealousy the motive and gone after you. It was too much coincidence for me.

"Setting that aside, I had to consider the possibility that my client killed Hendriks. That stuck me square in the middle. If I proved DeVries's story I established a motive. His alibi, that a woman who wouldn't identify herself called him to set up a meeting to arrange a payoff and then didn't show, stunk. The murder fit him too well so I set that aside too."

"Your logic is selective," Marianne said. Smoke from the abraded metal on the line enveloped his legs. We were standing directly under one of the ventilators mounted above the windows.

"That left Hendriks' second set of books. It pointed to any one of a number of multinational corporations he'd been fleecing, including the ancient and malevolent firm of Icepick & Garrote. Not that any of the higher profiles on Wall Street would be squeamish about murder either. They finance wars and foreign assassinations. A little domestic snuffing would come under the heading of minor adjustments."

"You're lying. Al was a lot of things but he wouldn't have sold out the company."

"Two point eight times," I said, "according to an accountant I had look at the two computer disks Hendriks had squirreled away. But in my business, evidence that comes that easy is automatically tainted. SOP in that situation is to look in the opposite direction."

Orlander said, "So far you've eliminated every suspect but DeVries."

"Not every one. Someone's still unaccounted for. Let's go back twenty years. We know, or we suspect, that Hendriks and Davy Jackson pulled off the actual heist of that armored car on Brady in 1967. DeVries torched the empty building to create a diversion, although he didn't know that's what he was doing. That leaves the wheel man. Hendriks would have had one. He was too practical to leave the getaway car unguarded in the middle of a riot."

"The broad," Orlander said.

"His girlfriend, Frances Souwaine, was a fellow student at Wayne State. She had priors for soliciting and possession of narcotics, which was part of the pattern back then, especially for an Alabama girl trying to make her way in the big northern city after the death of her parents. DeVries said she was a hippie. She looked like one and she was living with a man outside of wedlock and no doubt she had the standard things to say against the Establishment, but that prostitution record suggests she was more mercenary than the average run. So handling the wheel during the big caper wouldn't have seemed out of line. We may never know what she thought when Hendriks gunned down one of his own men during the getaway, or if she was in on that part of the plan from the start, or if she even saw it. The reason we'll never know is she was killed in an auto accident fifteen months later."

Orlander said, "Hendriks?"

"I thought about it. Probably not. If he were going to take her out he wouldn't have waited that long, and he might have been in England at the time. It could have been suicide. At least that's what her sister thinks."

Marianne kept his hands in his pockets. I'd been right about him. The tighter his situation the more casual he seemed.

"I looked up the accident," I said. "The newspaper account

didn't tell me as much as Frances Souwaine's obituary in the same issue. She left only one survivor, a sister named Edith."

"I suppose you got all hot and bothered over finding such a common name twice in one case," Marianne said.

"Don't knock hot and bothered. Sometimes it's the only fuel you've got. Mrs. Marianne told me her sister was killed in an accident that may or may not have been deliberate on the sister's part. It's conceivable that two transplanted Southerners named Edith lost sisters in accidents. Two named Edith Souwaine is stretching it. That was your wife's maiden name. I looked up the story on your wedding."

"You sorry trash."

"Her sister took part in the armored. Somewhere along the line she told Edith all about it, and then she killed herself on the road. It doesn't much matter if it was conscious or unconscious. She had helped Hendriks commit robbery and been an accomplice to murder and then he left her here to bog down in that drugged Morning After that her kind woke up to in the sixties while he went to England. Maybe he planned to give her her cut; probably not. He'd already killed to sweeten his end. She couldn't get to the money—it was with the Miskoupolis brothers getting scrubbed clean—and she couldn't threaten to go to the cops because she was just as guilty. He used her up and threw her over and she worried at it until she'd worried herself to death. But Edith was stronger stuff.

"She could have turned him in; Frances was dead and safe from repercussions. She didn't. Instead she put herself through a finishing course of some kind, shook the cottonseeds out of her hair, and became a model. She had the looks for it and more than her fair share of plantation charm. I'm not saying it was part of any master plan. More likely she was making her way after the example of her sister's mistakes and watching for her opportunity second. It came when an escort from one of the auto companies who employed her as a model introduced her to you."

He took his hands out of his pockets. It was starting to flake off now.

"She may have contrived that," I went on. "She'd have been watching Hendriks' stock rise since he took up with you, just as another of his victims would be later, in prison. Anyway she went to work, drawing on all that Southern heritage and Northern training, and before either of you was much older she became Mrs. Timothy Marianne. She must have especially enjoyed getting twenty percent of the corporation placed in her name. It made her Hendriks' employer."

"Edith loves me," he said. "You just can't accept that on its face. Your work's too greasy."

"No greasier than some of the people it rubs me up against. Just when your wife identified herself to Hendriks and put the squeeze on him to keep her from going public is one for the boys in the Securities and Exchange Commission. My guess is they'll find out the pair were partners in Hendriks' fast shuffle. It's the only thing that explains why she took so long before claiming her final revenge."

"No, Chester!"

"Watch it!" Orlander clawed under his sweater.

I ducked and something swished over my head. Then I turned inside the big foreman's follow-through and chopped at his throat. It was a glancing blow. He grunted and brought the wrench back the other way. I threw up a forearm to block it. Orlander stuck the Beretta in Chester's face and thumbed back the hammer. The wrench clanged to the catwalk.

"Kiss the floor, junior."

After a moment the foreman got down in push-up position. He had seen the confrontation from below, understood that his employer was in some kind of trouble, and climbed a different ladder from the one he had descended, coming up on our blind side. Orlander lowered the automatic.

"You didn't kill him, Mr. Marianne," I said. "If you did you'd have let your man bash my head in."

"You knew anyway." His tone was barely audible above the

noise from the floor. We had yet to attract any more attention from down there. Marianne's whole frame had subsided, not so much relaxed now as crumpled in on itself. He looked his age.

I said, "I didn't know how much you knew. I'm satisfied now you had no part in it. When Hendriks heard DeVries was out and paying me to ask questions about the robbery he got nervous. He went out driving with your wife that night to discuss a game plan. The jitters are contagious.

"The next day she invited me to lunch, letting you think it was your idea. She had more back-up plans than any of your people in engineering and design. She'd already called DeVries with a phony appointment to lure him someplace where he couldn't establish an alibi. It had to be her. Who else knew enough about the case to convince him? With your business contacts and their political contacts it wouldn't have been hard for her to find out where the state was putting him up. That was Plan B. If Plan A worked and I accepted your offer of cash or her offer of her—the cook coming in when she did to remind you of your errand downriver was perfect timing—the only thing lost would've been a couple more hours out of DeVries's life. When she found out I wasn't for sale for love or money she switched to the back-up."

I took a second to swallow. Between having to speak above the racket and inhaling smoke and sparks, I was getting hoarse. No one jumped in to fill the pause.

"She pretended to be insulted and threw me out," I said. "Actually she was in a hurry to get rid of me. If DeVries was going to be any use to her at all as a pigeon she had to get to the Detroit office of Marianne Motors and kill Hendriks before DeVries returned to his hotel."

"No one would risk a murder conviction to cover up simple extortion," Marianne said.

Orlander snorted.

I said, "It's been done. But you're forgetting her dead sister. Edith waited almost twenty years to repay that debt in full.

Ask DeVries and a guy named George St. Charles what that's like. The blackmail was just to make Hendriks squirm until she found an excuse to put him out of his misery. The possibility of his cracking made as good a one as any. Sooner or later there'd have been another if not that."

"All right, except the last part."

She hadn't raised her voice above normal range and should have been drowned out by the machinery. Maybe it was the drawl. Orlander jumped and started to turn, raising the Beretta.

"Don't." Louder now. He stopped.

I did turn. She had come out onto the catwalk behind us. She had on a raw silk top, burlap-colored, with straps over her tanned shoulders, a flared yellow cotton skirt, and cork-soled sandals. Sparks flying up from the floor reflected off her thick red hair and off the oiled finish of the .38 revolver in her right hand.

I kept my hands away from my body. "What'd I get wrong?"

"Edith's dead," she said. "She died in 1968 at the end of a short innocuous life. I'm Frances Souwaine."

30

"EDITH—" Marianne started forward. She moved the gun. He stopped.

"I'm not Edith. I never was."

"How'd you switch ID's?" I asked.

"Put the gun on the floor," she told Orlander. "Gently. We don't want it falling off the edge and alerting personnel. Kick it this way."

Orlander let down the hammer and complied. The Beretta scraped along the catwalk. She stopped it with a foot. Chester started to get up.

"Stay there." She looked at me. The tilt of her eyes was feline. "My apartment house was gutted during the riots. I was living with Edith on Chalmers, if you can call it living. She wouldn't have turned a dishonest dollar to keep from starving. The car was in my name. The police got the address off the registration and notified me. I identified her at the morgue, or rather I identified myself."

"Why?"

"Why not? Frances Souwaine had a record. Edith Souwaine didn't. Frances was an accomplice to an armed robbery and a murder that were still officially under investigation. Edith wasn't carrying identification and we looked enough alike to be mistaken for each other by people who didn't know us well, which no one did up here. She was between jobs. Of course the police had taken her fingerprints; but they hardly ever bother to process them when they've got a positive ID from the next of kin and no reason to suspect it. There wasn't a good argument not to let Frances die and go on as Edith. I started thinking along those lines when the officer who called asked me if I knew Frances Souwaine. I worked out the rest in the cab on the way to the morgue."

"No friend like a sister," Orlander said. He kept his hands in sight as well.

"We barely spoke," she said. "Our mother died delivering her and our father finally managed to drink himself to death when we were teenagers. In some families a thing like that brings the survivors closer together. Not us. The only thing we ever agreed on was to move up here, and even that was for different reasons. She wanted to support herself. I wanted everything. That meant education, and that took more money than I could make scrubbing toilets or answering telephones. Everything looked pretty far away in some of the filthy motel rooms I shared with filthier strangers an hour at a time. Drugs made it look a little closer. I got off them just in time for Edith, although it was already too late for Frances. Rest her soul."

"How soon after that did you dye your hair?" I asked.

"I went to a beauty parlor the morning after I visited the morgue. I was straight by then and had some trick money saved up. Getting a breezy good-bye and a promise from Al to see me when he got back from abroad shocked me into doing something with myself. Some minor plastic surgery, breast implants, and a little weight gained in the right places changed my appearance a lot more than you might think. Modeling school did the rest. I met Al several times after I started seeing Tim. He never recognized me until I told him who I was. By then I was Mrs. Marianne."

Marianne was shriveling. He looked nearly as old as the Commodore. "I love you."

"You love the Stiletto. I was an option to help you charm investors into getting it off the drawing board and into production. Stop posing for once."

The whine of the electric drills vibrated beneath our feet. Shifting my weight, I leaned closer to the foreman's chair. "Was Hendriks getting set to talk?"

"He discussed paying you off. He brought it up during that car ride you made so much about. I knew when you didn't accept my offer the next day that you'd keep at him until he broke."

"You killed him."

"Again, there was no good reason not to. Your client had made himself the perfect suspect. Failing that, there were all those investors Al had bilked into thinking they were buying original shares in Marianne. My percentage wasn't on record. I made sure of that."

"You were the one who put the disk in the computer," I said.

"I read them both and put one back in Al's desk. I didn't want to make it too obvious. He couldn't keep his access code a secret from me. Anyway the police couldn't overlook something in the machine with the signal on hold. All those other suspects would confuse the issue just enough, stop the investigation from progressing beyond them and DeVries. I did that afterwards."

"How'd you lure Hendriks into that elevator?"

"I was his partner, remember? I said we had to talk someplace where the watchman wouldn't overhear us."

"As the boss's wife you'd know when the watchman would be on the other floor. You took an awful chance on his not hearing the shots."

"Not really. You won't find a room with better insulation than an elevator."

"Or a noisy plant like this one," Orlander said. "Pretty cold."

She looked at him brightly. "It wasn't as if I hadn't done it before."

I broke the silence. "You killed Davy Jackson?"

"He was too slow getting back to the car. Al was already in the passenger's seat in front with the money. I shot Davy through the window. He shouldn't have turned around to see if anyone was chasing him."

"Hendriks in on it?" I asked.

"Are you kidding? To the end his style was to threaten a lawsuit or try to buy people off. It shocked hell out of him. I was high. If I'd been straight I might have known it would ultimately scare him away. At the time I thought it would bind us tighter."

"How straight were you the night your sister died?" I almost had a hand on the chair.

"I didn't rig the accident. An accident is just what it was. Letting people think it was suicide fit better with Frances Souwaine's record. My record. Death clears up so very much."

"Ours, for instance," I said.

"Just yours and your friend's. The police know you were harassing Hendriks. When you bulled your way in here and started on Tim, two armed men looking to shake him down—that's no box lunch under your jacket—he was forced to shoot in self-defense. This is his gun. He was given a permit to carry it when some crank started making threatening phone calls to the house last year. You know perfectly well that's the story you'll tell, Tim. Marianne Motors could survive the investment scandal. The other would kill it."

"What about Chester?" Orlander gestured at the foreman on the floor, who had started to make whimpering sounds.

"He got caught in the crossfire."

"I guess we never did know each other," Marianne said. "I won't cover murder to make cars."

"Sure you will. It's your life. Such as it is."

I threw the chair through the big window to my right. It took out a dozen panes, spraying glass glittering in the sunshine outdoors and turning heads along the assembly line below. Orlander's reflexes were good for his age, but not good enough. She fired as he charged her. He staggered but kept going, hitting her arm and throwing wide her aim. Her second bullet struck sparks off a girder near the ceiling. She spun out of his path and he piled into the railing, losing steam now. Dark drops the size of pennies pattered on the catwalk.

The rest was confusion. Marianne hung suspended, unable to move or comprehend what was happening. I tore the Luger out from under my jacket, but Chester stumbled to his feet just then, blocking my view. Then the entire catwalk bounded under the loping tread of a giant and two great arms tore Edith Marianne—Frances Souwaine—off her feet and lifted her over the railing, the gun going off one more time, and free-threw her in a tall arc that ended in front of one of the robots' welding torches six feet below. Her scream went on after the machinery had shut down.

When it ended she lay sprawled half-in and half-out of a Stiletto chassis with her skirt hiked up over her thighs and most of her face burned away. She wasn't moving.

"You all right?" I asked DeVries.

He nodded. His skinhead flickered under the track lights. "I blowed the horn when she came in, but I guess you didn't hear. I had some trouble with the guard. You said don't kill him. You didn't say nothing about not giving him a headache."

"What happened to your gun?"

He pulled up his shirt to look at it. "Forgot I had it."

I bent over Orlander, still hanging on to the railing with his other hand clutching his left side. The spots on the catwalk were blending into a puddle. "Where you hit?"

"I got shorter ribs than I took in here," he grunted. "Shit."

"Call an ambulance," I told the foreman.

"I'll last," Orlander said. "Reason I said shit, I never got shot once in eighteen years with the department. I knew retirement was going to be this rough I never would of let them kick me off."

Chester hadn't moved. I started to tell him again to call an ambulance, but he was staring down at his employer. Mrs. Marianne's last shot had made nearly as much of a mess of her husband's face as the torch had of hers. But he was breathing. I left DeVries to take care of Orlander and made the call myself from the floor of the silenced plant.

31

I WAS A ROBOT in the Marianne plant, high-tech as all hell and I didn't care who knew it. At the moment I was engaged in trying to weld Frances Souwaine's face back together. I wasn't making much progress, but that didn't faze me because emotions weren't a design feature. The bell rang, ending the shift. I lay there a while before I realized it was the telephone. I swung my feet to the floor—human feet, with sore arches—and sat in darkness, wondering where I was. Then I dug the empty Scotch bottle out of my back and remembered. I'd fallen asleep on the sofa in my living room.

The telephone kept ringing. As I lifted the receiver, the antique clock struck two.

"Walker?" The thin old voice had crack to spare. It was the beginning of his two-hour working day.

"Here, Commodore."

"Raf gave me your message a few minutes ago. I need details."

I gave him some. The whole thing had happened less than twelve hours ago and they were still sharp. There was complete silence on his end and for the third time in our acquaintance I wondered if he was dead.

Not dead, he said: "I must have those computer disks. Name your price."

"I gave them to the police."

"That was foolish."

"It was that or jail on more charges than even you could afford to listen to over the telephone. The cops downriver take a dim view of Detroiters coming down committing trespass, assault and battery, borderline impersonation of police officers, and illegal discharge of a firearm inside city limits. The cops up here take just as dim a view of withholding evidence and harboring a fugitive. I split the disks up between the two departments. They can fight it out without me."

"The company can declare bankruptcy and settle the claims for fifty million or so," he said, thinking aloud. "As chairman of the board Marianne will have to answer fraud charges in his general manager's absence. He can beat those. We'll pull something out of this yet."

"Marianne's got other worries. Last I heard they were still working on removing that bullet from his brain."

"I called the hospital. He's out of surgery and in intensive care. Generally speaking, if you survive the operation under those conditions you're already ahead of the odds. If nothing vital was destroyed he has a chance."

"He won't want it."

"What of the officer, what's his name, Orlander?"

"The bullet transfixed his side. They pinned his ribs together at General and sewed him up. He'll be released in the morning. His wife and daughter and son-in-law and their two kids were coming into the building when I left. Generally speaking, if you survive visits from loved ones under those conditions you're already ahead of the odds. Mrs. Marianne died more or less instantly," I added. "The pain and shock stopped her heart."

"What about your client?"

Richard DeVries and I had parted company downriver, where the cops were holding him before turning him over to Detroit. Floyd Orlander and Chester, Marianne's foreman, had agreed to provide statements corroborating mine on the subject of Frances Souwaine's confession. The whole process would take forty-eight hours and then DeVries would be free.

I told him I'd take my fee for five days and expenses out of his retainer and send the rest to him at the Alamo. I'd asked him if he still wanted the two hundred thousand. He stroked his short beard.

"Yeah."

"Get in line."

"I'm used to it." He shook my hand. There was nothing more anyone could teach him about that.

"He'll be fine," I told Commodore Stutch. "When the story gets out he'll be up to even *his* neck in lawyers wanting to sue the state for damages in his behalf."

"He was better off among thieves and killers." His tone changed. "Thank you, Walker. I'll send Gerald to your office tomorrow with a fee for your services."

"Have him mail it. I'm heading north tomorrow to pick up my car."

"Would you like a brand new Stiletto? It will be a collector's item in a few months."

"I'd just see Mrs. Marianne lying inside every time I looked at it."

He said good-bye and we hung up. Two weeks later Leland Stutch, aged one hundred years, three months, and twenty-seven days, died in his sleep. At that he outlived Timothy Marianne, who expired at fifty-two after ten days in a coma. The *News* ran a spread the following Sunday on the history of the automobile industry in Detroit from Stutch to Marianne. It didn't sound like either of them and it made me wonder about all the others.

Superior looked flinty under a low overcast, the waves pointy and sharp-edged like the shattered rocks on the beach. Three ore carriers sat low and black in a line on the horizon, resembling silhouettes on a navy chart. Tiny long-legged birds stilt-walked in and out of the tide looking for whatever the lake had served up. The air had a fresh metallic chill.

I dropped the Renault where I had rented it and walked three blocks to the garage where my Chevy was supposed to be ready. It was out being test-driven. I drank unspeakable coffee out of a Styrofoam cup and read a display of fan belts until it returned. I wrote out a check for six hundred and change, put away the receipt for the insurance company, and drove from there to sheriff's department headquarters. The inside of the car smelled like an aquarium with ammonia added.

Major R. E. Axhorn was sitting in a captain's swivel behind a gray steel desk in an office with his name on the door. He looked big and solid in his buff-and-brown uniform with his black hair going gray, and out of place with a ballpoint pen in his hand. He recognized me right away. "See Henderson in Fraud if you got a complaint about the garage," he said.

"No complaint. I thought you might want to know what it was you had a piece of last week."

"That big convict with you?"

"Ex-convict. I left him in Detroit."

He pointed the butt end of his pen at the open door. I closed it. The hinges squeaked.

"First time it's been shut since they promoted me," he said. "Suppose you start in with how you wound up in the lake."

I took a seat in an upright chair with a steel frame and told the story again. I gave him what I'd given the cops and what I'd given the Commodore, and in the giving realized it was the first time I'd told it all the way through without holding anything back. He sat rocking his chair back and forth on its swivel with his hands resting on the arms, looking like a chief hearing the terms of a treaty. When I was finished I lit a Winston and drew in smoke to fill the emptiness the story left behind.

"Figure this St. Charles fellow has shot his wad, do you?" he asked.

"They all have. Him, DeVries, Orlander, Davy Jackson's parents. Even Frances Souwaine came off tired after killing Hendriks and telling about it. It's one reason we were able to get around her. Poison builds up only so long and then it's got to find an outlet."

"Trouble is it don't leave you feeling no better afterwards."

"The shrinks don't think so."

"The shrinks don't know anything about anything. If they did they wouldn't be committing suicide twice as often as cops. Comes a point where the poison's the only fuel you got. Blow it off and die."

"How are the Wakelys?"

"Lurleen dropped her kid Saturday. A boy. Looks a little like Burt and Hank both. Whoever's sitting here sixteen years from now's going to know him pretty good. Hank just bailed Burt out of County after Burt broke a window and two fingers in the Gitchee Goomee Saturday night. Celebrating their new cousin. Hank paid cash. I expect a B-and-E report on this desk by next weekend."

"Seems the only difference between what you do up here and what the cops do where I come from is you don't have to ask for names."

"Only when the summer people are up." He watched me, his eyes black in their dark copper setting. "You fish?"

"It's been years."

"We ought to go down the Seney some Sunday. They tell me the salmon downriver's big as dolphins this year."

"Is there ever a year they don't say that?"

"I don't guess there is."

"Maybe next trip."

"Yeah." He rocked back and forth. "We never will, will we?"

"Never's a long time."

"Too bad. A man finds his soul fishing. Appreciate you coming in, Walker. You didn't have to."

"Sure I did."

We shook hands and I left. I didn't see him again. The next time I got up there, several months later on a wandering husband job that went sour in St. Ignace, a young sheriff's lieutenant told me Bob Axhorn had left the department. I wanted to ask if he'd gone fishing. I didn't.

DOWNRIVER:

A WORD AFTER

by

Loren D. Estleman

AMOS WALKER'S VENUE BEING the Motor City, it's inevitable that his cases will sometimes bring him into close contact with the automobile industry. However, I take satisfaction from the fact that none did until the eighth book in the series.

Although I can't claim that I made a conscious decision to defer using this obvious setting, I maintain a dim view of the Hollywood convention of having every potboiler based in New Orleans take place during Mardi Gras, every thriller with a Seattle locale end in a fight atop the Space Needle, every night-in-a-haunted-house creature-feature come complete with an electrical storm and a character named Penelope. The targets are too fat and conceal a multiplicity of sins, not the least of which is a lack of research. I'd as soon watch a western where the Indians are always saying "How," or read one of those murder mysteries in which the bodies fall like K-Mart stock prices and no one makes any attempt to leave.

Fortunately, Detroit is an ancient city with a complex personality, and like one of those holograms that decorate tickets to a Rolling Stones concert, presents a fresh picture each time you alter the angle. Whereas a pasteboard paradise like Las Vegas must needs provide the obligatory montage of stuttering neon signs in order to establish its identity, this French settlement, discovered by nomadic tribes and alternately owned by England, Chief Pontiac, the

U.S., abolitionists, Irish wardheelers, Henry Ford, southern-bred blacks, and Mayor Coleman A. Young's business partners, bleeds thick bright blood wherever one pricks it. The first seven titles in the series dealt with the pornographic underworld (*Motor City Blue*), the animosity of nearby small towns toward the big ugly city (*Angel Eyes*), racial tensions (*The Midnight Man*), juvenile delinquency in the affluent suburbs (*The Glass Highway*), the city's deep ethnic roots (*Sugartown*), local Vietnamese War veterans (*Every Brilliant Eye*), and Detroit's rich jazz tradition (*Lady Yesterday*).

But if the city is more than just cars, it is also most emphatically cars. Were I to avoid writing about the industry forever, I would be guilty of an omission as great as a contemporary history of Congress without pederasty.

The problem had to do with a dearth of situations necessary to create conflict. The universe began with friction. For want of an irresistible force to strike sparks off an immovable object, there is no place for the storyteller to start. Since the demise of Studebaker in the 1960s, and until the incursion of Japanese imports in the 1970s, American auto manufacturing consisted of the Big Three: General Motors, the Ford Motor Company, and the Chrysler Corporation of America. (American Motors, never a significant force, dried up unnoticed on someone's windowsill sometime around Disco's last gasp.)

Japan's innate arrogance, unfettered by union interference, caught the bloated U.S. triumvirate sleeping: The substandard American product of the mid-to-late seventies, whose only advertising feature worthy of mention was the ball-bearing ashtray, and the fact that the industry had faced no serious competition since the early twentieth century, made the domestic market a prime target for a society that had learned the value of mass production at the hands of Henry Ford's B-24 Liberators during World War II.

Honda, Toyota, and Datsun (later, Nissan) battered the Big Three from three sides, left them swollen and hemorrhaging, and forced the posturing Lee Iacocca to run to Washington, whining about increasing the tariff and begging for a handout to prevent Chrysler from sinking out of sight.

The climate had suddenly become promising for the kind of writer who enjoys a good scrap. Still, it lacked pathos. Tokyo was too smug, industrial Detroit too hypertensive for either of them to present the tragic hero the situation demanded. But history is a master of timing, and introduced John Z. DeLorean square on cue.

This former General Motors exec, trim, tanned, and handsome (with some surgical assistance), roared into the Reaganeighties at the wheel of his brainchild, the gull-winged, stainless-steel-jacketed DeLorean, posing the first real challenge to the automotive establishment from inside the U.S. since Preston Tucker rolled out his ahead-of-its-time product in 1948. DeLorean's go-devil sold briskly, abetted by his ubiquitous charismatic presence all over the TV dial and in every Sunday supplement. (The silver bullet even entered the enduring popular culture when it served as the time-traveling vehicle in the *Back to the Future* motion picture franchise, produced by the period's other golden boy, Steven Spielberg.) These were palmy days for individual enterprise. As the saying went, the only thing that could stop DeLorean was DeLorean himself.

Consumers are children, easily distracted, and even more easily bored into stupefaction. Once the novelty wore off, DeLorean's sales flagged. The *Wünderkind* might have overcome this setback with some sexy new features and a generous finance plan, as Detroit had been doing for decades. But a second whammy came when he was arrested and placed in federal custody on suspicion of trafficking in illegal narcotics. As alleged by prosecutors, DeLorean had enhanced his venture capital by selling controlled substances on a grand scale.

Although today his guilt is widely assumed, the fact is the government, as so frequently happens when handed what appears to be an airtight case, failed to prove its charges. The jury hung, and Washington decided not to retry. While the argument may convincingly be made that this was the point at which the United States officially lost the war on drugs, DeLorean was clearly finished. His car disappeared from the road and his name does not even appear in Merriam-Webster's otherwise exhaustive one volume desk encyclopedia, published in 2000.

Here was sustenance for the literary forager. John DeLorean's rapid rise and even steeper fall was the stuff of high tragedy, complete with the Aristotlean heroic flaw and with the added benefit of a Wang Chung soundtrack. *Downriver* had found its direction.

The creative process is synaptic and largely subconscious, with a pinch of magic, and once it's run its course it's almost impossible to track. I'd long wanted to revisit the 1967 Detroit race riots through the reminiscences of a survivor, but how that survivor developed into the character of Richard DeVries is a mystery to me now, an alchemic event. Beginning his story with his release from Marquette Branch State Prison in northernmost Michigan gave me the opportunity to spin a narrative that continues in a linear pattern ever downward, climaxing in the murky mists of Detroit's downriver section south of the city and reversing itself only in the epilogue, when Walker reconnects with Major Bob Axhorn, a might-have-been-close-friend and one of my better inventions. No one—not the reviewers, not casual readers, not my friends or family—seems to have noticed this downward structure, but I'm proud of it nonetheless; it smacks of *The Adventures of Huckleberry Finn, The African*

Queen, and *Deliverance*. So close to complete control of an organic thing like a novel is rare, and even more rarely successful.

I jettisoned the drug-pusher subtext from Timothy Marianne's story, which while it was suggested by DeLorean's was not directly based on DeLorean. I detest traffickers in human misery (the protagonists of *Easy Rider* and *Blow* got their just desserts, for all Hollywood's attempts to present them as misunderstood rebels), and could no more bring myself to make one of them sympathetic than I could forgive myself afterward. Further, the question of DeLorean's innocence was a complication that would only have derailed the plot.

Stock swindle is a different animal altogether. No one really cares except the stockholders, and since the market is fueled by greed and ignorance of the jaw-dropping, Who-Wants-to-be-a-Millionaire kind, whoever takes them to the cleaners is halfway to canonization. The flap copy on the Houghton Mifflin edition referred to the scam as "really innovative," but I suspect the editor responsible was being kind; selling more than one hundred percent of something is primitive stuff, employed by Mel Brooks's characters as far back as the original *Producers* and practiced on a daily basis by the airline and hotel industries. Moreover, it's easily understood and quickly explained, even by an old algebra flunkee like this writer. Stir in a *femme fatale* on the order of Edith Marianne and you get something almost operatic, begging the fiery finale.

I received one disappointed letter, from a reader residing in a Downriver community, complaining that very little of the action took place Downriver, and that the region's unique character did not appear to full advantage. I sympathized with the letter's author, and in my reply I attempted to explain that "Downriver," in the sense in which I applied the term, referred not so much to a place as to a state of mind: The territory farther down the Detroit River has always been looked upon by Detroiters as a mysterious land where dragons dwell, and where they themselves would no sooner travel than they would penetrate the Brazilian rainforest with its population of headhunters and man-eating alligators. This was Timothy Marianne's world, a literary response to Roman Polanski's Chinatown. The letter-writer never wrote back, so I have to assume that there is a reader lost. But I will continue to claim those who didn't complain in the first place.

Leland Stutch was pure self-indulgence, a throwback to the dawn of the automobile age, and not so far-fetched, as a not-inconsiderable number of these pioneers lived to observe their centenaries. Frail old men with limitless power are fascinating foils for a powerless character like Walker, and so it was fun to add a touch of Howard Hughes. I continued Stutch's story post-mortem in *Sinister Heights* (2002), the fifteenth book in the series.

In 1987, the Michigan Council for the Arts honored me as Author of the Year. At the ceremony I was asked to encapsulate twelve years of publishing into a five-minute speech. I chose to read the scene in the Alamo Motel, wherein DeVries is the victim of an attempted scam by a member of his own race. A friend told me that as I was quickly setting up the scene, he saw a black man in the audience stiffen at the words "black ex-convict." However, when I read the line, "You'd better let him go now. He doesn't look black any more," the man laughed loudly. This gratified me, as the Amos Walker stories, in addition to being pretty good mysteries and (one hopes) serious fiction, are also intended to be funny.

SUNDAY

by

Loren D. Estleman

THEY WERE HAVING ONE of those runs for a disease on West Grand River. Most of the streets leading into it were blocked off with sawhorses and large Detroit Police officers in uniform, and some peace-loving soul had installed a loudspeaker on every third lightpole to blast a running commentary on the participants. I didn't catch the name of the disease but it was a cinch it wasn't a hearing disorder.

Normally on Sunday morning I'd have been sleeping through it all in my little cottage by Hamtramck, but my taxes were due the next day. So far I had located most of my canceled checks under the desk blotter in the office and was putting off pulling the file cabinet away from the wall to look for some missing receipts when the door to my reception room opened.

The buzzer was switched off, but the connecting door to the private office was ajar and I had a clear view of my visitor. I couldn't have seen any more of her if the door had been open all the way, because she was as naked as an onion.

She was a tall brunette with her hair swept up from a long neck that hadn't gotten much sun. Her breasts were small but self sustaining and she had athletic hips and legs with a little more meat on them than the current fashion allowed, which was okay with me because I hadn't caught up with it either. Her feet were pretty in a time that emphasizes hands and faces, the nails neatly pruned and unpainted. It was a pale body like you don't see any more—it shone in the sunlight canting through the window at my back—and she hadn't had any bikini waxes recently. She was in her late twenties.

For a beat after she closed the hall door she leaned against it, breathing in shallow gusts and looking around jerkily like a doe that had jumped the wrong fence. Then she saw me, standing half-turned toward the file cabinet, and seemed to realize her naked condition suddenly, because she blushed clear down to her bosom. It was like spilling red ink over a marble statue.

The loudspeaker under my window crackled and spewed some irrelevancy that gave me the best line I could dredge up under the circumstances. "The race is downstairs."

She started, as if the additional discovery that I was capable of speech was too much for her to take in. "Next door," she said; and fell on her face.

I couldn't have caught her on a moped. Still, I sprinted through the connecting doorway, knelt and felt her carotid for the strong pulse I found there, and lifted her up onto the upholstered bench where the potential clients were expected to sit, thumbing through copies of *U.S. News & World Report* from the Carter administration. She'd skinned her nose when she fell, but the rest of the inventory checked out. She'd only fainted. I took my raincoat off the halltree and spread it over her. Then I went out, locking the dead bolt behind me.

The office next door belonged that month to a graphic artist, a bitter-faced old mutterer still waiting for his one-man show at the Detroit Institute of Arts—or failing that, next month's rent—who hadn't said a word to me all the times we'd passed each other on the stairs. I nodded to the workman painting someone's name on a glass door down the hall, knocked at the artist's door, and tried the knob. It wasn't locked. Nothing about the workman's resigned expression told me he'd seen any good-looking naked women that day.

The office consisted of one room, slightly larger than my private tank. It had been converted into a studio, with unframed canvases covered with riotous slashes of paint hung on the walls and a sheet tacked over the south window to simulate north light. A foot-high wooden platform occupied one corner; across from it stood an easel holding up a canvas with the outlines of a nude human female form brushed on and a low zinc-topped table smeared all over with paint from half a dozen squashed tubes. A bouquet of brushes stood in a chipped coffee mug on one corner.

The air smelled of turpentine and something else even stronger, that didn't belong in a studio or an office or anywhere else except the firing range at Detroit Police Headquarters. I went over and wrenched up the window to let some of it out. The run was still going on below, with accompanying commentary from the loudspeakers. Every corner wore a cop in uniform.

The room where an artist works is never tidy. There are always things lying around, props and half-empty containers and yards of canvas tarpaulin and piles of paint-stained clothing. The pile of clothing at the foot of the easel contained a man.

He lay on his side with his legs drawn up and one arm flung across his face. When I moved the arm to get to the artery on the side of his neck, the collar of his old streaked shirt shifted, exposing a blue-black hole the size of my finger in the back of his head, just below the occipital bulge. There was no reason to expect any activity in the artery, but I looked for some anyway. No surprises there. The face was the one I knew from the stairs. It looked a little less bitter. Death will do that, even the violent kind.

His right fist was wrapped around a long-handled brush. I made a mitten of my handkerchief and grasped the brush and pulled. It slid easily out of his grasp. I slid it back in. I straightened, touched the paint on the canvas with a corner of the handkerchief, and looked at the cloth. No stain.

There was a sink, paint-splotched like everything else in the room, a square plank table covered with charcoal sketches on rough paper, and a wobbly kitchen chair, where presumably the next Van Gogh sat with his back to the door, drinking coffee and brooding over his dark visions. A split, empty Styrofoam cup stood on the table. It smelled of grounds and was still warm.

One corner of the room was obscured by a sheet hanging down like a drape from tacks in the ceiling. Behind it was another rickety chair, with a woman's dress folded on the seat. A pair of low-heeled pumps lay underneath and a bra and panties hung from the back. I touched the dress lightly with a palm.

I found the telephone on the floor under an open Little Caesar's box with a bit of crust stuck to it and a couple of flies stuck to that. I made a call.

The painter in the hallway was gathering up his equipment. According to the fresh legend on the door, I was about to be blessed with another lawyer for a neighbor. My building ate them like peppermints.

"See anyone today?" I asked.

The painter shook his head. "I hate working Sundays. Dull as a washtub."

My visitor was standing in the middle of my waiting room, wearing my raincoat with her hands in the pockets. It nearly wrapped around her twice. A little of the frightened-doe look had gone from her eyes.

"You locked me in." She sounded accusing.

"I didn't want to lose the raincoat. Put these on instead." I held out her dress and shoes and undies.

"You went–in there?"

"Uh-huh. You want to talk about it?"

"Turn around."

I admired the view of the inner office while the raincoat rustled to the floor behind me and hooks hooked and elastic bands snapped.

"I'm a model," she said. "I work nude."

"I know. I'm a detective."

"I didn't see it. I was posing with my back to him. I heard the door open and close, but I didn't turn around. In my work you learn to stand still no matter what. I heard a sharp crack. Just a crack, like a brush dropping to the floor. I thought guns made more noise than that."

"Depends on the gun. Also whether it's wearing a suppressor."

"Suppressor?"

"Silencer to you. It was probably a twenty-two automatic, which is one of the few guns you can suppress successfully. It's a pro's weapon. What happened then?"

"He made a little noise and fell. I turned around then, just in time to see someone going out the door. It was a man–I think. That's all I can tell you. All I saw was his back."

"What was his name?"

"I told you, I didn't see his face. I wouldn't–"

"Not the shooter's, the artist's. I like it when the dead men I find have names. It helps me sort them out."

"Oh. Tontine. Victor Tontine." She hesitated. "He's really dead?"

"Didn't you check?"

"No. I just ran out. I didn't even bother to dress. I was

afraid he'd come back and kill me. Don't they do that to witnesses? I panicked. I knew I couldn't go outside all undressed. Yours was the first door I came to. Thank God it wasn't locked."

"If what you say is true, you aren't much of a witness. Do you know why Tontine was killed?"

"I know nothing about him. He hired me through the agency where I'm listed. Thirty minutes, that's how long we knew each other. That's how long I'd been posing." A zipper shrilled. "Can you take me to the bus stop? There's a crowd on the sidewalk and my legs are too wobbly to fight my way through. I need to go home."

"We need some law first. You can sit down till they're through with you. It shouldn't take long, since you didn't see anything." I started toward the inner office and the telephone.

"Turn around."

I did. She looked just as good with as without, a rarity. The dress was a simple blue frock with double-reinforced pockets sewn in. Some women just didn't like to carry purses. This one preferred to hold a gun. It looked familiar.

"You should have locked the door to your office, Mr. Walker," she said. "You never know who might walk in and plunder the arsenal."

"Poor judgment. You didn't have any pockets when I left." I raised my hands.

"It was going to stay in my pocket until we got away from the crowd; but I never make plans that won't stand alteration. You're going to take me to my car, arm in arm, just like we're going steady. This gun's going to be in your ribs just in case you can't stand commitment."

"You should've wet down the paint."

She frowned. "What?"

"The paint on the canvas Tontine was working on. It was

dry. He wasn't painting when he was shot. He was sitting at the table drinking coffee. After you shot him you pried the cup out of his fist, splitting the Styrofoam, dumped it out in the sink, dragged him to his easel to make it look like he was working, and stuck a brush in his fist. It was looser than it should have been if his muscles had contracted the way they usually do at the moment of death, but that wasn't evidence. The dry paint was. Also your clothes. They were still warm from your body. They wouldn't have been if you'd been posing for a half hour, like you said."

"Well, well. You *are* a detective."

"You were working under a deadline, or you wouldn't have hit him with a charity run going on down in the street and cops hanging from the lightpoles. You like your anonymity, or you wouldn't worry about being seen by one of them, a woman alone leaving a building where a murder was committed. And then there was the painter in the hall. He didn't see you slipping in; painters take breaks, just like everyone else. But you couldn't go back downstairs without passing him. You could have killed him, too, but that's one too many bodies on the same premises for a true professional. What's a girl to do?"

"What, indeed?" She seemed to be enjoying herself. She had the weapon.

"Easy. You shucked your clothes, ditched the gun somewhere in the clutter–the cops will find it, but it won't have prints or a serial number or a past history to spoil a job well done–waited till the painter wasn't looking, and slipped down the hall and through my door. Chances are you saw me through the window from the street on your way here and took a chance that I'd be working on a Sunday with my door unlocked. If you were wrong, you could always go back for your gun and kill him. He wouldn't be likely to run from a good-looking naked woman."

She laughed. She really was having a good time. "Thanks for the compliment. I work out. You have to stay in shape in my line, but I'm a woman too. I like to look good. Good enough anyway to ask a handsome gentleman to see me to my car and keep his mouth shut."

"Permanently, of course. If the painter was worth killing, so is a detective. There can't be so many lady mechanics in this town the cops won't put two and two together."

"Here's where I say I prefer to be called a 'hitperson.' " She wasn't laughing now. Nothing like amusement had ever crossed that face. "On second thought, you may not be worth the commitment. Never let it be said I ever needed a man for any purpose, let alone slipping away in a crowd." She slid back the hammer on my revolver.

"Lose the piece *now!*"

She hadn't heard the hall door opening behind her. Now it swung around the rest of the way and Mary Ann Thaler charged in, accompanied by a pair of Detroit Police officers in uniform. They spread out inside the door, crouching, their service pieces clamped in both hands. The Felony Homicide lieutenant had on stone-washed jeans, black high-top Reeboks, a satin jogging jacket, and a baseball cap with a brown suede visor and her hair tucked up inside.

The game of cops and robbers was starting to require all new equipment: compacts and curlers and an extra pair of pantyhose for those pesky runs during high-speed chases. I was beginning to feel even more like an endangered species than usual.

The piece was lost. The officers flung Ms. Raskolnikov against the wall and put on the cuffs.

I lowered my hands and looked at my watch. "Twenty minutes for a murder. That's some kind of record."

"You try finding a place to park with barricades all over the neighborhood." Lieutenant Thaler returned her nine-millimeter to the shoulder rig under her jacket. “Where’s the cold cuts?”

“Next door.”

In the studio, she squatted on her heels to look at the dead man’s face. “That’s Tontine, all right. He’s wanted for questioning by the FBI for an art forgery scam with connections to the Benevolent Brotherhood of Sicilians. We got a flyer. I guess someone was afraid he could talk as well as he could paint.” She looked up at the embryonic painting on the easel. “That’s where she got the idea to impersonate a nude model, huh? She got a nice body?”

“If you like one with a murderer inside,” I said. “You’ll find my prints on the telephone when you dust the place. I called you from here.”

She stood up. “What are you doing at work on a Sunday, anyway?”

“What are you? I thought you had weekends off this month.”

“The IRS doesn’t recognize weekends.”

“You shouldn’t put things off till the last minute,” I said. “You can get in all kinds of trouble.”

THE AMOS WALKER MYSTERIES

MOTOR CITY BLUE

ISBN: 0-671-03898-2

Marla Bernstein is a pretty, dark-haired teenager . . . who also happens to be the ward of Ben Morningstar—a semi-retired mobster who prefers to keep family business out of the newspapers. When Marla suddenly disappears, the gang boss is forced to call in private eye Amos Walker, who quickly learns his new employer doesn't take "no" for an answer when he offers a job opportunity.

Unfortunately, the only clue to Marla's whereabouts is a pornographic photograph that clearly proves she's become part of a world that disgusts even her criminal guardian. The photo, in turn, leads Walker into the seedy world of Detroit's porn shops and blue movies, where Marla's trail becomes even murkier . . . and increasingly more dangerous to follow. As first cases go, Walker could have asked for one less challenging. . . .

ANGEL EYES

ISBN: 0-671-03900-8

Ann Maringer is a go-go dancer with a problem: her life is in danger, and she's certain that her end is coming soon. Her only hope is Walker, a guy who "sticks like a nuclear fallout," according to a former client.

When Ann disappears, Walker is hot on her trail. But this is no ordinary case, as the private eye soon learns—not when a union boss, a corrupt judge, a vengeful son, and a concerned mistress are just some of the players involved. And not when all of them want him dead. . . .

THE MIDNIGHT MAN

ISBN: 0-7434-0002-X

In the private eye business, mistakes can fatal. Just ask Amos Walker.

First, he pulls his gun on a man he thought was a member of a group of potential truck hijackers. Even goes so far as to fire a round at the suspicious driver to make him step from his car. Only trouble is, the guy—Van Sturtevant—is a cop.

Then, after Sturtevant is crippled in a shootout with a gang of black militants, Walker—figuring he owes the cop for letting him off the hook—offers his investigatory services to the officer's pretty, blond wife, Karen. At no charge.

If Walker had been paying attention, he would have seen the warning signs. But now bodies are going to start piling up, with politicians, private eyes, and members of Detroit's Finest on the giving and receiving ends.

Yes, mistakes can be fatal. And if Walker doesn't watch his back, the next one will definitely be his last. . . .

INCLUDES THE BONUS AMOS WALKER STORY "REDNECK"

THE GLASS HIGHWAY
ISBN: 0-7434-0729-6

Television newscaster Sandy Broderick seems to be the type of guy who has it all: good looks, good hair, a deep voice, and great ratings. Unfortunately, he's also got a son who, more often than not, tends to find himself in the sort of trouble that only someone like private eye Amos Walker can fix.

And so Walker takes the case, with its two objectives: find Bud before all the illegal drugs he's been consuming and the women with whom he's been sleeping make for a fatal combination; and keep Bud's actions from ruining Broderick's sterling reputation.

What Walker finds, though, is more than he bargained for—in a case that tests this terrific P.I. to his very limits.

INCLUDES THE BONUS AMOS WALKER STORY
"CIGARETTE STOP"

SUGARTOWN

ISBN: 0-7434-1293-1

Spring has come to Detroit's Sugartown enclave, and Amos Walker would like to feel kindly toward the human race. Unfortunately, his first case of the new season immediately leads him into trouble among the Polish settlers of neighboring Hamtramck, when old Martha Evancek hires him to look for the grandson she lost nineteen years ago. But even before Walker gets a chance to investigate the almost two-decade-old disappearance, a second case presents itself. This time, it's an eminent Russian novelist, exiled and famous, who fears that someone is trying to cancel his next book by canceling its author.

Something connects the two cases; Walker knows it. But finding that elusive link might just wind up costing him his life. . . .

INCLUDES THE BONUS AMOS WALKER STORY
"NECESSARY EVIL"

EVERY BRILLIANT EYE

ISBN: 0-7434-1325-3

To hear him tell it, Amos Walker is an unsuccessful man in an obsolete profession. Still, even P.I.s have a sense of honor, and Walker has always been a man who believes in paying back favors that people have done for him over the years. He owes his old friend Barry Stackpole a big one, for saving his life in a Cambodian shell crater a lifetime ago.

Now Stackpole, lately a good, hard-scrounging reporter, has vanished. And finding him is the job Walker's been hired for–not once, but twice: first by Stackpole's newspaper, then by an attractive literary editor hot to track down an even hotter book the missing man's been writing.

The investigatory trail becomes littered with a bewildering assortment of fresh dead bodies. Walker nearly joins the clutter when somebody rigs his steering and brakes. And a final revelation explosively narrows the distance between the tropical jungles of Asia and the concrete jungles of Detroit–and between one brand of war and another. . . .

INCLUDES THE BONUS AMOS WALKER STORY
"THE CROOKED WAY"

LADY YESTERDAY

ISBN: 0-7434-3495-1

Tracking down a runaway wife is run of the mill. That's yesterday's blues. But finding the trombonist father of black, beautiful, reformed hooker Iris threatens to blow up into the case of a lifetime.

The trail Amos Walker follows through Detroit's smoky music clubs leads him to dens of hard crime and harder drugs—where Iris and Amos will be lucky to escape with their lives, much less the truth about a past packed with menacing secrets. And that's no jazz.

INCLUDES THE BONUS AMOS WALKER STORY "DOGS"